# ERICA LUCKE DEAN

*For the Love of Katie*
*The Katie Chronicles*™
A Red Adept Publishing Book

Red Adept Publishing, LLC
104 Bugenfield Court
Garner, NC 27529
http://RedAdeptPublishing.com/



First Print Edition: April 2017
ISBN-13: 978-1-940215-90-7
ISBN-10: 1-940215-90-0

Cover and Formatting: Streetlight Graphics

*To Colleen*
*For keeping Cooper alive...*

# The City of Light

J UST OVER A MONTH AGO, when Cooper and I boarded the plane for Paris, I figured I'd make the best of it. While Cooper worked, I would stay out of trouble—take in the sights, maybe shop a little... oh, and eat. I fully expected to devour as many pastries as I could get my hands on. When I hit four months pregnant, the cravings had gotten out of control, and I had an entire French dictionary of delights I wanted to sample. But never in my wildest dreams—and trust me, I had an impressive imagination—did I envision I'd end up shackled to a cold metal chair in a dingy Paris police station. Yet, there I was, cuffed to the armrest and engaged in an epic stare-a-thon with the hairy, fishnet-wearing cross-dresser across the room.

"Excuse me!" I rattled the steel bracelet to get someone's—*anyone's*—attention. Meanwhile, all around me, the room hummed with conversation, but I couldn't understand a single word. My French was limited to "*Ou sont les toilettes?*" and "*Puis-je avoir un autre croissant, sil vous plait?*" So unless I had to pee—an occupational hazard these days—or someone came around with a pastry tray, I was out of luck.

Tearing my attention from Dr. Frankenfurter in the corner, I sucked in a breath to calm my jangled nerves. I caught a whiff of what smelled like week-old curried french fries and stale cigarettes, a lethal combination to a pregnant woman's stomach. Where were the fresh-ground coffee and the hot buttery pastries? It had been hours since I'd last eaten, and I would've flat out *killed* for a baguette right about then.

Instead, I was surrounded by a veritable sea of crumpled McDonald's bags and ancient tacos, reminding me of the Atlanta police station and destroying every notion I'd ever had about the City of Light. Not that I'd spent that much time being interrogated by police. There was just that once—not counting the time one of my clients tried to blow up the bank—but I'd definitely expected the Paris experience to be a little more... *I don't know... fancy?*

Middle-aged police inspector Henri Gaspard—apparently the only person on duty in the *4th arrondissement* of Paris who spoke English—swept into the room and dropped into his chair with more than just a little exasperation. He bounced the business end of his pen against a blank pad of paper, tapping out a jagged rhythm. He stopped mid-motion to glare at me from the opposite side of his desk.

"Do you mind?" His French-accented English came out in a rich baritone as his beady brown eyes flicked from my face to my wrist and back again.

Following the path of his eyes, I glanced down to the steel bracelet I'd been absently banging against seat of my chair and froze mid-swing. "Actually, yes, I do." I gave the handcuffs another shake. "Are these really necessary? I'm hardly a flight risk." I was far from graceful before the baby bump got in the way. And with the scary four-inch heels strapped to my swollen feet, I'd be lucky to make it halfway across the room without breaking my neck.

"*Bien sûr que non.*" He flashed a halfhearted grin but didn't make a move to release me. "Are you ready to tell me who you *really* are and why you felt compelled to elude an entire security team to gain access to a restricted area?"

"Take a closer look at my face. Are you *sure* you don't recognize me?" My picture—well, Cooper's picture, but I'd been standing next to him in most of them—had been splashed across all the local papers.

"Hmm." He squinted as he scanned me from top to bottom, swishing his thick rodent-like mustache back and forth beneath his enormous nose.

I looked bad. I knew I did. Partly by accident—I didn't intend to get my hair caught in that gnarled bush—but partly by design. The goth makeup, the tight black cat-burglar leggings, and matching turtleneck were all meant to conceal my identity. It was the perfect disguise on the set of a vampire movie. But Gaspard's intense scrutiny made me squirm.

"I think I have seen you somewhere before. Ah, yes." He tapped his upturned lips with a long finger. "Turn around."

"What?" I blinked at his amused expression.

He made a circular motion with his finger, and I twisted my body as far as I could while still tethered to the chair. Several feet behind me, chained to a long bench against the back wall, sat six women, all dressed in black with varying degrees of dark goth makeup.

"Mr. Maxwell's other admirers." Gaspard's voice drew my attention from the row of doppelgängers, and I turned just in time to see him wipe the grin from his face.

"I must admit you're the only one who claims to be his wife, though at least five of the six have named him as their sire. I assume you know what that means."

I rolled my eyes. *Is he serious?* Of course I knew what it meant. I'd been Elizabeth Jayne's biggest fan before I realized *she* was really *Cooper*. I knew all about vampires and their sires.

"Now, where were we?" He cleared his throat and repositioned his pen above the notepad. "I believe you were about to tell me who you really are."

I let out a huff, ruffling his salt-and-pepper comb-over. "I've already—"

"Humor me. I'd like to hear it again." He relaxed into his seat, folding his arms between us. His judge-y eyes burned matching holes into my forehead. "You have no identification, no phone. You don't appear to have bathed—"

I speared him with an icy glare. *So much for my disguise.* "I told the arresting officer I left my purse at the hotel. I only brought the room key with me."

He covered his chuckle with a cough. "Why don't we start with what brings you to Paris?"

"Fine." I shifted my weight in the uncomfortable chair. "As I've already stated, my husband and I arrived—"

"And who is your husband?" Mr. Impatient interrupted.

I blinked a few times before answering. This was getting ridiculous. *Where's the trust?* "Coo-per Max-well." I stretched out the name to be sure he understood me this time. Maybe his English wasn't any better than my French.

His dubious expression annoyed me as he jotted down something I couldn't make out. "The author?"

"Yes!" I started to jump to my feet before remembering I was chained in place. "I've already told you this at least a dozen times."

"*Mais oui*, but I'm still as unconvinced as I was at the start. Let's pretend you really *were* traveling with Mr. Maxwell."

"Because I *was!*"

"Why prowl around, watching him from the shadows? Someone might suggest you were spying on him."

My temper flared just as my stomach gave a rumble of dissatisfaction. "Hell, yes, I was spying on him. He's my husband!"

Gaspard rolled his eyes toward the ceiling and muttered something that sounded suspiciously like "*Americans,*" then dug a finger into the hair above his ear and scratched. "I think I have a simple solution to our dilemma." He picked up the cracked handset of his antique desk phone and punched in a series of numbers. "We'll just ask Mr. Maxwell—"

"Noooo!" This time, I did bolt out of my seat, nearly snapping my wrist in half in the process. My insides plummeted to my toes, and the bread I'd only dreamed of devouring threatened to make an appearance. Cooper couldn't find out about my covert mission, not until I figured out exactly what he was up to. My voice shook as I shrieked at Gaspard from across the desk. "You can't call Cooper. He'll *kill* me!"

Inspector Gaspard's bushy brows jumped toward his hairline as his breath whistled in and out past parted lips. "Kill you? Explain."

I froze at the expression on Gaspard's face. He still gripped the phone in his hand. "Oh. Um. I didn't mean *kill* kill. No, he's not—" A nervous laugh escaped my throat. "It's not like he's an assassin. I mean, I did *think* he was. Once. But that was a just great big mistake, a colossal misunderstanding." If I had a dollar for every time I'd heard *that* little phrase... but in this case, it also happened to be true. In my defense, the evidence had been stacked against him. Random dead bodies, mysterious bank deposits, and a high-powered rifle were pretty compelling by themselves. But added together? *What other conclusion is a girl supposed to come to?* How was I supposed to know he simply wrote *books* about killing people? Of course, I knew better *now*. Cooper Maxwell was no killer. But he was definitely hiding something. Of that, I was certain.

Gaspard screwed up his face and dropped back into his chair. "Relax, *mademoiselle*. Sit down."

I gulped in a lungful of air, willing my trigger-happy hormones to stand down. I blew out the breath and settled into the chair again. "I'm sorry. It's just... well, it's a long story."

"Aren't they all?" He sighed. "Perhaps you should start from the beginning."

*The beginning?* If I was going to delve into this story, I'd need sustenance first. "Could I get a glass of water? And can you please remove the cuffs? They hurt."

The inspector crooked his finger, and a uniformed man who looked a few years younger than me walked over. Gaspard whispered in his ear, and the man pulled out a key and unfastened the shackles at my wrists. Then Gaspard dug through his bottom drawer, reaching out to me with a room-temperature bottle of water he'd pulled from the chaos.

"Thank you." I unscrewed the cap and took a swig.

He waved off my gratitude. "Continue, *sil vous plait*."

If he wanted the beginning, he'd get the beginning. With one last deep, cleansing breath, I launched into my story. "Cooper and I had been dating for less than a month when everything came crashing down around me. He might not've been an assassin, but he lied to me about who he really was."

"And who was he?" Gaspard leaned forward, abandoning his pen to rest his elbows on the desk in front of him.

"As I'm sure you know, he's world-renowned author Cooper Maxwell, the son of British diplomats. And unbeknownst to me, I was his biggest fan. I should have been delighted. I loved those books. But instead, his admission made me furious. I'd made a complete fool out of myself in front of everyone I knew. I'd even managed to involve my mother—the absolute *last* person I'd ever want involved with my love life."

"And what happened after you found out?"

"I left him. What else is a girl to do?"

Gaspard smiled. "What else, indeed?"

"That was just over a year ago, but I remember it like it was yesterday. I said my last good-bye and stormed out of the bank, leaving Cooper openmouthed and brokenhearted. I left my whole life behind, never to look back."

Gaspard popped up an eyebrow.

"Okay, so maybe I looked back through a blur of tears. But I still did it..."

I'd barely cleared the main doors of the bank before the hyperventilating started. I'd done it. I'd taken charge of my life. Why did I feel so damned empty?

After hiccupping and shaking my way across the parking lot, praying Cooper hadn't followed me out the door—yet secretly hoping he had—I climbed into my car, cranked up the radio, and rested my head on the steering wheel to have a good cry. Etta James almost managed to drown out my sobs while I struggled to get the train wreck that was my emotions in check. I knew I'd never make it home in this condition.

*What have I done?*

*Did I really just quit my job and break up with my boyfriend?* My fingers ached, tingling as I tightened my grip on the wheel. My whole life was in that bank. I'd just walked out on everything—and everyone—I'd known for the past year.

At the sudden realization, I picked up my head and stared at the building in my rearview mirror. What sort of idiot walks out on the only man she ever loved because he *wasn't* an assassin trying to kill her? Me, that's who. *Poor pathetic Katie James.* My mother would be so ashamed.

I closed my eyes, and Cooper's devastated face waited for me behind my lids. *Why did I have to be so stupid? Why couldn't I just forgive him for his little white lies and live happily ever after?*

My driver's-side door flew open, and before I could get a scream out, a pair of warm hands reached for me, dragging me from the car.

"If you think for even one damn minute I'm letting you leave me like that..." Cooper growled, gripping the tops of my arms as if I might flee if he let go. Determination lined his handsome face. "What do I have to do for you to believe how much I love you?"

I opened my mouth, but no sound came out.

"Katie, please say something." Desperation clouded his voice.

"I-I love you too?" I felt the tension drain from him at my whispered words.

His face split in a wide grin, and he used his thumbs to wipe the tears from my cheeks. "Damn right, you do."

"I'm sorry." I didn't know what else to say. I was as much to blame as he was.

He rested his forehead against mine. "You have nothing to be sorry for. This is my fault. All my fault."

I wound my arms around his neck, weaving my fingers into his thick, dark hair. "I forgive you."

"I promise I'll never keep anything from you again," he murmured as he placed light kisses on the corners of my mouth.

"And did he keep his promise?" Gaspard asked, at the edge of his seat.

I had to shake myself to clear the memory. "Would I be here if he had?"

# We Now Return to Your Regularly Scheduled Program

EXACTLY THREE WEEKS FROM THE day I'd nearly kissed my perfect life good-bye, everything seemed, well... *perfect*—at least on the surface. The weather had taken a turn for the better, and Cooper had finally finished *An Immortal Heart*, the last book in his Immortal Blood vampire romance series, secretly written under his mother's name, Elizabeth Jayne. That very same book had caused so many of the misunderstandings between us. Naturally, I hated it before reading even a single word.

Oh, Cooper had no idea I harbored such negative feelings toward his latest masterpiece, and if I had my way, he'd never find out. Unfortunately, finishing the book was only the beginning. Little did I know, I'd still have a rival for his attention.

"Can't you just meet with her over Skype? Is it really necessary for you to fly all the way across the country?" Immature or not, I pouted as Cooper tossed clothes into a suitcase.

He gave me a pointed glare, but his lips quirked into a smile, despite his attempt to hide it. "It's work, Katie. Nothing else."

"Humph." I pulled a pillow over my face. I could hear my mother now. *That's what they all say. Just ask Vicky.*

He bent down to tug the pillow away and planted a kiss directly on the furrow between my brows. "Didn't your mother ever tell you you'd get a wrinkle if you made that face?"

*Did he really just bring up my mother?* My mouth dropped open like a bigmouth bass. "You promised."

"Uh, sorry. I... forget I said that," he muttered then went back to packing. "All I'm saying is it's silly to worry about Vivian. If I didn't know better, I'd think you were jealous."

"I'm *not* jealous." Despite my claims to the contrary, I was far from over my irrational jealousy of Cooper's publicist, Vivian.

"Good." He zipped his bag then slid into the bed beside me, pulling me into the circle of his arms. "You have absolutely no reason to be."

That's exactly what Silvia said. My coworker, who was arguably more of a mother to me than my actual mother, didn't pass up any opportunity to remind me where my lack of trust had gotten me last time. His secrets, coupled with my suspicions, had nearly been our undoing. I probably should've heeded the warning in "curiosity killed the cat," but after eavesdropping on several of their conversations, I'd convinced myself Cooper had a *thing* with Vivian and, at her urging, was planning to kill me. Then again, blowing things out of proportion had always been one of my specialties. "I know. I trust you." And despite everything, I did. It was Vivian I didn't trust.

"I really have no idea where you get all your crazy ideas." He nuzzled his face into my hair and chuckled. "It's like you're living in another world. *I'm* supposed to be the one with the vivid imagination."

He could laugh all he wanted, but I knew it would only get worse. He was going to Los Angeles for a meeting with her. Rationally, I knew he couldn't get out of it. He'd already postponed the trip once, when I had him arrested for trying to kill me. But honestly, how was I supposed to know that instead of being an assassin, he was a world-famous romance writer? I couldn't be mad at him for working, but I hated to see him go. And his return flight wouldn't get him home until Saturday morning.

"Do you know what Saturday is?" I infused as much nonchalance into my voice as I could.

"Hmmm?" He slid his hands into my hair, massaging my scalp in a way that sent tingles down my spine.

"Saturday. You know, Valentine's Day?" I tried not to sound too eager. It was only Thursday, and I was already keyed up.

His fingers stopped moving for a second before he picked up where he'd left off. "Is it really?"

"Wait, you really didn't know?" I sat up quickly, dragging my hair through his fingers. He sounded genuinely surprised, which worried me a little. It wasn't like Cooper to pass up an opportunity for romance. *Unless...*

Maybe he thought it was a stupid holiday. I mean, it wasn't a real holiday, after all, just another day blown out of proportion by Hallmark and the candy companies, but I was a woman with her first real boyfriend in I-couldn't-even-remember-how-long, so I clung to hope.

"Yes, Katie. I know Saturday is Valentine's Day." He kissed my open lips. "And before you ask, I'll be back in plenty of time. Obviously, I have something planned, but don't ask what it is. Our previous agreement aside, I'm not divulging this particular secret."

"I wasn't going to ask," I fibbed, relaxing into his arms again, secure in the knowledge that Cooper had a secret agenda. Of course he did. I was silly to worry. He was a romance writer, after all. *And what better day for a romance writer to propose than Valentine's Day?*

Friday morning found me alone and oddly hungover with Cooper gone. Strange, since I hadn't had a sip of alcohol after I'd singlehandedly downed an entire pitcher of margaritas the last time my mother was in town—another reason to push thoughts of her out of my head—but that was weeks ago. I groaned at the memory. It hadn't been one of my better moments. I'd since sworn off alcohol completely. I wasn't just a lightweight. I was a *featherweight*.

I crawled out of bed, past the cold, empty spot on Cooper's side. It was ridiculous for me to miss him already, but I did. I missed him in the shower, and since he usually drove me, I missed him on the ride to work. Though, without the distraction of morning sex to slow me down, I was actually early for once, so early that I parked my car near the front door and managed to slink unnoticed into my office.

Work had lost some of its magic since Cooper and I had become practically inseparable. I used to rush to work with the hopes of seeing him, and now, rushing to work meant leaving him behind. Oh, he still popped in from time to time to see me, under the thinly veiled guise of studying his bank accounts, but no one was fooled by that in the least. I doubted they ever were. Not like I was.

It wasn't that long ago I believed Cooper came to see me for his banking needs and nothing more. Since the cat was out of the proverbial bag, he didn't spend as much time in my office. It had become more of a precursor to lunch or going home—his home.

We hadn't officially moved in together yet, but it seemed inevitable. I hadn't set foot in my townhouse in over two weeks. Cooper insisted on going to get the mail and checking things out every few days, but I had no desire to leave his house other than for work and really, not even then.

My branch manager, Phil—who, for some strange reason, refused to call me by my first name—poked his freshly shaved head into my office with a cheeky grin. "James, I left you a few notes. Since you're not likely to have anything better to do today, I thought maybe you could squeeze in some actual work?"

"Oh, sure. Definitely." I forced a cheery smile, watching until he vanished around the corner before falling into my chair with a sigh. One by one, I read the messy jumble of sticky notes posted around the perimeter of my monitor without detaching them. Everything I had forgotten—or, more likely, ignored—was neatly spelled out on its own brightly colored square and tacked up for me.

In an attempt to tackle the most difficult matters first, I reached for the neon-pink square marked number one— Phil had labeled them by importance—and focused on the task. My main goal for the day was to keep busy. I wrote up a few proposals, and per his new requirements, copied Phil on the emails. I was sure it was another way to keep tabs on my progress, but I didn't really mind. It actually forced me to get things done.

As usual, my enthusiasm withered as the morning went on. Just after ten, I wandered off, desperately in need of coffee. What I really wanted was an excuse to see what everyone else was up to.

In the break room, Phil and June—the most senior employee at the bank—glowered at each other. This, in and of itself, was nothing new. Phil rarely made it through an entire day without saying something to piss her off. He was the boss, but June never failed to remind him she'd been with the bank almost since he was born.

"Did I miss something?" The tension in the air threatened to choke me.

"Not you, dear." June's sugary smile crumpled, making the velvety brown skin around her mouth pucker into a sour frown. She put her hand to her heart in a remarkably well-played Scarlett O'Hara gesture. "Apparently, *I'm* the one missing things."

I was afraid to ask.

Phil threw up his arms and rolled his eyes in an over-the-top expression that made his entire face morph into a cartoon. "Oh, here we go again."

June turned her back to him and huffed. We all knew that meant the subject was closed for the moment.

As far as I knew, they'd barely spoken in days. According to Silvia, Phil gave June a less-than-stellar performance review because she failed to follow procedure to the letter. One time. It was a simple mistake, but Phil believed things needed to be done right the first time, every time. And he liked to get under June's skin. But today was different. June once told him he was just one step away from being an asshole, and apparently, he'd finally taken that last step. And I'd missed the whole thing.

I supposed it was my own fault. Lately, I'd effectively disconnected myself from the gossip chain. I'd traded all after-work social interactions to spend every free moment with Cooper. I didn't even go for margaritas and *señoritas* anymore. Back when all I had was my stack of romance novels to keep me company, they'd drag me to the bar every Friday against my will. But now I had Cooper, and dragging me wasn't as easy. For once in my life, I had a real boyfriend to keep me busy.

Silvia held a steaming cup to her lips, blowing on it as she stepped out of the little kitchen. She probably knew exactly what had happened between Phil and June, but I wasn't about to ask, not when she eyed me over her leopard-print reading glasses as if I'd grown a tail or something. "Oh, you *are* here. I'm so glad Cooper didn't kill you before leaving town."

"Ha. Ha. Very funny." Three weeks after our little falling out, things were finally back to normal, meaning Silvia never missed a chance to poke fun at me for believing Cooper was an assassin.

She took a loud slurp of her coffee. "I slay myself."

"Enough with the assassin jokes, please. You're never going to let me live that down, are you?" Despite her relentless teasing, it was impossible to stay mad at Silvia. I figured if I could forgive Cooper for lying, I could forgive her for keeping his secrets.

"Nope."

While I waited for Silvia's cackling to die down, I glanced at Vicky digging through the picked-over donut box. "How is she?"

"Eh." Silvia gave a noncommittal shrug, but her eyes told me there was far more that she wasn't saying.

Our little group had been walking on eggshells since Vicky's husband left her for a missionary—the church kind, not the sexual position. Though, according to Vicky, the woman had impressive flexibility in just about every position. I refused to ask how she knew. Her husband didn't even have the decency to let the dust settle after Dean, my former client and Vicky's pretend boyfriend, went crazy, taking us hostage and trapping us all in the vault. Later, we learned Dean was the one leaving the trail of bodies I'd attributed to Cooper. *What are the odds?*

Some might say poor Vicky brought it on herself with the pretend boyfriends and fantasy threesome lists, but even with all that, she was a friend, so I decided to cut her some slack. Instead of getting angry or begging her to stop when she brought up inappropriate topics, I listened to her strange fantasies about bizarre sexual appetites and mate swapping—no matter how much it freaked me out. I even let her wax philosophical on... *waxing*. As in Brazilian. I wouldn't admit this to anyone, least of all Vicky, but I secretly considered giving the whole waxing thing a whirl. I even picked up a home waxing kit but hadn't worked up the courage to use it.

After getting my own coffee and the last half of a glazed donut, I parked myself against the copy machine. "I'm going to hate myself for saying this, but maybe a night of karaoke would bring her out of her funk?" I'd barely gotten the words out when Vicky sauntered up beside me.

She flipped her flame-red hair over her shoulder and let out a sharp exhalation—her preferred form of communication lately—but this time, the tiniest of smiles threatened to disrupt the melancholy set of her lips.

"Well, go on." Silvia gave Vicky a nudge then perched on the edge of June's chair. "I can see that wicked sparkle in your eyes. You obviously have something to share with the group."

Vicky studied her bloodred fingernails as she dropped her little bombshell. "I've decided to give up men."

"Ha. Ha." Phil rolled his eyes and gave Vicky a slow golf clap. "Congratulations, you almost had me there. Not."

"No, really." Vicky abandoned her fingernails and turned her laser focus on me. "I mean, look at what happened to poor Katie. Her whole life turned upside down, all because of a man. I've decided they're just too much trouble."

There was a unanimous jaw dropping across the room. Despite her recent relationship status, we all expected her to mourn her losses then get right back out there. I couldn't imagine Vicky taking up reading or needlepoint to keep her occupied.

"But Cooper turned out to be one of the good ones." June stuck up for my boyfriend.

I waited for Silvia—or anyone really—to join the Cooper bandwagon, but there weren't any takers.

"Men? As in all of them?" Silvia shook her head, making her spiky caramel hair dance. "No, I don't believe you."

"I'm dead serious. *All* men. They're just too... unpredictable." Vicky seemed calm, but a spark of fire lit up her eyes. "One minute they love you, worshiping the ground you walk on and encouraging you to indulge in your wildest fantasies, and in the next, they're spouting off Bible verses while balls deep in the benediction. And let me just say, what I walked in on was about as far as you can get from the *missionary* position."

"You just need time." June smiled, her dark skin crinkling around her eyes. "You're still in shock."

"No, I'm done with the lot of them. But don't you dare feel sorry for me. I'll be fine. I'm happy." Vicky stopped to stare at the ceiling for a long moment. Then, as if she'd gotten the answer to a question she hadn't asked aloud, she nodded. "I'm switching to women."

June broke the silence. "That's nice, dear."

"Thanks, June." Vicky beamed. "I mean, why wouldn't I, right? If anyone knows their way around a pus—"

"Okay then!" Phil shot up from his chair. "As enlightening as this conversation is, I'm now certain I know more about your sex life than I legally should." He didn't waste any time exiting the break room.

"I guess I'd better get back to work before you convince me to give up men too." Silvia followed closely behind Phil, shaking her head and laughing.

June got up and wrapped Vicky in a bear hug. "That boy will rue the day he hurt you." Then June left Vicky and me standing by the copy machine.

Ordinarily, I avoided spending alone time with Vicky. Since her marriage fell apart, she'd been much less acerbic, but that didn't mean I wanted to let my guard down. Her biting wit was sharp enough to cut through the thickest of skin. And she had the uncanny ability to leave me speechless.

Case in point. "Uh..." I couldn't think of anything to say. The idea of Vicky giving up men simply didn't compute. Yet, I had to admit, I was all for it if it meant she'd stop fantasizing about Cooper.

She tipped her head to the side, piercing me with her bright-blue eyes, and I knew she was about to say something I didn't want to hear. The long pause would've been the perfect opportunity for me to escape like the others, but *naturally*, I froze like a deer in headlights.

Finally, a crooked little smile broke across Vicky's face,

and she leaned in close enough for me to smell her powder-fresh deodorant. "You know what I'm thinking, don't you?"

"I... not really. No. Why would I know what you're thinking? I'm not a mind reader, you know." I stammered through the words.

"Oh, come on, Katie. You have to know I've always had a bit of a thing for you."

A quick blast of hysterical laughter escaped my throat, and my hand flew up to cover my mouth. She *had* to be kidding. *Of course* she was kidding.

Her sly smile didn't waver. "I'm not kidding." Her eyes locked on mine, and I focused on her wide pupils.

Oh. My. God. She *wasn't* kidding! I didn't know whether to be horrified or flattered. I mean, God only knows where her mouth had been, let alone her... this was bad. When I made plans to go dress shopping with Silvia after work, I figured that would be the worst possible thing to happen to me all day. Oh, how wrong I was. The only thing worse than having Vicky declare herself to me would've been Phil making a pass. *Gross!*

After a long minute, I finally pulled my gaze from hers and took two quick steps backward, crashing into a filing cabinet. "Why me?"

She rolled her eyes as if I'd asked a stupid question. "You have to admit, it's so much more convenient this way. We already work together. We have the same friends." She listed the benefits as if she'd suggested we carpool together. "I can't think of anything more perfect."

I could. In fact, I could think of a lot of things I'd rather do, like have my appendix out or get a root canal.

"Did you know that before Jim decided to shack up with a missionary, he listed you as his first-round draft pick on the fantasy threesome list?"

I shook my head.

"Oh, yeah, he came up with the most elaborate scenarios. And I have to tell you. It was some of the best sex of my life. So can you just imagine how jealous he'll be when he finds out I actually nailed you?" Her self-satisfied smile frightened me almost as much as her words. She reached out to snag the edge of my sweater.

I jerked away from her wandering fingers. Still speechless, I pulled my eyebrows together in a tight pinch and managed to squeak out, "Please. Stop. Don't tell me anything else. I-I really don't want to hear about your sex life." I pressed my chilled hands to my face in an attempt to cool the flush in my cheeks.

"Oh, don't get your panties in a twist. I wasn't going to invite you home with me." Her eyes flashed as she took another step toward me. "Not yet, anyway. That is, unless you've gotten tired of Mr. Romance already."

"Don't call him that," I barked, instantly irritated. "And no, I'm not tired of him."

Ever since Cooper's secret identity had come out, everyone called him Mr. Romance. Never to his face, but thanks to me, he knew. And I didn't think he took the insult seriously enough. As far as I was concerned, he wasn't nearly as offended as he should've been. I had to be insulted for both of us.

"Oh, stop being so sensitive, Katie. You're a grown-up now. Live a little, why don't you? Who knows—you might even like it." Vicky laughed as she walked out of the back and disappeared around a corner.

# I Didn't Know I Was Even in the Closet

IT TOOK MORE THAN A few minutes for my pulse to slow down as I processed what had just happened. Why did these things always happen to me? And it wasn't just because Vicky was a woman—I would've been equally freaked out if Phil had decided to pursue me, possibly even more so—but if I'd wanted to change my sexual orientation, Vicky would've been the last person I'd want to be involved with. We just weren't compatible. I could barely stand to work with her, let alone... I shuddered hard enough to crack my teeth. *Ewww.*

As soon as I was sure my legs wouldn't give out, I sprinted for Silvia's office.

"Silvia!" I whispered with every ounce of breath I had left. "Do you know what Vicky said to me?"

"You mean *after* she said she was switching teams in the middle of the game? Sweetie, this is Vicky we're talking about. I can only imagine." She didn't look up from her monitor, but I could tell she struggled to keep from laughing. It didn't take long before she broke, letting out a loud guffaw. "Better you than me. That's all I've got to say."

I gasped with righteous indignation and what I could only imagine was a horrified expression. "If you knew, why didn't you warn me?"

She looked up with one eyebrow raised. "I didn't know. I suspected. Big difference. I saw that glint in her eyes when she looked at you back there and figured something was up. I only knew for sure when you slid around the corner just now as if a horde of zombies was chasing you."

I couldn't decide what was worse: Vicky or the zombies. I fell into the chair across from Silvia's desk, my heart still pounding. "What should I do?"

Silvia gave up pretending to work and leaned back in her chair. "Well, did you tell her you're not interested?"

Apparently, my expression was all the answer she needed.

"*Are* you interested?"

"No!"

"I'm sorry." Silvia laughed at the strangled sounds emanating from my throat. "I had to ask. But if you're not interested, tell her thank you but no thank you. I'm sure you've had to shut down unwanted attention before." She waved a hand in the air as if it were that easy.

"Do you think that will work?" I had hope. Not a lot, but a girl could dream.

"Knowing Vicky? Probably not. But it might make you feel better."

"Thank you, as always, for your invaluable advice," I hissed. "Maybe if I just pretend nothing happened, she'll go away."

"Don't bet your next paycheck or anything."

Another fit of hysterics hit her, so I turned on my heel and marched straight back to my office, shutting the door behind me. With a groan, I dropped into my chair and spun around to face the window. Snow flurries floated through the air, and I shivered at the sight. *So much for warm Atlanta winters.* I should've gone to California with Cooper when I had the chance. He'd offered, but he had no idea about my little *issue.* I would've never been able to go to California with him, not with my paranoid, irrational fear of flying. The mere thought of getting on an airplane had me completely paralyzed with terror.

I never flew. Not anywhere. On the rare occasions I

visited my parents, I either drove or took the train. And that was not a subject I wanted to broach with Cooper just yet. It could wait until later. *Much later.* Until then, I had more important issues to deal with.

I reached for my iPhone—a gift from Cooper after I managed to destroy the last one—but it wasn't there. After digging through the empty candy wrappers and spare napkins in my purse with no luck, I ran back to the break room, but it wasn't there, either. While back there, I grabbed a fresh cup of cream and sugar with a splash of coffee then headed back to search my office again.

As I walked out of the break room, I heard Silvia laughing at something across the lobby and glared in her direction. So much for forgiving her—the woman was unforgivable. And to think I considered her a second mother. Hell, half the time, I liked her *better* than my own mother. Unfortunately, it was the similarity between them that drove me crazy at that particular moment.

Vicky stood in the doorway to my office, swinging something shiny in front of my face. "Looking for something?"

"Yes." I snatched my phone from her outstretched hand. "Where'd you get this?"

"You left it in the back." Vicky sucked in her cheeks but wouldn't make eye contact with me. She couldn't fool me. She needed to start practicing her innocent expression in the mirror. "You need to be more careful next time. You're lucky you didn't leave it where someone else could find it."

Mesmerized by the incoming text notification staring up at me, I nodded. "I've been searching everywhere for it. Thank you."

"You're welcome. What are friends for, right?"

She emphasized the word *friends,* and a sudden twinge of guilt hit me square in the chest. I felt worse than I had the time the teenage grocery store bagger invited me to his prom. "Listen, I'm sorry for overreacting earlier, but you have to know I'm not interested in you like that. I mean, most days I really do like you as a—you know—a friend. But that's it."

"Hey, I totally understand, friend." A slow, sinister grin spread across Vicky's red-lacquered lips. Before I had a chance to consider what that meant, she leaned in. "You know, friends with benefits is my absolute favorite arrangement."

As if having some sort of seizure, I jerked away from her, spilling my coffee down my front. "Shit!"

"Oh, please let me." Vicky reached for the wad of fast-food napkins on my desk and made a move to mop my coffee-drenched chest.

"No!" I grabbed the napkins from her and pressed them to my now-see-through blouse. "I'm good."

Vicky purred, as in actually *purred.* "I'm counting on it."

"Katie?" Silvia poked her head into my office.

My breath let out with a *whoosh.* "Oh, thank God!"

"What happened to you?" Silvia lifted her eyebrows as she looked me up and down.

"Vicky... *coffee!* Spilled. Just being clumsy. Nothing else going on." The words came out in a jumble, and I slapped a hand over my mouth to stop the flow.

"Only you, Katie." Silvia chuckled. "Only you."

Glaring at Vicky's smug grin, I chucked the wet napkins into the trash and grabbed more.

Silvia squinted as she darted her eyes back and forth between Vicky and me. I could almost see her trying to solve the puzzle in her head. I needed to shut that down before she had it figured out. I'd never live that down. "So... did you need something?"

"Oh, right." Silvia shook her head as if to clear it. "Cooper's been trying to reach you. He's blowing up my phone with texts. Would you please put the boy of out his misery?"

In all the commotion, I'd forgotten about my phone. I quickly retrieved the text and stared at it, confused. This was why he'd been blowing up Silvia's phone?

*Cooper: Do you have something you'd like to tell me?*

"What does—" I looked up from the screen, but both Silvia and Vicky had gone. Instead of typing out a reply, I hit the speed dial for Cooper and waited while the call connected.

"Katie?"

The mere sound of his voice calmed me, and I heaved out a sigh. "Hey. Silvia said you were trying to reach me. Why didn't you just call?"

Cooper made a strangled sound but didn't answer.

His long silence made the back of my neck prickle. "Cooper? What's going on?"

"I was actually hoping you'd tell me." He threw out the statement and got quiet again.

I perched on the corner of my desk, completely exasperated. "What does that mean?"

"I knew when I left you weren't happy about my trip, but I chalked that up to jealousy. I never imagined you'd..."

"I'd what?" My tongue seemed to swell into a giant ball of mush in my mouth.

Cooper exhaled loudly. "Are you breaking up with me?"

"What?" I jumped to my feet. "No! Why would you ask that?"

"I feel like a complete tool saying this out loud, but—" He let out a nervous chuckle. "I saw what you posted on Facebook, and I just... I kinda lost it."

*What?* "Um, Cooper, I have no idea what you're talking about. I haven't been on Facebook in days."

"You're sure you didn't post... *something* as payback for me going to see Vivian?"

I had no idea what he was talking about, but I was beginning to appreciate the genius of the whole thing. I wished I could take credit for it, whatever it was. "No, but I'll admit I'm curious."

Cooper let out a relieved sigh as a sultry female voice called his name. "Listen, they're calling me back into my meeting. Go check your Facebook, then do me a favor and change your password. If you didn't change your status, someone else did. And I have an idea of who that someone is." The voice called out to him again, this time more urgently. "I, uh, I'll call you later."

"Okay. I love—" The line went dead in my hand. I tossed my phone onto my desk, and a low growl rolled up my throat, surprising me a little. Yeah, the jealousy wasn't going away any time soon.

Cooper's words echoed through my brain until curiosity got the best of me, and I grabbed my phone from where it had landed. I'd barely gotten my finger in position above the Facebook app when my mother's resting bitch face flashed across the display. I tried to stop the motion before it was too late. I really did, but the heat from my skin hovering over her icy demeanor must have been enough to make the connection. The next thing I knew, Mom's voice barked up at me.

"Katie? Katie, are you there?"

*Shit.* Instinct told me to throw the phone and run in the other direction, but years of dealing with my mother kept me rooted in place. With a quick steadying breath and a fake smile plastered across my face as if she could actually see it, I pressed the phone to my ear and braced myself for the coming storm. "Hi, Mom."

"Why did it take you so long? What were you doing? Oh, never mind. Don't tell me. I'm sure I don't want to know." My mother had the uncanny ability to sound curious and condescending at the same time. "I don't know why I ask, anyway. It's not as if you tell me anything."

"I tell you things."

"Oh, you mean like the time you told me you were dating a killer?"

I couldn't stop the groan. She would never let me forget I'd kept my relationship from her for all of a week. And she'd never let the whole assassin thing drop. "Mom, Cooper isn't a killer. He never was."

"You keep telling yourself that, dear. Not that it matters anymore."

"Exactly... *wait.*" My mother never dropped anything. Ever. She still brought up the disastrous crush I had on my eighth-grade science teacher every chance she got. *"Remember the time you set off the sprinklers at the Science Fair? I'll bet Mrs. Evans still avoids white blouses."* My mom and her running litany of every mistake I'd ever made... "Why doesn't it matter?"

She huffed as if the answer were obvious. "Well, now that you've decided to join the lesbians, of course!"

"What?" I choked on a laugh.

"Oh, I suppose I should just count myself lucky they're allowed to get married now. We'll probably be considered trendsetters at the country club. I can't wait to see the look on Bette Wilcox's face when she finds out. You know, she's still in denial about her nephew. He's an interior decorator, for Heaven's sake! It's not like everyone doesn't know what *that* means."

"Mom, stop." I swallowed barely contained laughter. I'd never get an answer out of her if I lost it. "What are you talking about?"

"For goodness's sake, Katie." Mom sounded exasperated, and I knew exactly how she felt. "I can read. Did you forget we're friends on the Facebook? Oh, I hope Bette McGrath doesn't see it before I have a chance to tell people. You know how she is. I'd never live down the gossip."

"Wait, did you say...?" What had started out funny suddenly took a sharp turn toward disaster. Cooper's words came back to me in a rush, and the anxiety swelling below the surface threatened to bubble over. "What did you see posted on Facebook?"

"Are we really playing this word game again? I'm not upset about it. I'm really not. I'll admit it came as a bit of a shock at first, but your father reminded me what century we're living in. And as he said, if you want to join the lesbians, who are we to stop you?"

"Mom, you don't *join* the lesbians. It's not a-a gang. They don't have matching tattoos and a secret handshake."

"Well, of course not." She scoffed. "I know that. I'm not stupid. I watch *Orange is the New Black*, you know. But you're the first in our circle to come out. I wasn't sure how to refer to it."

*Orange is the New...*

"I didn't come out!" I tamped down my rising panic.

"Now, Katie, you don't need to be ashamed. There's nothing wrong with being a lesbian, though you're not planning on getting one of those short haircuts now, are you? Because your ears are much too large for that. I'm afraid it wouldn't be at all flattering—"

"Oh my God!" I shrieked. "Would you stop talking and listen to me? I am *not* a lesbian. If I was, I wouldn't be ashamed of it. But I'm not, and I have no idea why you think I am."

My mother finally let loose with a shriek of her own. "Because you posted about it on—"

"Mom, I'll have to call you back." Without waiting for a reply, I hung up on her. The weight of her accusations, coupled with Cooper's strange behavior, had finally sunk in.

*Note to self: change Mom's picture to something more fitting with her personality.*

Circling back to where I was before my mother interrupted, I opened the Facebook app and searched my status updates. I didn't see anything out of the ordinary, but I knew something had warranted both my boyfriend and my mother losing their minds, so I kept digging. As I was about to give up looking, I found the catalyst to their madness. With my heart pounding in my ears, I fell into my office chair, every drop of air in my lungs rushing out in a *whoosh*. There, right before my eyes in bold print, were the offending words.

*Katie James is in a relationship with Vicky Dixon.*

Before I could gather enough brain cells to fix what she'd done, I dropped my phone as if it had bitten me. And in a way, it had. I certainly felt the sting keenly enough. My mouth opened and closed like a fish on the deck of a boat, but I couldn't pull in enough air to breathe. Why would Vicky do that?

Oh, I knew why, and yet I still couldn't wrap my head around it. This was more than a simple prank. This was... it was... *devious* and demented but also, in a Hannibal Lecter "I want to eat your face" kind of way, undeniably brilliant.

# Does My Insecurity Make Me Look Fat?

"TELL ME AGAIN WHY I can't have a cheeseburger?" I picked at my barely-there salad with its green tea chaser then glanced over at Silvia's greasy slice of pepperoni pizza and Vicky's bean burrito.

Ugh. *Vicky.* How I managed to get roped into inviting her along for the ride, I would never know. *That's a lie.* I knew exactly how Vicky ended up tagging along, and her name rhymed with shmilvia.

Though, I had to admit, Vicky did seem genuinely sorry for having upset me. And even if I hadn't quite forgiven her, I did feel bad that her husband jilted her for someone who obviously spent more time on her knees worshiping the one-eyed trouser snake than praying. Like Vicky'd said, *"She didn't get those scabby knees from saying Hail, Marys all day and night."*

My capacity for compassion had been stretched to its limits, but when Vicky turned on the sad-kitty face and begged for a second chance, how could I say no? I couldn't. Because Katie James—non-lesbian with the undeniably gorgeous boyfriend and bossy mother—was a pushover. This was why I needed to grow a backbone.

After securing a seemingly heartfelt apology from Vicky—including the promise to keep her hands and assorted other body parts to herself and refrain from ogling me like chocolate lava cake *a la mode*—Silvia made us kiss and make up, figuratively, of course. My kisses were entirely reserved for one Cooper Maxwell.

"You can't try on dresses if you're full." Vicky held on to her burrito as if she were about to deep-throat it. "It throws off the lines, and they won't hang right." She opened her mouth wide and made half the burrito disappear. *How does she do that? And will she teach me?*

Silvia nodded her agreement as she stuffed a corner of pizza into her mouth and took a big bite. My stomach took that opportunity to growl. I wanted to disagree with their logic, but I was too weak from hunger. Besides, how could I argue when I was all but certain they were right? And as I'd already established, I had no power against their dark magic.

*Note to self: Acquire backbone... and a set of balls, for good measure!*

After my pathetically unsatisfying dinner and equally disappointing self-administered pep talk, we headed straight for Silvia's favorite department store.

First stop: the lingerie department.

"Katie, grab a few of those lacy thongs." Silvia pointed to a rack filled with frilly silk and lace.

I reached for the safest pair I saw.

"Not the white ones." She shook her head and chuckled. "I know it's hard, but try to think sexy for a minute, okay?"

"White can be sexy," I argued as I eyed the rack. The lace looked scratchy and uncomfortable.

"Under a wedding gown, maybe." Vicky snatched the white pair from my hand and shoved a scary red lace pair in its place.

"Tell me again why I need new underwear? I do actually own nice panties, you know." I dangled the barely-there thong from my index finger and tried *not* to imagine where the micro-string would end up—or how I'd get it out.

Silvia rolled her eyes as if I should know these things. "You can't wear the same underwear with every dress."

"Really, Katie." Vicky snickered as she plucked a pair of black lace knickers—a word I'd picked up from one of

Cooper's books—from the rack and added it to the red pair in my hands. "Don't you know anything?"

After shooting an icy glare in Vicky's direction, I turned to Silvia for the rest of my "lesson."

"Surely your mother must have schooled you on the importance of foundation garments. Even at your age, you need to make sure everything stays where it belongs. I'd never leave the house if it weren't for my Spanx." Silvia wove through the racks, building an armload of said foundation garments. "And as for bras, you have your plunging neckline... your strapless... your backless..."

And apparently, a terrifying push-up number that would surely obstruct my view of my feet, putting me in grave danger of tripping, not to mention all the other dangerously sexy unmentionables that looked like they belonged in Christian Grey's Red Room of Pain.

"Come on. We don't have all day." Silvia clapped, and Vicky and I jumped like a pair of her trained Yorkies. After hanging the lingerie in the changing room, we set out to find the perfect Valentine's Day dress.

Silvia was like a wraith, ghosting around the department, plucking her choices from the racks and piling them into Vicky's outstretched arms. I stood, dumbfounded, in front of the open changing room with a mountain of delicate fabrics weighing down the swinging door and several more hanging on the hooks designed for that purpose. Out of all the dresses in front of me, I'd chosen three. Silvia had picked at least twelve.

"In you go." With a firm shove from behind, Silvia propelled me into the room then shut the door behind me, but not before Vicky squeezed in with me.

It took a second for her presence to sink in. "What are you...?"

"I'm helping you try things on." Vicky grabbed what looked like a torture contraption from the pile and held it out to me. "Kinda looks like a straitjacket, doesn't it?"

"Oh, no." I flattened my back against the icy mirror. "I don't need help."

Vicky rolled her blue eyes. "Stop being such a baby. I'm not going to put the moves on you. Silvia made me promise to be good."

I waited for her signature smirk to come out, but after nearly half a minute, her sincere expression hadn't changed. Slowly unfolding my arms from in front of me, I let myself relax. "You promise? No inappropriate comments? No copping a feel?"

"Not even if you begged me." Vicky shot me a smug smile.

I stared her down, looking for the chink in her armor. If she was lying, I'd see it. "No sexual fantasies about doing it in a dressing room?"

She winked. "I'll never tell."

"I'm serious." I kept my eyes locked on hers and pointed toward the door. "You clear that dirty mind of yours right now, or you can get out."

Vicky blew out a breath. I could almost see the white flag waving over her head. "Fine. No inappropriate comments, no copping a feel, and no sexual fantasies about doing it in a dressing room."

"And no using any visual memories later for spank material." I had her that time. No way would she agree to that without a fight.

"Oh, come on. You're killing me here." She threw up her arms, stealing all the extra space in the tiny room.

It was my turn to flash the smug grin. For the first time in... maybe ever... I'd gotten the upper hand where Vicky was concerned. I crossed my arms in front of me. "Hey, those are my terms. Take 'em or leave 'em."

"Damn it, you drive a hard bargain. Fine, I'll bleach my brain if I have to. Are you happy now?"

I couldn't contain my happy. "Ecstatic."

"Good, now, put this on." Vicky shoved the strapless

contraption into my hands. "But I'm afraid with those great big balls of yours, you won't be able to try on the underwear, so we'll just have to imagine what the dress looks like without panty lines."

And so began my official truce with Vicky and the frightening task of trying everything on.

After climbing in and out of lingerie and dresses until my skin went numb, the excitement had worn off. "I'm too tired to go on." I peeled off the latest reject and dropped it into Vicky's lap with a sigh. "We're never going to find the perfect dress."

"Oh, sweetie," Silvia spoke through the crack in the door. "You can't give up now. I know the first few were horrible, but you have to soldier on. Here, try these." She opened the door to shove another stack of dresses at Vicky, closing it before I could protest.

I'd already tried a few of *her* choices and felt as if my fear of the unknown was justified.

"Try the black one." Silvia paced outside the door.

"Which black one?" Vicky and I asked at the same time.

I surveyed the half-dozen black dresses in front of me, clueless as to which one she meant.

Silvia poked her head in again. "The one with the strappy things."

Vicky held up the dress with multiple thick black straps crisscrossing the back. "I'm pretty sure I saw Houdini escape from this in a movie."

"Wait... there's a cross-dressing Houdini movie?"

She shrugged. "Maybe it was *Rocky Horror.*"

"Tim Curry played Houdini?"

"Would you two stop arguing about movies, and put on the damn dress?" Silvia barked through the crack.

Vicky and I glanced at each other tried not to laugh.

After strapping me into the Houdini dress, Vicky winced. "That looks like it hurts."

I wrinkled my nose at my reflection. "It's a little...

constricting." More like it pushed my chest up so far, I looked like I'd had a horrible allergic reaction to something.

"It's a good thing I'm here, because I don't think you'd be able to escape this one on your own." Vicky laughed.

"Yeah, this one's a definite no. What about the blue one I picked out?"

Silvia said, "No," at the same time Vicky said, "It's Valentine's Day. You can't wear blue."

*Of course not. Silly me! Who wears blue on Valentine's Day?*

"What about this one?" Vicky pulled a dress from the bottom of the pile.

"Red?" That was the understatement of the day. The dress wasn't just red—it was fire engine, cherry tomato, and Satan's jumpsuit red all rolled into one. "Isn't that a bit obvious?"

"It won't hurt to try it on, right?" Vicky shrugged. "Besides, nothing wrong with going traditional. And it's a step up from the asylum chic of the last one."

As much as I hated to admit it, Vicky had a point, so I swapped out the itchy backless one-piece bra thingy for a pretty strapless black bustier and shimmied into the red dress. I had to bend forward to rack myself into the bodice. I stood tall, turning from side to side to get a good look before showing Silvia. The dress was snug but not tight, more like a glove—a ruby-red strapless glove.

"Nice!" Vicky let out a wolf whistle and lifted her hand to slap me on the ass. She stopped right before making contact.

I shot her a glare.

She laughed. "Oh, give it a rest. I said I'd be good. You really do need to loosen up a little."

"Not in this dress, I don't. Okay, here goes." With one last peek in the mirror, I stepped out of the dressing room.

Silvia took a sharp intake of breath and motioned for me to turn. I did a slow spin in front of her. "Oh, Katie."

She put a hand over her mouth, and her eyes teared up. "That dress is fabulous."

"She's gonna need a damn bodyguard to wear that," Vicky said. "And for the record, I volunteer."

"It's fabulous, isn't it?" I squealed as I checked out my reflection in the three-way mirror. "It makes me look so thin."

Vicky rolled her eyes. "Katie, you *are* thin."

"I really like it." Silvia turned me around again to check out the back. "And Cooper will love it."

"I hope you know CPR," Vicky said. "Because Cooper's gonna have a heart attack when he sees you in this."

We fell into a fit of giggles. Cooper would *definitely* have a heart attack. I couldn't imagine a more perfect dress for a Valentine's Day proposal.

"Okay, this is it." I reached for the tag then changed my mind, letting it fall to the side. "I don't care how much it costs. I'm getting this dress."

Vicky bumped my shoulder. "If you don't, I will."

"Oh, no, this one's mine." I tapped my index finger absently against my lips as I ran accessory choices through my head. "Red or black shoes?"

"Red," Vicky said.

Silvia nodded. "Definitely, red."

"And you know what they say about red shoes, right?" Vicky flashed one of her trademark evil grins.

I groaned. I knew exactly what that smile meant. "I'm afraid to ask."

"Red shoes..." She trailed off, letting the moment drag on. "Oh, don't tell me... you seriously don't know?"

Silvia and I both shook our heads.

"I thought everyone knew the saying 'Red shoes, no underwear.'"

"That's ridiculous." Silvia waved her hand as if swatting away the thought. "I've never heard of that."

"It's true!" Vicky insisted.

"Well, red shoes or not, I'm wearing underwear tomorrow night." And thanks to Silvia, I had a wide selection of black lacy thongs to choose from.

After paying for my dress, shoes, and assorted lacy underthings, I checked my phone for messages. Cooper hadn't left a single one, but I had six messages from my mother. Her questions ranged from grooming habits to sexual mechanics. Someone needed to take away her Netflix.

"Look what you've done!" I shoved my phone in front of Vicky's face. "Apparently, my mother and her friend Bette Wilcox would like to know if I prefer oral sex or dildos!"

Vicky smirked. "It's not an either-or thing. It's more of a both, preferably at the same time. And as for dildos, my personal favorite is the double-headed pleasure wand. It lights up when both heads are—"

"It's not funny! I'll never live this down. My mother's bad enough, but you don't know Bette Wilcox. You may as well have put a front-page ad in *USA Today*. The woman has a memory like an elephant, and she's already planning a garden party in the spring to announce my coming out."

Vicky exploded into hysterics. "I'm sorry. I had no idea your mom would find out. I swear!"

"Yeah, well, she did. So now you owe me."

Vicky leaned in and dropped her voice to a sultry whisper. "I know a perfect way for you to collect."

"Don't even go there." After the day I'd had, I wasn't in the mood.

"Speaking of going somewhere..." Silvia jumped into the conversation, effectively changing the subject.

I turned in time to see the mischievous look Silvia gave me. I eyed her with suspicion. "What?"

"It's only eight thirty. We still have time." Her face lit up, and I knew instantly where her thoughts had gone.

With a resigned groan, I threw up my hands. "We may as well." When Silvia wanted something, resistance was futile. Besides, she'd driven.

Vicky already had her phone pressed to her ear. "I'll call Phil. You call June."

# Margaritas and Señoritas

S ILVIA DROVE LIKE A MANIAC to get to our Friday-night karaoke spot, and once we arrived, I stood outside the door, staring through the glass into the smoky bar. I hadn't set foot in Don Juan's in weeks. The place brought back a lot of memories, both good and bad. The first time I'd sung on that stage marked the beginning of my relationship with Cooper. My last time was memorable for entirely different reasons, most of them bad.

"Go ahead. I'll be right in." I had a sudden and overwhelming urge to hear Cooper's voice.

They disappeared into the bar while I hit the speed dial and waited on pins and needles for the call to connect. He should have been finished with all his meetings by now.

One ring... two rings... *If he doesn't pick up after the third ring, hang up.* I'd just about given up when a woman's voice said, "Hello?"

"I'm sorry. I must have dialed the wrong—" I checked the display to find Cooper's face grinning up at me. "Wait, who is this?"

"Vivian Allen," the voice purred. "And who am I speaking to?"

*Why is she answering Cooper's phone?* My stomach plummeted. "It's Katie."

"I'm sorry, Kathy—"

"*Katie.*" I spit out my name as a sudden jolt of jealousy kick-started my heart. "Katie James. Cooper's *girlfriend.*"

"Right. Well, *Katie,* I'm sorry, but Cooper can't come

to the phone right now. He's a little... um, tied up," she whispered the last two words as if letting me in on a big secret.

*Tied up? What does that even mean? And why did she have to say it that way? Like he was tied to the bed naked. Not naked. Don't think like that. He wouldn't do that. He loves you.*

"Katie? Are you still there?"

"Oh, yep, still here. So, um, Vivian... why are you answering Cooper's phone?" I didn't know why I asked, but like that stupid cat, the curiosity ate away at me.

"Maybe you should ask Cooper." Her voice dripped venom. She knew she had me rattled, the viper. I could almost hear her smile. "But since now obviously isn't a good time, can I take a message?"

"Just have him call me when he's untied... I mean when he's not too busy. Uh, working. Because you work together, so you'd know when he was done. Working. Anyway... so, yeah, thank you. Bye." I quickly ended the call before I said something I'd regret.

Or something *else* I'd regret. I sounded like a complete idiot. And the best remedy for a devastating blow to the dignity was margaritas and karaoke. So I took a deep breath—my last breath of fresh air for a while—and stepped into the smoky bar.

It didn't take me long to find June and Vicky beside our usual table, screaming in the direction of the stage. I immediately turned to see what had them so excited and did a quick double take. A man wearing a red sequined dress worthy of *La Cage Aux Folles* and the largest pair of patent-leather black stilettos I'd ever seen strutted around the stage, doing the world's worst Cyndi Lauper impersonation.

I stared with my mouth hanging open. "Oh my God, is that Phil?"

"Yep." Silvia kept her back to the stage as if she couldn't

bear to watch while Vicky recorded the spectacle on her phone, and June clapped and cheered like a teenage girl at a Justin Bieber concert.

On stage, Phil waved his sparkly arms around as he belted out "Girls Just Wanna Have Fun" at the top of his lungs. As usual, he was completely off-key and not even close to keeping up with the beat. It was the most pathetic display Don Juan's had seen since the last time I was there. That time, it had been me making a fool of myself.

By the time he reached the chorus, I had to turn away. "How drunk is he?"

"Oh, he isn't drunk yet," Vicky shouted over the music.

My eyes went wide. "He picked this song sober?" I didn't even want to know about the outfit.

"*He* didn't pick it," June said with a sadistic glimmer in her eye. I'd never seen her look so devious before. Maybe Vicky had rubbed off on her.

"Well, if he didn't pick it..." I studied each of their faces in turn. "Who did?"

Silvia snickered. "The better question would be: what bet did he lose?"

"What bet?" I slid into the booth beside Silvia.

June smiled but didn't give anything else away.

"He and June had a bet that he was just as fallible as anyone else. And the man didn't just *lose*—he lost *spectacularly*." Vicky gleefully watched Phil humiliate himself.

Things were getting interesting. "What exactly did he do?"

"He broke one of his precious rules. And now he's getting payback for every dirty, underhanded thing he's ever done and a few he hasn't thought of yet." June ground out the words. "Vicky's going to post it on YouTube so he'll never forget."

Finally, I could ask the question I'd been dying to ask

all day. "Is that why you were so mad this morning? What rule did he break?"

A dark cloud crossed over June's features.

I waited, but when she didn't answer, I turned to Silvia. "Oh, come on, you can't leave me hanging. I know it's bad if Phil willingly got up on stage in a dress and high heels with Vicky recording him."

Silvia bit back a laugh. "Someone broke the toilet in the men's room, so Phil decided to use the ladies' room."

"Oh." That didn't seem all that bad. I would have ignored the damn rules if I'd been in his shoes. "Did he leave the seat up or something? Oh no! You didn't fall in, did you?"

"Oh, it was a little worse than that." Silvia chuckled.

"Much worse," June said.

"What could be worse than falling in the toilet?" I glanced to the stage, where Phil had gone all out for the final chorus.

Silvia put her hand over her mouth to hold back the laughter. "Leaving the door unlocked for just anyone to walk in."

"No."

"Oh, yes. June walked in while he was..." Silvia couldn't get the words out before she dissolved into convulsions.

"While he *what*?" My eyes darted between them. "Silvia!"

Vicky turned to me over her shoulder. "June saw more of Phil than his wife has in months. I wish I'd gotten *that* on video."

I bit my lip, unfortunately visualizing the scenario, and broke into nervous giggles. No wonder June was so upset. "I guess that'll teach him to pee in the ladies'."

"Oh, he wasn't, uh, using the toilet, exactly," June stammered.

I widened my eyes, psychically trying to pull the rest of the sentence from her. "Well, what exactly *was* he doing?"

When no one else answered, Vicky blew out an

exasperated breath. "Oh, for Chrissake, he was rubbing one out on the company dime."

"Oh, yuck!" I swallowed down a dry heave. I didn't think I'd ever be able to look at Phil the same way again.

"For the record, I was *not* rubbing one out, as Vicky so colorfully put it." Phil slid into the booth, half out of breath and covered in a sheen of sweat. He grabbed the pitcher of beer and downed half of it without taking a breath.

Vicky waited for Phil to catch his breath before tossing another accusation at him. "Really? You always moan and groan when you pee?"

Phil almost laughed but caught himself in time. "I was sighing with relief because I'd been holding it so long."

"So if your back was to the door, how'd June get an eyeful of your junk?" Vicky kept the camera rolling while she questioned him.

Phil threw up his arms, clearly exasperated. "Because she screamed when she walked in. I turned around. It was instinct!"

Vicky smirked and cocked an eyebrow. "With your dick still in your hand?"

Phil groaned. "That's where it was when she screamed. It's not like I had time to put it away. I just reacted."

June smoothed the front of her bright-fuchsia blouse before sliding into the booth beside me, looking as smug as I'd ever seen her. "And *that* is why we have rules."

Phil searched everyone's face before settling his gaze on me. He shot me a look that said he knew I was completely out of the loop. "You know what, James? Payback is a bitch, and her name is June."

"Okay, enough about payback. It's time for margaritas!" Silvia trilled in her terrible Spanish accent.

The waitress brought a tray with two pitchers and three glasses—Phil still had half a pitcher of beer on the table— and June did the pouring. I held out my glass for a toast.

"To the best friends a girl could have." I clinked my

glass to each of theirs and took a long pull on the straw until my head ached with the familiar brain freeze.

Vicky leaned across the table to shout, "So when is Mr. Romance going to pop the question?"

"Stop calling him that." I groaned. After my brief chat with Vivian, the nickname suddenly took on a whole new meaning. And I didn't like it.

"Fine. When is Cooper going to pop the question? It's been weeks since he confessed his sins and professed his undying love." She rolled her eyes, her voice echoing into the margarita glass as she poured the last of her drink into her open mouth. At that moment, the word *sins* stuck out in my head more than *love*.

"Oh, that's enough." Silvia waved her hand. "I'm sure he'll propose when he's ready."

"Tomorrow night!" I blurted, trying to convince myself as much as them. "He's going to propose for Valentine's Day. He practically told me so. He has something extra-special planned, something he had to do covert shopping for. What else could that mean?" I sucked down the last of my drink with a loud slurp and waved for a refill.

"Slow down, Katie," Silvia warned. "Have you forgotten what happened the last time you drank margaritas?"

I cringed, remembering all too well. But that time, my mother had been in town, driving me to drink.

"Valentine's Day, huh? I wouldn't expect him to go the cliché route, but hey, a ring is a ring, right?" Phil mused. I found it difficult to take him seriously with his hairy legs poking out the bottom of a sparkly dress.

"It's going to be perfect," I muttered to myself. "Silvia helped me pick out the perfect dress. I have the perfect lingerie and the most *perfect* boyfriend in the world." Perfectly unreachable. Perfectly far away, with his perfect publicist answering his perfect phone.

"Katie, are you drunk?" June patted my hand.

"No." I sucked the last of my drink through the straw with a loud slurp. "I've only had one."

"Two," Silvia and Vicky chimed together.

I gazed down at the remnants of my frozen concoction with a frown then shrugged and picked up the glass. *Waste not, want not, right?*

One and a half margaritas later, Silvia took my glass and wouldn't give it back. After singing his favorite song, I drunk-dialed Cooper's voice mail not once, but twice, and she took my phone too.

"This is your fault," I slurred.

Silvia slid her reading glasses down her nose and looked at me over them. "My fault you can't reach Cooper?"

"No. Your fault I'm all Drunky Brewster again. You made me eat rabbit food for dinner. If I'd eaten a cheeseburger like I wanted, I'd be fine."

Vicky laughed. "Katie, you could've eaten two cheeseburgers, and you'd *still* be drunk after three margaritas."

"Three and a half," Silvia added.

"That's what it was... that extra half." I picked at my cuticles. "I probably should have stopped at three."

"One," Silvia said. "You should have stopped after one."

Across the table, my phone chirped, and we all stopped what we were doing to stare at it.

"Is that..." I reached for it at the same time as Silvia, and this time, she let me have it. With my heart pounding and a level of dexterity I shouldn't have been able to master, I pulled up my messages only to have my hopes dashed.

"Well?" Silvia leaned forward, trying to read over my shoulder.

I let out a loud sigh. "My mother wants to know if it was her or my dad who drove me to join the lesbians."

"Wait." Phil screwed up his face as he studied mine. "When did you become a lesbian?"

Silvia dropped me off at Cooper's at a quarter to twelve, but by then, I was wired with anxiety. I hadn't heard from Cooper since the whole Facebook thing that afternoon, and after talking to Vivian, my imagination had gotten the better of me. Visions of Cooper tied to a bed naked—something I didn't have to try all that hard to imagine—danced through my head. Only this time, Vivian controlled the ropes, not me.

Jealousy spread through me like a virus until a light bulb went off in my head. It was a terrible idea, but after two more calls to Cooper went straight to voice mail, I needed something to distract me.

Taking the stairs two at a time, I ran all the way to the CRWAT, or chandelier room with adjoining toilet—the nickname I'd given Cooper's ridiculously opulent bathroom—and dug through the linen closet until I found the waxing kit I'd stashed there earlier in the week. With the kit in hand, I headed back to the kitchen to prepare everything.

While heating the wax in the microwave, I skimmed through the instructions. It looked simple enough—as easy as ripping off a Band-Aid. Just three basic steps: wax on, wax off, wipe off the residue. *How hard could it be?*

If I'd been sober, I might've reconsidered smearing what looked like boiled peanut butter anywhere near my girl parts. But I wasn't. The directions suggested dusting the area to be waxed with baby powder or cornstarch, but since I didn't have either, I searched the dark walnut cupboards for something similar. We were out of flour, but we did have a box of pancake mix. *Close enough.*

In an effort to save steps, I dropped my pants right there in the kitchen and set to work. After pulling on the rubber gloves that came in the kit, I sprinkled a little pancake mix on my crotch then dusted off the excess. *So far, so good.* I dipped the giant Popsicle stick into the hot wax and spread a thick layer over my bikini area. *Smells like Waffle House in here.* I gave the wax a few seconds to cool then attempted to flick up the end like the instructions said. *What does that even mean?* I had no idea how to "flick" the end of the wax, especially with sticky goop stuck to my fingers.

"This isn't wax. It's glue," I muttered as I picked at the edge of the hardened wax strip.

After several minutes, I only managed to chip away at it like old nail polish, if old nail polish had the consistency of tree sap. I had wax molded to the seam of my leg and a sticky trail all the way from my knees to my elbows. It felt like I'd rolled around in flypaper. And no matter how hard I scrubbed, it wouldn't come off, even after using the entire vial of oil specifically designed to remove the residue.

*What do I do now?*

Nothing. Not in the middle of the night, half drunk and barely able to keep my eyes open. I tossed the gloves onto the granite island, then without bothering to put anything away, I dragged myself up the stairs and crawled into Cooper's bed, tucking the blankets around me like a cocoon. The wax would still be there when I woke up.

# Hair Today, Goo Gone Tomorrow

SOMEWHERE IN THE BACK OF my pounding head, I knew it was morning. Vague images from the night before floated behind my eyelids, but none of them made sense to my fuzzy brain. I couldn't imagine why Cooper would be tied to railroad tracks or why someone in a Waffle House would be tugging on a fistful of my pubic hair. Then I remembered the phone call with Vivian, the three point five margaritas... and, *oh God*, the wax.

I groaned, silently chastising myself for drinking that third margarita and half of the fourth. After saying a quick prayer for my head to either stop pounding or just go ahead and explode, I nestled back into the pillows for a few more minutes. I'd almost drifted back to sleep when I heard a loud noise from downstairs.

I bolted upright in bed and let out a bloodcurdling shriek of pain as something vital ripped in the vicinity of my groin. *I'm on fire. My pubic bone is on fire!* That was the only explanation I could come up with.

I pulled back the covers to inspect my injured lady bits. "What the hell?" I was naked from the waist down—I had no idea why—with a strip of thick dark hair attached to my inner thigh and a very obvious bald spot where my pubic hair used to be. "No, no, no... What did I do?"

And it wasn't just my pubic hair stuck to me, either. Tufts of blue fuzz from the fleece blanket clung to the dozens of sticky patches on my skin, and one of the rubber gloves I *thought* I'd thrown in the trash had managed to glue itself to my ass. I even found an earring—one I'd lost weeks ago—stuck to my leg. "I look like I escaped from Madame Tussauds Wax Museum."

Once I finished reciting every swear word in my personal vocabulary, I heard another bang from downstairs. Something or someone was inside the house! *How is that possible?* I was sure I'd set the alarm. And after my ordeal with gun-wielding security guards in the middle of the night, I knew all too well how sensitive that alarm system was. I shuddered. *Where is the security team now?*

I heard it again—this time not a bang but footsteps on the stairs. I recognized the creak on the fourth step from the top.

*Oh. My. God!*

Someone was only four steps from the top!

I grabbed my phone and sprang from the bed with my legs still tangled in the covers. I hit the carpet hard, knocking the wind out of me. With my nose deep in carpet fiber, I struggled to pull in a breath. After what seemed like forever, I managed to scramble to my feet and made a mad dash for the bathroom.

As I rounded the corner, I heard the doorknob rattle and let out another bloodcurdling scream that echoed loudly against the marble in the CRWAT. I locked the bathroom door before running to the water closet and locking myself in. Sitting on the toilet seat with my feet perched on the rim, I loosened the death grip on my phone to dial 9-1-1. Before I entered the first digit, it rang in my hand.

"Cooper!"

"Katie?"

"Oh, thank God. Someone's in the house!" I blurted out in a frantic whisper.

But instead of reacting with horror as I expected, he laughed.

"I'm not kidding. I heard a noise. Well, more of a bang. Then I heard someone on the stairs. And now they're outside the bathroom door!" My whisper cranked up a notch, raw panic seeping into my voice.

"Katie..." he said calmly.

I was so *not* calm. In fact, I was this close to losing it. "What should I do?"

"Open the door."

"Are you crazy?" I shrieked.

"It's me." He chuckled. "I'm outside the door."

It took a few seconds for his words to sink in. "You're here?"

"Yes, I took the red-eye home. Now please let me in. I've missed you."

"I missed you too, but..." I glanced down at myself. White carpet fibers had joined the blue fuzz, making me look like a balding Muppet. And the damned rubber glove was *still* attached to my ass. I ripped it off, swallowing a squeal as it took the top layer of skin with it.

"Katie?" Cooper interrupted my mini breakdown. "Can I come in?"

I shook my head, making myself dizzy. If he saw me now, he'd take one look and run the other way. "No."

"What?" He sounded as surprised as the time I'd accused him of being a hired killer.

"No," I said more firmly. "You can't come in."

Cooper went from lighthearted to concerned in a nanosecond. I could almost hear the vein in his forehead pulsing. "What's wrong?"

"Nothing," I lied unconvincingly. I was a terrible liar.

"Don't tell me 'nothing.' I can tell something's wrong. Let me in." Cooper must have slammed his fist into the bathroom door, because I heard the sound through the phone but also through the wall.

"I can't." I tried to keep calm, but I was far from it.

"Katie..." Cooper raised his voice until I could hear him in stereo. "If you don't let me in, I'm breaking down this door."

"No!" I jumped up from the toilet and held on to the doorknob as if that would keep him out. "You can't."

"Why?" Cooper's temper was a rare and glorious thing. I almost wished I could watch him pacing like an angry lion.

"Because I, uh..." *Think, Katie. Think.* "Because I'm naked!" *No, not that!* I clamped a hand over my mouth to stop the stupid before it escaped again.

He chuckled, and the tension drained from his voice. "You know, I've seen you naked before. And honestly, it's been too long since the last time."

I groaned. It *had* been too long. But no way in hell would I let Cooper see me when I looked like a leper from the Yankee Candle colony. "Cooper. Please. I'm, uh..." I sucked in a ragged breath while I thought up another lie and thought it up quick. "I don't want to spoil the surprise. It's Valentine's Day, you know."

"Oh." He didn't say anything else for what seemed like a long time. "You have a surprise for me?"

*Boy, do I ever!* I dropped down onto the toilet lid again, relieved that he'd fallen for my ruse. "Yes. But if you don't let me, uh, finish preparing it, you'll ruin it. You don't want to ruin my surprise, do you?"

"I don't know. That depends." He sounded suspicious but unconcerned. "Does it have anything to do with the mess in the kitchen? It looks as though you were building a bomb down there."

"Yes. Err, no. I mean, it does have to do with the mess, but no, I'm not building a bomb." Though that non-bomb had spectacularly blown up in my face.

"Do you know how long this surprise will take?"

"No more than a few hours." *I hope.* "Why don't you pick me up at my townhouse at seven? It'll be like a real date."

"A real date, huh? I suppose I can do that. And I have a few last-minute details I need to attend to while you're tied up."

*Tied up?* His unfortunate word choice sent my thoughts reeling. For the briefest moment, I considered telling him about my phone call with Vivian and demanding an explanation. But my rational side quickly took over and refused to allow me to wander down that dark path. In fact, I decided I would completely put it out of my mind. For now. "What kind of details?"

"Well, for starters, I have a special dinner planned, so be sure to wear something nice. I expect it to be a night to remember."

Vivian no longer mattered as his words hung in the air, and I got caught up in the spell of his voice. *A night to remember...*

He let out a nervous laugh. "You still there?"

Trying to clear the fog, I gave my head a little shake. "Uh, yeah. Yes. I'm here."

"I missed you last night," he whispered.

"I missed you too."

More than anything, I wanted to hang up the stupid phone and let him into the bathroom. And I would have, if I hadn't remembered one horrible little detail.

*I'm still covered in wax.*

The instant Cooper backed his BMW out of the garage, I called for reinforcements. I could think of only one person to help me with my dilemma. Yet, somewhere in the deep recesses of my mind, I knew I'd regret what I was about to do. In a big way.

Twenty minutes later, Vicky answered her door wearing a black leather mini skirt and a red silky blouse. "I knew you'd come around." Her crimson lips curved up at the corners as she took in my oversized gray sweats and Converse sneakers. "But I sort of hoped you'd be dressed a little nicer when you showed up."

I exhaled the breath I was holding. "Don't make me regret calling you."

"Whatever." She rolled her eyes. "Do you want my help or not?"

I bit my lip, debating whether I should step through the gateway to hell or call Cooper and come clean about my little problem. It took less than thirty seconds to decide. "Yes. I need your help, okay?"

She swung the door wide to let me in. "It's more than okay. I'd say it makes us even."

"Not quite. But if you can de-sticky me before my engagement dinner, I'll consider it."

Vicky pursed her lips and nodded. "I can work with that. Deal."

"So where do we begin? And please, don't start with the sexual comments. My nerves are already stretched about as far as they'll go. I had to lie to Cooper to get away. I told him I was working on a special Valentine's Day surprise for him, but if I don't fix this, the surprise will be on me when he dumps me for someone who doesn't manage to tar and feather herself on a semi-regular basis."

"Fine. I'll be on my best behavior, but you're going to have to drop your pants, so you'd better leave modesty at the door."

"I was afraid you'd say that," I muttered as I followed Vicky up the stairs to her tiny yet spotlessly clean bathroom.

She rubbed her hands together with a bit too much glee. "Okay, let's see the damage."

"It's pretty bad."

"I'll be the judge of that." Vicky leaned against the sink and waited.

I kept my eyes focused on the black-and-white octagonal tiles as I let Cooper's sweatpants fall to the floor.

She gasped. "Jesus, Katie. You only have half a bush!"

"I know..." My cheeks burned as I felt Vicky's eyes rake over me.

Her warm breath fanned out over my hip, making me shudder. "Holy shit, the other half's stuck to your leg!"

"Yeah. I'm aware of that too." My stomach flip-flopped at her proximity, and not in a good way. I felt like a failed science experiment.

She circled me like a shark sizing up its dinner. "And what the hell happened to your ass?"

"Glove," I mumbled the word, hoping she'd let it go. I should've known better.

I flinched as she fingered the raw skin where the rubber glove had spent the better part of the night. "Glove? What glove?"

"Can we not worry about that right now? I have bigger issues to deal with."

"Right. Like the bald spot where your bush used to be. You weren't kidding when you said it would be a special surprise. That"—she drew a circle in the air in front of my girl bits—"is something special, all right. How in hell's half acre did you pull that off?"

"Literally? Apparently, I glued myself to... *myself*. In my sleep."

"Did you actually use glue?"

I scowled. "No, I didn't use glue! I used wax."

"What kind of wax?" She continued her perusal of my sticky places, plucking the occasional bit of blue fluff.

"I don't know? The hair-removal kind. I bought a kit about a week ago and decided to pull it out of the closet after I got home last night."

"Didn't your mother ever tell you not to drink and wax? If waxing-while-intoxicated isn't a crime, it should be."

"Ha. Ha. Very funny. Trust me, I'm paying the price."

"Yeah." She laughed. "It cost you half a bush."

"Would you stop saying *bush*?" I whispered the last word as if it had mystical powers.

"Bush, bush, bush," Vicky chanted.

I glared at her, and she rolled her eyes. "Can you help me or not?"

"That depends." She stood straight and crossed her arms.

"On what?"

"On what exactly you mean by *help*. I can help you get the wax off, most of it, anyway, but I can't glue your bush back together." Vicky sat on the edge of the tub so she was at eye level with my crotch.

"Let's start with the wax first. I'll deal with my... with *the rest* after that."

"Okay." She reached behind her and opened the tap to fill the tub.

"What are you doing?"

"Isn't it obvious? I'm letting the water get hot."

"I already tried washing it off."

"Oh, I don't want you to take a bath. We're going to run hot water over your crotch until the wax melts right off."

I yanked up my sweats and backed into the wall. "Oh, no, we are not! My skin'll melt off long before the wax does."

"Oh, right. You've got a point. Wait. I have an idea!" Vicky jumped up and bolted from the room. She came back less than a minute later with a bottle of Goo Gone. "We'll use this."

The smell—a cross between artificial orange candies and motor oil—hit me the instant she opened the yellow bottle. "Is that even safe to use on skin?"

"Sure, why not?" Vicky poured some onto a jumbo cotton ball and rubbed at a spot on my forearm. "I use it all the time."

When the wax came off after a minute or two, she moved to the next spot and then the next until we were working together on the thick patch glued to my thigh.

"It's not coming off."

"Yeah, no shit." Vicky dumped Goo Gone directly on the spot. "It's too thick." Using her fingernail to get under the wax, Vicky chipped it off, one chunk at a time.

While she picked at the wax, I followed behind her, scouring away the sticky residue. "Is it supposed to burn?"

"That's just because you're scrubbing so hard."

After nearly forty-five minutes and a bottle and a half of Goo Gone, I'd rubbed my fingers raw, but the wax—and several patches of skin—had vanished. Unfortunately, thanks to the Goo Gone, I smelled like I'd bathed in a chemical cocktail.

"Well, step one was a success." Vicky washed her hands. "Time for step two."

A nervous laugh rolled up my throat. "I'm almost afraid to ask."

"Well, you can't leave it like that." She darted her eyes to my exposed nether regions.

I didn't waste any time pulling my sweats back on. "Leave what like what?"

"You can't be that clueless." When I didn't reply, she huffed. "Your hooch. You need to finish what you started and remove the rest of that hair."

"I'm not sure about that..."

"Don't be stupid." She grabbed her phone from the vanity. "I'll call my girl at the Brazilian place. I'm sure she can squeeze you in."

"Thank you, but I'd really rather not. I'm done with wax for a while. Maybe forever."

Vicky looked up at me with her eyebrow cocked. "It's either get the Brazilian, or go to dinner with half a bush."

"I can just shave—"

"You can't just shave the other half. You'll end up with a five o'clock shadow on one side. And trust me, that's the last thing you want if Cooper ends up up close and personal with your goodies. You want the man to get razor burn on his gorgeous face?"

"No... no, I don't want that." *How could I subject the man I love to razor burn?*

As the reality of the situation began to sink in, I got that sick feeling in the pit of my stomach—the one usually reserved for my mother. I wasn't sure if it was from the solvent fumes or because I was about to submit to an honest-to-goodness bikini wax, the full Monty of bikini waxes, in fact. The idea terrified me. I'd just freed myself of my waxy shackles, and now I was about to willingly allow someone else to start over again from scratch. And after the one strip I'd inadvertently pulled, I knew how painful it would be: infinitely more painful than pulling off a Band-Aid.

"Fine." I sighed. "Make the appointment."

# Bedazzle My Heart

VICKY HAD ME FOLLOW HER to the spa so I wouldn't get lost—or chicken out—and she stood impatiently beside my car while I worked up the courage to unbuckle my seat belt and get out. To be honest, if she hadn't, I was pretty sure I would've turned around and driven right out of the parking lot.

Vicky knocked on the glass. "You've stalled long enough. Get out."

With my knees shaking and every drop of color draining from my face, I stepped out of the car.

"How is it you look even more pathetic than you did before?" Vicky tilted her head to the side. "If I didn't know better, I'd swear your cat died."

If I'd had the energy, I would've been offended. But since my cat was perfectly fine—and entirely imaginary—I let it go.

"Come on, you big chicken." Vicky linked her arm with mine, and I flinched. She laughed as she towed me toward the door. "I'm not going to bite you."

I didn't believe her. I had the distinct feeling she *would* bite me given the opportunity. But since I didn't have any other options, I let her drag me inside anyway.

Women of all ages packed the reception area. Clearly, I wasn't the only one with a hairless Valentine's Day in my future. Vicky found us two chairs near a miniature waterfall cascading down the wall. The soft sound of waves crashing against the shore played in the background, and essential oils scented the air. The Zen-like setting was meant to be calming, but I wasn't calm. Not at all. Every muscle in my body tensed like a giant mousetrap ready to snap. And I had to pee.

Vicky leaned in and whispered in my ear, "If you clench your jaw any tighter, your teeth'll crack."

I sucked in a lungful of lavender and tried to relax, but it was useless. "Remind me why I'm here again."

"Because you handle your liquor about as well as a fifth-grader?"

I shot her an icy glare.

Vicky pressed her lips together in a horrible attempt to hide her smile. "Don't blame me! I'm not the one who decided to pull out the wax kit after four margaritas."

"Three and a half." I knew I was pouting, but I didn't care.

"Oh, cheer up." Vicky bumped my shoulder with hers. "At least now you'll have an excuse to give Cooper the Valentine's surprise that keeps on giving. Sex is so much better with a bare—"

"Okay, I get it!" My little outburst attracted the attention of everyone over the age of thirty, and I slumped down in my chair. As much as I hated to admit it, and as misguided and insane as it was, she did have a point. Planned or not, getting waxed would add an element of surprise to the evening. After Cooper slid that ring on my finger, I'd have something equally shocking to give him in return. He wouldn't be the only one with a few tricks up his sleeve.

Before I knew it, a tiny woman in a white lab coat called my name in a thick German accent. "Katie James?"

With a faint whimper, I shot a panicked plea to Vicky. The acute memory of hair ripping from my lady bits kept me frozen in place.

"Come, come." The woman—who had to have been close to eighty—motioned for me for me to follow her.

Vicky nudged me with her elbow. "Get going."

"I changed my mind. I'm going to leave it as it is. Maybe Cooper will think I'm being trendy."

"Half a bush is *not* trendy. It's stupid." Vicky got up and yanked me from my chair while Lab Coat Lady watched from the open doorway. "You're going with Helga to get your hooch waxed if I have to carry you and hold you down while she rips your hair out!"

I gasped. "You wouldn't dare!"

"Just watch me."

Staring into Vicky's flinty eyes, I knew she meant what she'd said. Without giving her a chance to make good on her promise, I swallowed hard and nodded.

Helga led me to a quiet little room reeking of patchouli and vanilla. Candles burned on every flat surface, and the same ocean sounds played softly in the background, but nothing could distract me from the table in the center of the room. Flashing back to my last gynecologist appointment, I instinctively clenched my pelvic muscles.

"Here." Helga handed me a paper drape, the same kind they used at my doctor's office. "Take off your pants, and lie on the table."

My eyes darted between Helga and the drape, and I gulped. *What am I doing, besides exposing myself to a total stranger while she forcibly removes my body hair? Right. Just another Saturday.*

She must have seen the fear in my eyes because she smiled and patted my hand with an icy one of her own. "Don't worry. It'll all be over soon."

*It'll all be over soon.* Why didn't her promise comfort me in the least?

Keeping the drape in front of me, I dropped the sweats and climbed onto the table as instructed. White paper crinkled beneath my rear as I worked to find a comfortable position.

When I hadn't stopped fidgeting after the better part of a minute, Helga gripped my thighs and dragged me to the end of the table. For an old lady, she was incredibly strong. "Relax your knees."

*Relax?* I almost laughed, but the stern expression on Helga's face stopped me cold. Instead, I dropped my head back against the cushion and said a silent prayer that my ordeal would, in fact, be over soon.

Helga moved with clinical precision. The wax was incredibly warm but not at all pleasant. It tugged on my hair as she spread it in the hollow where my leg met the V. I tensed, using every last drop of my control to stay still. She hummed a familiar tune as she smoothed a strip of cloth over the hot wax then, without a word of warning, ripped the hair from my already-abused skin.

My ass came off the table as a string of obscenities I'd never put together in a sentence flew out of my mouth like I was possessed. "Holy-fucking-shit-guzzling-mother-fucker-that-hurts!"

Helga winked. The bitch actually winked!

The next thing I knew, Vicky stood beside me, brushing sweaty tendrils of hair from my face. I hadn't even realized she'd followed me into the room. "If you're a good girl, I'll take you for ice cream when she's finished."

Unless she'd planned on spreading mint chocolate chip over my injured crotch, I had no interest in ice cream. Or being a good girl, for that matter.

"Let's just go. I don't even care if my girlie bits look like a yin yang symbol. I'll keep the lights off. Or I'll... I'll tell him I'm on my period!" I tried to sit up, but she pushed me back down.

"No, you won't." Vicky kept her palm pressed to my chest. "You'll suck it up and let her finish."

"But it hurts." I whined like a five-year-old getting a tetanus shot.

"Oh, it doesn't hurt that much." Vicky clucked her tongue in a remarkable impersonation of Silvia. "You're just a baby."

My lips curved into a frown. I had to admit, it was entirely possible I was being a baby.

Vicky turned to Helga. "Give us a minute?" As soon as Helga stepped out of the room, Vicky fished through her purse and handed me a prescription bottle.

I turned the bottle over in my hand. "What's this?"

"Xanax." She took the bottle from me and opened it, pouring a pale-blue oval into my hand. "Take this. It'll help you relax."

"Is it safe?"

"Sure." She shrugged. "It'll just take the edge off."

"I-I don't know." I studied the pill.

She walked to the door, tossing me her water bottle. "Here. You might need this."

After washing down the Xanax, I dropped back against the table with a renewed sense of courage and waited for Helga to return. I didn't have to wait long.

Helga perched on the edge of the stool between my legs, holding the wax-covered stick like a weapon. "Ready?"

With a slow, steadying breath, I nodded.

*Rip!*

For the record, I wasn't ready. Not at all. And the Xanax didn't help. The ripping was just as brutal the second time. And the third, and the forth, for that matter. Swallowing scream after scream, I chanted, "This is for Cooper, this is for Cooper..." until somewhere after the fifth wax strip, I drifted into a beautiful oblivion.

After what could've been days for all I knew, I woke to Vicky's face hovering over mine.

"Oh, good." The lines in her forehead smoothed out. "I thought you were dead."

"What happened?"

"You passed out."

"How long was I out?"

"Uh, just long enough to finish."

*Finish?* As the fog lifted, I remembered why I was lying

on a table with a strange woman between my legs. "Oh, right. So I'm done?"

"All done." Helga peeled off her rubber gloves and flashed her stained teeth in a wide grin. Then she climbed off her stool and slipped from the room with a grace I wouldn't have expected from someone so old.

As soon as the door shut behind her, I hopped off the table and reached for my pants. That's when I noticed the sparkle.

"What the hell?" My heart skipped and stuttered as I darted my eyes between Vicky and the red-jeweled heart taking up nearly every inch of skin between my legs. "You roofied me and bedazzled my... my...?"

Vicky held up a finger. "First of all, I didn't roofie you. I offered you a Xanax, and you took it. I can't help it if you handle your sedatives as well as you handle your liquor. And as for the heart, it's called vajazzling, and yes, I had her vajazzle your hooch. It'll help hide the wax residue and cover up the missing skin."

"I can't go home like this!"

"Sure you can!" Vicky beamed as if she'd just won the Golden Dildo Award in Las Vegas. With the paper sheet pooled at my feet, she was able to openly stare at Helga's handiwork. "All you need is a big red bow, and this can be your special Valentine's Day surprise."

With my modesty effectively stripped away, I took my time pulling on my sweatpants. Despite Vicky's enthusiasm, I wasn't sold on the vajazzled heart, but I didn't have time to argue. "Well, I don't have a choice now, do I?"

"I guess you'd better get used to it then."

# How many glasses of champagne do I have to drink before finding a ring at the bottom?

FTER SETTLING UP WITH THE spa and thanking Vicky for rescuing me from myself, I raced back to my townhouse in a panic. Ready or not, Cooper would be picking me up in two hours. With the Prius parked and my overnight bag in hand, I headed upstairs to get ready. I only tripped twice as I took the stairs two at a time.

At six thirty-five, I applied the last swipe of mascara to my lashes. Chocolate-brown curls tumbled over my forehead in loose waves, the caramel highlights making the green in my eyes pop. That left nothing to do but get dressed.

Fishing through the shiny pink bag, I freed my pretty new undergarments from the tissue paper and stepped into the sexy black panties. I squirmed against the unbearably scratchy fabric. "Oh... no, no, no." I readjusted the crotch panel to no avail. In a cruel twist of fate, it seemed new lace and freshly waxed skin weren't compatible. "This isn't fair!"

Careful not to snag them on the jeweled heart, I slid the panties back down my legs, where they stayed in a puddle at my feet while I fastened the strapless push-up bra. After several attempts at positioning my breasts in the flimsy cups, followed by a brief struggle with the matching black lace garter belt and a pair of shimmering stockings, I finally managed to shimmy into the snug red dress.

Zipping and adjusting the bodice until I was spilling out just enough to make it sexy without being naughty was almost impossible. Somehow, I pulled it off. I stepped back to gaze at my reflection. Twisting my lips to one side, I studied the dress in the full-length mirror. It was shorter than I remembered. The hem barely skimmed the tops of my knees, and I had to keep tugging the skirt down to keep it from riding up any farther. But I couldn't deny I looked good. In fact, I almost didn't recognize myself.

A cold draft chilled my freshly waxed and jeweled bits. Stupid Vicky and her stupid ideas. *I'm never drinking again! And this time, I might actually mean it.* Scooping my expensive panties from the floor, I contemplated putting them back on and suffering through the discomfort, when I heard a knock at the door. I stuffed the scrap of scratchy lace into my purse for later. Hopefully, I'd find a way to put them on, with just enough time to take them off again.

Cooper knocked again, this time more insistently, and I grabbed the brand-new pair of stilettos sitting beside the bedroom door. *Stupid red shoes.* Vicky would never let me live it down if she found out I'd ended up wearing them without underwear after all. *But what she doesn't know can't come back to haunt me.* Shoving Vicky from my thoughts—hopefully for the last time—I made like Cinderella and ran down the stairs, stepping into my ruby slippers at the bottom.

My stomach dropped to my toes as I slid the deadbolt out of the way and eased the door open. Cooper stood frozen in the glow of the porch light. I drank in every effortlessly stylish inch of him, starting with his thick, dark waves and ending with his shiny black shoes. His tie matched my dress. "You look amazing."

My deliciously handsome boyfriend stepped inside with a smile that lit up the night. His suit—a color that landed somewhere between dark gray and navy—brought out the blue in his eyes. And those eyes were locked on mine. "Me?"

The way he looked at me—like I was about to be dinner, dessert, and breakfast all rolled into one—sent a rush of heat up my neck. My face must have been as red as my dress. "Yes, you. You're—"

"No, Katie," Cooper whispered, wrapping his long fingers around my wrist and tugging me forward to rest his cheek against mine. "You're the one who's stunning."

I took shallow breaths, drawing in his spicy cologne, and ran my fingers along his smooth jaw. "You shaved."

"It seemed like the thing to do." Cooper shrugged and pushed a hand through his hair. He seemed nervous, which made me nervous.

My legs were actually shaking. I almost wished he'd drop to his knees right there in the entryway and propose, just to get it over with. The suspense was killing me. I cleared my throat. "So... where are we going?"

"That, my love, is a secret." His lips brushed mine, making my knees go weak.

I bit back a smile. It was all I could do to keep from clapping like a five-year-old. I already knew his secret.

"Are you ready?" He helped me into my coat.

I nodded. "More than ready."

Cooper put his arm around my shoulder and escorted me to the passenger side of his BMW. He opened the door and waited while I carefully climbed in.

"Is everything okay?"

"Fine." I quickly forced a bright smile to cover my fear of exposure. I struggled to get comfortable on the chilled leather as flashes of celebrity crotch shots, courtesy of *TMZ*, filled my head. I gave another tug on the hem of my dress then tried, and failed, to cover myself with my coat. The last thing I needed was to flash my vajazzled nether regions before dinner.

Cooper slid into the driver's seat and fumbled with the keys. It was almost as though this were our first date, rather than our engagement night. There'd never been a more awkward silence between us. Despite the quiet, I felt the nervous excitement rippling from Cooper in the seat next to me. I could tell he was struggling to keep the smile from his lips.

"Okay, you have two choices... either close your eyes and promise to keep them closed until I say so, or I blindfold you so you aren't tempted to peek. I would really hate to mess up your pretty hair tonight, so it would be better if you could promise not to peek. Though, knowing you, that'll be almost impossible."

It took no time at all to decide. I gave him a resolute nod. "You'd better blindfold me."

"I figured as much." Keeping his eyes on the road, he reached across me and pulled a delicate silk scarf from the glove box. "Can you at least be trusted to put this on?"

"Ye of little faith," I huffed, snatching the scarf from his fingers. I carefully wrapped it around my eyes and tied it loosely in the back. "There. You have me where you want me. Whatever will you do with me now?"

He leaned in until his breath tickled my neck. "I guess you'll have to wait and see. Won't you?"

I laughed, but my insides rippled, twisting into knots. I was afraid my legs wouldn't hold me when it came time to stand.

The car accelerated, speeding through the city streets if the wind rushing past the window was any indication. Less than twenty minutes later, the tires crunched over what must have been a gravel drive, and my stomach fluttered with a fresh batch of butterflies.

"Don't move," Cooper said as he parked the car. Then he got out and ran around to open my door. "Hold on to me so you don't fall."

"I'm not that clumsy." I almost stumbled as I struggled to protect my modesty in the too-short dress.

He laughed. "You're *every bit* that clumsy."

I elbowed him hard in the ribs. He let out an *oof* but didn't say anything more on the subject.

Cooper wordlessly led me into the unknown. We crossed a long stretch of uneven pavement before coming to a stop on a smooth surface. In the distance, water splashed into a pool of some kind. "We're here."

He removed the silk scarf, and I gasped. We stood at the mouth of a cavernous glass atrium filled with hundreds of white flowers. Roses, tulips, snowdrops... even orchids. I couldn't begin to identify all the different varieties of flower in front of me. And in the center of the vast room, under a blanket of stars and thousands of twinkling lights, was a small table dressed for dinner. Dinner for two.

I'd never expected him to outdo our first date, but somehow he had. He'd blown it out of the water. The stunning scenery combined with the sweet blend of fragrances short-circuited my senses, leaving me completely speechless.

"You don't like it?" His eyebrows furrowed as he searched my face.

I blinked up at him. "No."

His mouth dropped open for a moment while I collected my thoughts.

"No, Cooper." I threw my arms around his neck, choking the life out of him based on the strangled sounds he made. "I-I love it."

He set me on my feet again and ushered me to our table. The *only* table, in fact.

Once we were seated, an older man in a black tuxedo wheeled out a cart. He pulled a chilled bottle of champagne from a silver bucket. After making a point of having Cooper inspect the vintage and offering him a sample, he filled the fluted glasses in front of us.

"This is so beautiful. How did you...?" I asked, unshed tears in my eyes.

Cooper smiled, but his eyes softened. "I'll never tell."

"I had no idea the botanical gardens could be rented."

Cooper sipped his drink with a shrug. "You just have to know who to ask."

I caught a glimpse of the bubbles in his glass and picked up mine, inspecting it from several different angles in the faint light before bringing it to my lips for a careful sip.

He watched me with a sparkle in his eyes. "Is everything all right?"

I hoped the dim light would hide the flush as my face went up in flames. "Oh, you know, just looking at the pretty bubbles." I took a big gulp to put out the fire.

*How many glasses of champagne do I have to drink before I find a ring at the bottom?*

I posed the question again after my third glass—to myself, that was. Cooper was blissfully clueless as to my motives. I didn't even like the taste that much. And the bubbles tickled my nose. But I kept drinking. Any more, and I'd need to use the restroom. But after three glasses of the pricey Dom Perignon, I knew if I stood up, there was a good chance I'd fall right back down again.

I caught a glimpse of Cooper in the bottom of my glass.

"Katie?" Deep concern furrowed Cooper's brows as he analyzed my behavior across the table. "Are you okay?"

My lips wouldn't cooperate as I attempted a smile. "I'm wonderful. You're wonderful. Valentine's Day is *wonderful.*" I trilled like a songbird, drunk on life, or in my case, champagne. "Pour me another?"

*Nothing* was wonderful.

My bladder was so full, I sloshed. At this point, I was more than just *slightly* tipsy. And the fourth finger of my left hand was *still* naked. Because despite all the champagne splashing around in my belly, I was pathetically unengaged.

"If you're sure." His eyes narrowed slightly, and he hesitated before filling my glass again.

I wasn't sure of anything anymore. Was I wrong about his intentions? Or maybe... just too early. Maybe his proposal would come later in the evening.

A genuine smile lit up my mood at the thought. The night was still young, after all. And Cooper was nothing if not resourceful. I had no idea what he may have planned for after dinner. Dessert was still to come. Maybe I'd find my ring in a piece of cake.

After checking the bottom one last time, I picked up my glass yet again and touched it to his. "To us."

He flashed his lopsided grin. "To us."

Three excruciating courses later, I forced down my last mouthful of crème brûlée with a shudder. Cooper gaped at me with astonished appreciation as I devoured every last bite of my dessert and my fifth glass of the sickeningly sweet champagne. We'd officially killed the second bottle, leaving me fuller than I'd ever been in all my twenty-nine years.

So stuffed, I was afraid to move, but desperate to visit the restroom. I felt sick. I recognized my symptoms all too well. I was drunk and probably very close to throwing up.

*On Valentine's Day.*

Forcing a smile, I reached across the table to take Cooper's hand in mine. My fingers didn't register the sensation. Never a good sign. "Do you happen know where I might find the ladies' room?"

His horrified expression told me I'd failed at keeping the hysteria out of my voice. "I'll walk you." He offered his hand, and under the circumstances, I had no choice but to accept.

The red shoes teetered ominously as I stood, so in a flash of genius, I kicked them off under the table.

"Have I mentioned how beautiful you look tonight?" Cooper tucked me under his arm without once mentioning how drunk I was. And there was no way he'd missed the signs.

"I wanted tonight to be special." I leaned into him, fighting the urge to cry. How could I have miscalculated the evening so completely?

"It *is* a special evening," Cooper murmured into my hair. "It's our first Valentine's Day, and I haven't even given you your gift yet."

*My gift?*

My body thrummed back to life, sending an exhilarating thrill through me. I practically dragged Cooper to the restroom, leaving him openmouthed at the door. I wasted no time relieving myself of at least a gallon of champagne. And less than two minutes later, Cooper was still waiting where I left him.

"Better?"

I laughed. "Much."

"Ready to go?" He took my hand to steady me.

"Where to now?"

"Home."

He shook his head at my pitiful pout and touched his lips to the tip of my nose. "That's where your present is."

"That's convenient." I flashed a wicked grin. "I have a present for you too, and I can only give it to you at home."

The ride home was excruciating, partly because I'd slipped the sadistic lacy panties back on while I was in the ladies' room—they were more uncomfortable than I'd remembered— and partly because I'd been forced to stuff my feet into my red shoes to traverse the parking lot. But more importantly, I was horribly drunk. *Again.* What I really wanted was to hang my head out the window for fresh air, like a golden retriever. Instead, I opened it a crack and laid my cheek against the glass, trying to discreetly breathe in the cool air.

*How do I get myself into these things?*

I should've stopped after the second glass. *Who waits*

*until the second glass to add the ring anyway?* If he were going to put a ring in my drink, surely he would've done it on the first pour. I didn't need to drink five glasses to discover there was nothing but champagne in the flute.

*But I did.*

And maybe I should've simply stirred the damn crème brûlée to see if it had a diamond hidden in it, instead of eating the whole thing.

*But I did.*

Two hours later, it was all I could do to hold back a fountain of two-hundred-dollar-a-bottle champagne and crème brûlée, and my grip was slipping. And right before my big moment too. *My mother would be so proud.*

I barely noticed as we pulled into the garage, and Cooper turned to me with a look of concern. "You don't look so good. You drank too much, didn't you?"

I fought to focus on his handsome face and flashed a watery smile. "Uh, I don't think so. I had just enough."

"Oh, you've definitely had enough." Disappointment rolled off him in waves, or maybe that was just the room spinning. "There's no doubt about that. Do you think you can get out of the car by yourself?"

I had no idea why that struck me as funny, but I couldn't stop laughing. In between fits of giggles, I managed to drag myself out of the car without incident.

Cooper laced his fingers with mine to lead me into the house. He never let go of my hand as he guided me up the stairs. "Are you ready for your surprise?"

A jolt of electricity shivered through me. I was more than ready. I'd been ready for my surprise for weeks. I nodded. "Mm-hmm."

Cooper trembled like a little boy lining up to see the newest *Star Wars* movie. "Good."

I kicked off my shoes as he dragged me to the bed, walking me backward until I had no choice but to sit on the edge.

"You have no idea how hard it's been waiting to give you this." He knelt at my feet, still gripping my right hand in his. "I've been bursting at the seams since I got it."

I sucked in a shaky breath and held it to keep from hyperventilating. The scratchy panties had me squirming where I sat, and I tucked my left hand under me to keep from wiggling my ring finger in his face. I froze as he reached under the bed for something.

The word *yes* sat on the tip of my tongue, itching to burst free. *Yes, yes, yes!* I pulled my left hand from under my leg and rested it on my knee.

My poor stomach lurched like a boat tossed around at sea as Cooper reached for my hand, grasping it gently in his. He rested a heavy object in my palm, and my head swirled.

"Yes!" The word was out of my mouth before I could stop it. It took a full minute before reality caught up with me. It wasn't a ring he'd handed me. It was... *A book?*

# Hurricane Dom

WITH MY HEAD TILTED TO the side, I attempted to dissect the book in front of me. *An Immortal Heart.* When I said I wanted Cooper to give me his heart for Valentine's Day, that was not at all what I'd meant. And to make matters worse, he'd wrapped it with a fancy red ribbon. *Like a box of chocolates.*

I flipped through the pages quickly then lifted my eyes from the dark and broody cover to Cooper's jubilant face. *Why is he smiling?* Had I missed a secret compartment just big enough for a ring box?

Cooper took the book from my hands and opened it to the first page. "To Katie, with love. You are my inspiration, the beating of my immortal heart. I've loved you since the day I met you, and will love you until the day I draw my last breath."

The dedication was sweet, but I'd already seen it. I might have even cried the first time I read it. The only tears I'd be shedding tonight would be tears of disappointment. I blinked them back and forced a smile.

"What do you think?" Cooper beamed, and the guilt hit me like a cardboard box filled with sad-eyed puppies.

I swiped my tongue over my lips, but my mouth had gone dry. Under normal circumstances, the sweet gesture would have thrilled me to my core. I mean, a few months ago, I would've been over the moon to get a special copy of one of Cooper's books. And back then, I didn't even know he'd written them. But I wasn't ecstatic. I wasn't thrilled.

I was mortified. And the guilt was killing me. I'd told everyone at the bank I was getting engaged for Valentine's Day, but instead, Cooper gave me a book. "It's beautiful."

"You inspired me to write this, you know?" He gathered my hands in his. "This very special copy is only for you. Promise me you'll read it."

"Tonight?"

"Not tonight." He chuckled then squeezed my hand. "But soon."

"I promise." I gave him my word, and he sealed it with a kiss so tender, I lost it. I wrapped my arms around his neck and cried. I only hoped he thought they were tears of joy. *Why ruin Valentine's Day for both of us?*

After I'd cried myself out, he untangled my arms from his neck and cupped my face in his hands. He pressed his lips to mine. This kiss started slow but quickly left me breathless.

"Too tight." I worked the skirt up my legs as I panted between kisses.

Cooper reached behind me to slide the zipper to my waist. "You're so beautiful."

I shuddered as he slowly lifted the dress over my head then tossed it aside to crush his lips against mine again. As he devoured me with his mouth, he lowered me to the mattress, murmuring my name with each breath he took.

Warm hands slid across my shoulders and down my back, making quick work of the strapless bra, then made their way down my arms to the soft swell of my hips. Cooper toyed with the straps on the garter belt before unsnapping the first clip with a *pop*. The next clip snapped free, and he rolled my stocking down my leg and over my foot, dropping it over the side with my dress. Then he switched legs, popping the clips and sliding the other hose down my leg. He glided his hand up my thigh again, resting it against the small of my back.

He pulled his lips from mine, and even in the dark, I

could see the sparkle in his blue-green eyes. "Should I even ask why you're inside out?"

I sat up too quickly, and my stomach swirled like a flushing toilet. I had to lie back down. I was almost afraid to ask, but I had to know. "What do you mean, I'm inside out?"

He kissed the corner of my mouth, and whispered, "Your panties. I don't think the tag is supposed to be on the outside, is it?"

"No. I don't imagine it is." I laughed.

Cooper hooked his thumb in the waistband of the flimsy inside-out panties and tugged them down my thighs. "You don't need them anyway."

I flinched as the lace scraped against my tender flesh, and he froze.

"Did I hurt you?"

A hot flush moved from my chest, past my neck, to my face. "Just ticklish."

He tossed my panties with the rest of my clothes, and I waited for him to continue where he'd left off. But he didn't. My eyes snapped open to find him gaping at the V between my legs.

I put my hands over my face.

"That's, uh, festive?" He rested on his haunches, still fully dressed. His jaw strained with the effort to keep from laughing.

"It's your present." I peeked at him from behind splayed fingers.

"My present?" He trailed a finger along my inner thigh on a straight path to the red-jeweled heart. He wrapped his free hand around my wrist and pulled my hand away from my face.

I took a deep breath. "It's a really long story."

"Does it have anything to do with why you smell like Goo Gone?"

My mouth fell open, but not a sound came out.

"I, uh..." He cleared his throat. "I have a remarkable sense of smell."

The words tumbled out all at once. "I accidentally waxed off half my, uh, you know... so Vicky took me to the spa. She gave me a Xanax—and I know, I should've just said no, and believe me, next time, I will—but when I woke up..." I glanced down at the sparkly heart. "And after all the suffering my poor tortured, uh, lady bits endured, I didn't dare take it off without professional help." As soon as the words were out, my hands flew back to cover my face again.

The bed shook with his quiet laughter.

Nothing had gone the way I'd planned. Valentine's Day was officially ruined. And in two days' time, I would have to go back to work and tell everyone I *didn't* get engaged. I got a book.

The sobs I'd been trying to hold back all evening came ripping out of me like claps of thunder.

Before I even registered his movement, Cooper had scooped me up in his arms. His thumbs swiped my tears away as he murmured against my hair. "Oh, baby, don't cry. I kind of like it."

"It w-w-was an awful present." I hiccuped. It was as much a statement on the vajazzling as the book. But I'd never tell *Cooper* what I really thought of his Valentine's Day gift. How could I?

"It wasn't an awful present." He brushed my hair away from my face, pressing a kiss to my forehead. "It's actually a very sexy present." He growled softly in my ear.

"You really like it?" I whispered.

He answered by trailing his lips down my jaw. "Oh, I *definitely* like it. The whole package, actually." He cupped me down *there*, and the warmth of his hand sent a shiver through me. *Maybe Valentine's Day isn't ruined after all.*

Or maybe—my stomach swirled with an ominous rumble—I'd entertained that thought too soon.

"Katie?" Cooper's eyes widened. "Are you okay?"

Before I could answer, another growl sounded from deep within me as the champagne volcano prepared to erupt. I threw my hand over my mouth, clipping Cooper on the chin as crawled to the edge of the bed.

I hadn't made it more than a few steps when my gag reflex kicked in, and everything I'd ever eaten came back to haunt me in all its Technicolor glory. After emptying the entire contents of my stomach, I remembered Cooper's question. "No. I'm most definitely *not* okay."

Sunday brought with it the most spectacular hangover I'd ever experienced: *the champagne hangover.* It wasn't a pleasant discovery. On the upside, I felt too horrible to think about the disastrous night before and the marriage proposal that wasn't.

"I brought you food." Cooper set a plate on the nightstand then stepped back while I sniffed at it like a wounded dog. *Tuna. Blech.*

I grumbled out a response, and Cooper grinned. He'd worn a perma-smile since the wee hours of the morning, as if he found my misery amusing. And despite spending half the night kneeling on the heated marble floor in the bathroom, holding my hair back, he looked downright edible in a pair of faded jeans and a black-and-navy flannel button-down.

"You're enjoying this, aren't you?" After vomiting all night long, my scratchy voice sounded foreign to me.

He approached the bed slowly, as if I might bite, and sat on the edge of the mattress just out of my reach. "Now, why would you think that?"

"Oh, I don't know. The Crest-bright smile, maybe? And don't think I missed that sparkle in your eyes when you look at me." I threw in a low growl for good measure.

"That's absolutely ridiculous. Of course I don't enjoy

your suffering." He scooted close enough to rub my back, and the heat from his hand felt wonderful against my clammy skin. "That being said, I wouldn't mind in the least if your discomfort served as a reminder of sorts."

"I knew it!" I sat up too fast, and my head spun. "You're hoping I take this as some sort of sign from above."

He pressed his lips together in a failed attempt to hide his smile. "I wouldn't be disappointed if you did."

"Well, you can stop wishing." I groaned and dropped back into my nest of pillows. "I've definitely learned my lesson. I'm never drinking again."

Cooper resumed my massage. "If I'm not mistaken, you've said that before."

"Well, this time, I really mean it."

He didn't bother to hide the grin. "We'll see."

Several minutes passed in silence before Cooper's hand stilled on my back. "How do you feel today?"

"Like my head's about to explode. In fact, you'd probably better get back. I'm a danger to anyone within a ten-foot radius."

"I'll take my chances." Cooper stretched out on the bed beside me. "You know what would make you feel better?"

"A blood transfusion?"

"No, but close." He laughed as he reached for something behind his back. He placed the novel he'd given me between us and patted the vampire on the cover. "You should read this. It's guaranteed to raise your spirits if nothing else."

I buried my face in the closest pillow, muffling my voice as I spoke. "Don't even *think* the word *spirits* until all the alcohol's out of my system."

"Just a few pages? I know just the right place to start..." He opened the book and flipped to the middle.

Despite his persistent coaxing, I wasn't in the mood to read. In fact, I wasn't in the mood to do anything other than curl into a tight ball and wait for death to take me. And that's exactly what I did.

"Maybe tomorrow. If I don't die before then." I shoved a pair of cracked sunglasses I'd found in the nightstand on my face to block out the light and buried myself in Cooper's magnificent sheets until Monday morning.

My alarm went off far too early, and I nearly dislocated my shoulder silencing it. The hangover—or Hurricane Dom, as Cooper liked to call it—still brewed just off the coast. After thirty-two miserable hours, I'd finally shed the broken glasses and managed to keep dry toast and green tea in my stomach, but I was far from cured, especially when Cooper waved the plastic cup of vanilla yogurt under my nose. It would be a long time before I ate anything even remotely resembling crème brûlée.

After vanishing so I could get ready, Cooper reappeared to drive me to work. He insisted, convinced my blood alcohol hadn't yet slipped below the legal limit—a ridiculous notion that I actually considered. I didn't think I'd ever been so miserable in all my life.

Cooper pulled into a parking space a few spots away from the door and cut the engine.

"You don't have to walk me in." I'd planned on bailing out the instant the car came to a complete stop, but my inability to manage the release button on the seat belt forced me to abort the mission.

He ran around to the passenger side and opened my door for me. "I don't mind."

The instant we stepped through the door, I felt Silvia's eyes boring into me from across the lobby. I stopped dead in my tracks to stare her down in what could've been a scene from *Tombstone*. Her triumphant smile told me I had about thirty seconds before my humiliation was complete. Cooper couldn't find out I'd told everyone he was going to propose. I had to stop Silvia before she walked over to congratulate us on our engagement. *Why did I have to open my big mouth?*

Silvia took a step in our direction, and an icy jolt of panic shot through my veins.

"Come on." I put a hand on Cooper's shoulder blade and shoved until I felt him moving in the direction I needed him to go.

The furrow between his brows deepened. His expression told me he was confused but curious as I pushed him forward until we were inside my office.

With a loud huff, I pressed my back against the glass door, blocking his view of the lobby beyond. No doubt my coworkers were watching us like fish in a bowl.

Cooper's lips curved up at the corners. "What was that all about?"

"Oh, nothing." I shrugged, stepping away from the door, drawing his attention away from the lobby, and sat on the edge of my desk to catch my breath.

His eyes narrowed, and he looked at me sideways. "Nothing?"

"Nope. Not a thing."

"Hmm." He gave a thoughtful nod then joined me on the desk. Our thighs pressed together from hip to knee, and he stared into my eyes without blinking. "I think you're lying."

My mouth fell open with a gasp, not because I was insulted—I wasn't—but because he was right. I was lying. Big time. "H-How did you know?"

"Where Silvia's involved, there's always *something* going on." He looked deeper into my eyes as if solving a complex riddle. "And, I love you, but you'd make a lousy poker player."

I groaned. *I knew it.* My face gave me away. Every. Single. Time.

He chuckled. At least he found it amusing.

"Well..." I hopped off the desk to escape his built-in lie

detector. I decided I'd better keep as close to the truth as possible. "It's nothing for you to worry about. They just like teasing me. Silvia's probably waiting for a, uh, play-by-play of Saturday night. I'm sure Vicky told everyone about my—" I stared down at my crotch and squirmed. That damn heart was beginning to itch. I really needed to find out how to get it off with the least amount of damage to my... person.

"Everyone?" Cooper's eyebrows shot up toward his hairline.

"Probably. No one around here can keep a secret, and Vicky is the absolute worst."

Cooper stood, eyeing the lobby with growing suspicion. "I don't think I like the idea of everyone picturing..."

"I need to say something to Silvia. You stay here." I pointed at the chair directly across from my desk, and he sat down without a word. "Don't move. I'll be right back."

I slipped through the door and took several long strides across the lobby to where Silvia stood, watching me with something akin to admiration.

"What on earth has gotten into you?"

Instead of answering, I hooked my arm in hers and towed her toward her office, keeping Cooper in my sights the entire time.

Once we were behind closed doors, she grabbed my left hand and frowned. "Where's the ring?"

"There is no ring," I hissed, yanking my hand back. "No ring. No engagement. No wedding."

Silvia tilted her head to the side like one of her dogs. "I don't understand."

"Oh. Well, allow me to enlighten you." After a dramatic pause, I laid it out for her in a clipped staccato. "Cooper... didn't... propose."

Silvia's eyes widened, and her mouth dropped open. "But I thought..." She trailed off, tapping her lips with one finger.

"Yeah, me too." I peeked around the corner to check on Cooper. He was still there, watching me with rapt attention. I pressed out an awkward smile and waved. He waved back with a look of utter bewilderment on his beautiful face.

Silvia peeked around the corner, and she waved at Cooper too. "So what happened?" she whispered as if he could hear us across the room.

"Before or after I drank five glasses of champagne?"

Silvia gasped. "You didn't!"

"Oh, but I did." I perched on the edge of her desk and let my head fall into my hands.

If anyone knew the potential ramifications of alcohol in my system, it was Silvia. She'd personally witnessed my descent into inebriation on at least two occasions and knew exactly what happened after *two* glasses of champagne, let alone five.

"You threw up, didn't you?"

"Eventually."

"He's going to think you're an alcoholic." Silvia clucked her tongue. "Is *that* why he didn't propose?"

"No!" I popped my head back up to stare daggers at her. "I only kept drinking because I thought he was going to put the ring in my glass."

"Oh, Katie." She scrunched up her face and shook her head. "Cooper wouldn't do something so cliché."

I threw my arms up in mock defeat, my tone flat. "Now you tell me. Where were you when I was looking for diamond rings in my champagne? And in the crème brûlée, too."

"There were diamonds in your pudding?"

"No. Definitely no diamonds in the dessert. But I ate every single bite just to be sure." I groaned again, my stomach rolling with the memory.

Silvia just shook her head, and then she broke out into loud laughter.

"It's not funny."

She pulled herself together and cleared her throat to cover another laugh. "You're right. It's not funny at all." Silvia was as bad a liar as me. If I didn't know better, I'd think she was choking on something.

"Just make sure everyone knows not to bring up rings and weddings, okay?"

"Fine. I'll take care of it." She pushed me toward the door. "Now go walk him out before someone says something before I have a chance to tell them."

After making a mad dash from Silvia's office to mine, I fell against the closed door, out of breath. "I'm back."

"You're up to something." Cooper narrowed his eyes. "Spill it."

"It's not important." I waved a hand between us as if I could knock the words out of the air.

"If you say so," he muttered then flashed an evil grin. "Your mother called."

My legs buckled beneath me, and I reached for the corner of the desk to steady me. *Oh, God. Please tell me he didn't...* "You didn't..."

"Of course I answered the phone. How else would I have known it was your mother?" He reclined in the chair, obviously pleased with himself. "Besides, I had to find out who'd earned the Imperial March ringtone and the Darth Vader screenshot."

I narrowed my eyes. "Right. Of *course* you did."

Cooper laughed. "She said to tell you, you shouldn't leave your phone on your desk when you leave your office."

*Excellent advice.* I grabbed my phone and slid it into my pocket. Then without taking my eyes off Cooper, I cleared my throat and lowered myself into my chair. "So, uh, what did she say?"

He bit down on his bottom lip, and the innocent gesture made my stomach lurch.

"Cooper?"

The beginnings of a grin tugged at the corners of his mouth.

My heart hammered behind my ribs. The suspense was killing me. "Would you *please* tell me what my mother said?"

Cooper wiped his hand over his mouth, effectively removing all traces of humor. "She asked about the wedding."

I succumbed to a coughing fit after inhaling my own saliva. I couldn't breathe, but at least that meant I couldn't say anything if Cooper asked.

Cooper came around the desk and patted me on the back until the spasms passed. "For some reason, she's convinced we're getting married."

"W-What did you say?" My voice came out shrill and unsteady.

He shrugged one shoulder. "I told her we weren't even engaged, and she called me a liar."

*Oh. My. God. Why did I tell my mother I was getting engaged for Valentine's Day?* "Why would she..." I spluttered as my throat threatened to close up again. My face went up in flames. I had to tread very carefully. I was all too aware of Cooper searching my eyes for the lie in my words. "What did you say?"

Cooper scratched behind his ear, shifting his weight from one foot to the other as he studied my blank computer screen. He licked his lips as if he were about to say something but didn't answer.

Squinting my eyes into narrow slits, I scrutinized his out-of-character behavior. "Why do you look so guilty?"

His head snapped up, and he smirked. "I, uh, told her we got married last night."

The floor could've swallowed me up, and I wouldn't have noticed. My eyes popped wide, and I let out a strangled laugh. "You what?"

"I'm sorry, I just couldn't help myself." He laughed,

looking only mildly contrite. "You'd better call her back before she gets on a plane."

*Fabulous.*

My mother didn't pick up when I called. I left a short message then dialed her number again. This time, she picked up, but the instant I said, "Mom..." she hung up on me. At nearly thirty years old, making my mother angry still freaked me out.

Cooper found the whole thing hilarious. He laughed while I paced back and forth over the low-pile carpet in the small space, my arms flailing around my head like a wild animal.

"This isn't funny. Do you want my mom showing up on your doorstep, demanding to see the ring?" I shrieked.

He shrugged again, cocking his head to the side with a lopsided grin. "I'm sure I could come up with a ring if I had to."

My racing heart faltered, and I lost my footing. Leaning against my desk for support, I gaped at him. *If he had to?* He had me at a complete loss for words. I didn't want to be the if-he-had-to girl. "So you'd put a ring on my finger just to drive my mother crazy?"

His smirk reappeared, and he rubbed his thumb over my bottom lip. "Oh, I don't know. I like watching your mother freak out."

Lowering my voice to just above a whisper, I said, "I'm going to forget you just said that." At least I'd try.

As I attempted to step around him, he reached out and grabbed my wrists. "Wait." He sat in my chair and tugged me into his lap.

"What?" I muttered, staring at the faint impressions his fingers made in my skin.

"Stop over-thinking this." He released my wrists and reached up to take my face in both hands, giving me no choice but to look directly at him. His blue-green eyes showed nothing but sincerity as they locked on me. Sliding his fingers between mine, he lowered his voice and spoke straight to my soul. "When I put a ring on your finger, it'll be the real thing."

*When... or if?*

# Someone Wicked This Way Comes

"VIVIAN'LL BE HERE TOMORROW." COOPER stood in the bathroom doorway, unbuttoning his gray flannel shirt. He avoided eye contact with me, something he'd been doing far too often lately. In the almost three weeks since Valentine's Day, Cooper's mood had mysteriously slipped into a dark place, somewhere I couldn't reach.

At first, I thought it was because I hadn't made a big deal about his Valentine's gift. Every night before bed, he'd ask, "Have you read it yet?" And every night, I reluctantly shook my head no while the guilt ate me up.

Long before I'd ever discovered Elizabeth Jayne was really Cooper Maxwell, I'd fallen in love with the Immortal Blood series. And I'd read each of his earlier books so many times, the pages had come unglued. I just couldn't bring myself to read the newest in the series. I'd allowed my disappointment to overshadow his sweet gesture. And that was entirely my fault.

So I lied.

Using my knowledge of the characters, and the bits and pieces of the story I'd read while he was doing edits, I convinced him I'd finished it. I probably went overboard raving about the book. But instead of making him happy, my proclamation seemed to push Cooper deeper into his dark mood.

He still hadn't proposed, and I seriously doubted he ever would. Instead, he sulked around the house, barely cracking a smile for days on end. And when he wasn't brooding, he locked himself in his office to finish his new book, a project that required him to meet with my nemesis yet again. But this time, instead of Cooper flying to New York to meet with his publicist, Vivian was coming *here*. I was determined to fix whatever was broken between us before she arrived. I just needed to figure out what that was first.

"Here?" He'd caught me off guard as I climbed into bed Tuesday night. "What do you mean by here?"

He ignored my question and continued to rattle off Vivian's flight information. "She'll catch a cab from the airport, but I expect her rather early. We have a lot to cover in a short amount of time."

"When you say here, do you mean at the house?" I was careful not to say *our* house, which was difficult, because that's how I thought of it in my head.

"Yes." He looked directly at me for the first time all evening. "I invited her to stay here."

"But..." I gaped at him, waiting for him to change his mind. "Wouldn't she be more comfortable at a hotel?"

"Traffic to and from all the nice hotels would be inconvenient." He spoke to me like I was his secretary instead of his girlfriend. Next, he'd ask me to change the linens in her room or make her a pedicure appointment.

She hadn't even arrived yet, and I already wanted her to leave.

"You must really like her." It seemed like an innocent enough statement. And I tried to keep my voice steady as I said it, but his response left me cold.

"I've known her for a long time." He didn't really answer the question, but he made it clear he was done with the conversation.

I didn't know what to say. I knew how he felt about my petty jealousy. We'd already explored that topic, and it hadn't worked out well for me. I was almost afraid to press the issue further.

*Almost.*

"So, if you've kept her around this long, you must like her a lot, right?" It took a great deal of effort to maintain my composure. What was supposed to be my cheerful voice came out mechanical.

He exhaled sharply, making the hair on the back of my neck prickle. "Katie, I'm tired. I don't want to fight about Vivian again. She's my publicist. I've never been involved with her. I'm not interested in her. She works for me. That's all."

"She won't be here for your birthday, will she?"

"I don't know. Why?" He looked exhausted, like he hadn't slept in days.

"Because it's your birthday. I wanted to plan something nice."

I couldn't decipher the pained look he gave me.

"You're going to have to help me out here. What's a girl supposed to get for the man who has everything?"

Cooper's eyes flashed, and his jaw clenched then relaxed. I could almost see him restraining himself. "You already know what I want."

And truly, I had no idea. I stared at him with my mouth hanging open.

Before I had a chance to decipher his cryptic birthday wish, he sat on the edge of the bed. His shoulders sagged, and he exhaled long and hard, like a man defeated. "Katie..."

He hesitated long enough for his eyes to meet mine, and what I saw in them terrified me. My heart jumped into my throat. He was about to break up with me. I just knew it.

Whatever he'd been about to say, he must have changed his mind, because he stood and shook his head. "I've lost track of how many times I've told you I love you. It's your choice whether to believe me or not."

Instinct kicked in, and I quickly crawled to the edge of the bed and reached out to him. "Cooper, wait! I love you too. So much, it hurts sometimes." I echoed the words he'd said to me in the vault.

He leaned in, lifting my chin with one finger. "I don't want it to hurt." And he bent down and gave me a soft kiss. "It should never hurt."

His breath fanned across my face as he rested his forehead against mine and smiled. It was the smile I'd fallen in love with all those months ago, and it felt like the lifeline I'd been waiting for. I grabbed on to it with both hands, throwing my arms around his neck, and pulled him into the bed with all my strength.

"I've missed you," I whispered as our lips moved together in that practiced way.

He tensed for an instant. Then a dam broke within him, and he grabbed a hold of me like a man possessed. I'd always been the impatient one, wanting all of him immediately, rushing things while he endeavored to slow me down, to savor every moment. This time, Cooper was impatient. He couldn't seem to get enough.

The man had a way of making me forget my name when he kissed me. His mouth devoured mine as he moved his attack down my neck and back to my lips again, tearing my pajamas from my body as he went. His kisses were needy. Desperate. And exquisite. And he murmured my name with each breath, making me breathless with anticipation. Nothing mattered when I was with Cooper this way.

Our bodies came together with that same desperation, and his frightening intensity took me by surprise. My skin went up in flames. I couldn't catch my breath. But I didn't want him to stop. He held me tighter than he'd ever held me, and I wanted him to hold me tighter still. I understood the fear behind his embrace—I felt it too—as if we were only safe where we touched.

"I love you," he murmured against my neck. His whispered words drove me to the edge, and we tumbled over together.

My senses completely overloaded, and we collapsed in a mass of tangled limbs.

The next morning, I opened my eyes to find Cooper, propped up on one elbow, smiling down at me, looking sexier than anyone should be allowed to. His eyes still held a trace of the sadness I didn't fully understand, but he almost seemed back to normal.

"Good morning," he purred in a husky voice. His roaming hands and the sparkle in his blue eyes told me exactly what he was thinking. And I couldn't have agreed more.

My body ached, but I would've gladly endured that sweet ache all day. "I think it's about to be."

"You would be right." He leaned over, taking my bottom lip between both of his.

The doorbell rang.

Cooper groaned but didn't pull his lips from mine. He stopped moving and waited. The bell pealed again, and he sighed, pressing his lips to mine one last time.

"Vivian?" I knew it must be her, but I held on to the hope that she'd get lost. The house wasn't easy to find, completely hidden from the road, sequestered behind a deep grove of trees and down a long drive.

"I'm sure it's her, but she's early." Cooper climbed out of bed and pulled on his jeans, commando. "I told her you didn't leave until eight."

"You..." I gaped at him while I struggled to form the words. "You told her to come after I left?" What was I supposed to think about that? I ran the possibilities through my head.

He scooped his gray flannel shirt from the floor where he'd tossed it last night. "It's not like that."

While holding the jealousy back by little more than a dangling thread, I halfheartedly dug for my pajamas in the tangled blankets. After just a few moments, I gave up the search. And the pretenses. "Why don't you tell me how it is then?"

"I didn't want her to ruin your morning." Slipping his last button through the hole, Cooper glanced at the clock by the bed. "You'd better get a shower. You'll be late for work."

The bell sounded again, and he hurried through the door while I sat in the center of the bed, completely stupefied.

Vivian's sultry voice rolled up the stairs like a dark fog, and I scrambled to my feet for a closer look. Getting as close as I could without exposing myself—and my crazy morning hair—I peered down the stairs. Cooper's scent was still on my skin as he greeted her.

Anger, hot and irrational, coursed through me. He might have been blind to her motives, but I wasn't. I wasted no time showering, and in less than fifteen minutes, I'd dressed in Cooper's favorite outfit—the low-cut champagne blouse with the curve-hugging chocolate-brown pants— and smoothed my hair back into a reasonable style. With a swipe of mascara and a dab of cherry lip-gloss, I was ready to go: a woman on a mission.

Hopping on one foot then the other, I shoved my feet into a pair of open-toe pumps and bolted for the stairs. Once I was firmly planted on the main level, I smoothed my blouse and my hair one last time before stepping around the corner into the kitchen.

"There she is!" Cooper beamed at me, and in that moment, there was no question he loved me.

I stole a quick glance at Vivian, and his words carried a completely different meaning. *There she is, indeed.*

Vivian was more beautiful than even *my* wild imagination

could've conjured. Her long jet-black hair hung in loose corkscrew curls that were far more exotic than my dull-brown hair could ever be. And her icy-blue eyes seemed almost unnatural against her dark hair and creamy-white skin. If only her beauty had been restricted to above her neck. Unfortunately for me, the rest of her was even more stunning. Cooper's publicist was built like a Victoria's Secret underwear model.

*Life isn't fair.*

"Katie..." Cooper's voice shook me from my thoughts, and I forced a half smile. "I'd like you to meet my *publicist,* Vivian." He put a strong emphasis on the word that defined her role in his life, as if a mere word would reassure me when the woman herself shot daggers into my heart with her inhuman eyes.

"N-Nice to meet you." I stumbled over the lie, reaching out numbly to shake her hand like a field mouse staring into the face of a hungry snake.

Vivian's eyes zeroed in on me like a target as she clasped my hand in both of hers and squeezed. "*Katie.*" My name sounded like a curse coming from her lips. "Finally, I get to meet the woman who's inspired Cooper to reach for bigger and better things. Cooper reminds me time and time again, money isn't everything."

Cooper threw his arm over my shoulder, extracting me from Vivian's grasp, and tugged me into his arms. "You do inspire me." He gave me a quick kiss, apparently unaware of the tension between Vivian and me.

She glowered behind his back, quickly schooling her features into a smile as he turned back to her.

"Cooper says you have somewhere you have to be this morning. That's such a shame." Vivian injected a dose of feigned sweetness into her velvet voice. "But don't worry, I'll make sure he's far too busy to miss you while you're gone."

I shuddered, and Cooper wrapped his arms even tighter around me.

"Oh, I'm sure I'll miss you. No matter how busy I am." He nuzzled my ear then released his hold on me with a grin. "But you'd better get going, or you're going to be late. You know how Phil gets."

Forcing the corners of my lips upward, I flashed a feeble smile in response. "Right. Phil hates when I'm late."

Feeling thoroughly dismissed, I went through the motions of gathering my things. I dragged my purse and keys from the kitchen island and grabbed my coat from the back of a chair. Before heading out the door, I paused in the doorway and turned around to say goodbye to Cooper, but he was already gone—with Vivian—most likely to the office that was just a few feet from the bedroom.

Cue the anxiety attack.

Before I changed my mind and stormed Cooper's office to tear Vivian's snake-hair from her head, I rushed out of the house. I climbed into my Prius, slammed the door, and squealing tires, backed out of the garage. I didn't care if they heard. In a way, I wanted Cooper to know how off-balance I felt with the dragon lady taking up residence in his house. How could he not notice the way she looked at me? How could he not see the venom in her glare?

*Men.*

Fifteen minutes later, the anger hadn't even begun to wear off. In fact, with time to think about Vivian's icy-blue eyes piercing my skin like pointed teeth, my mood had worsened. Somewhere in the back of my mind, I'd truly hoped meeting her would alleviate all of my apprehension. Instead, it bubbled over like the foam in a boiling pot of potatoes.

Phil stood just inside the front and opened his mouth to say something.

I held up both hands to stop him. "I am in no mood for your cute comments today."

"I didn't even say anything." He stared at me with his mouth open.

"You were thinking it." I glared at him as I passed. "And thanks to me, you've been saved from yourself."

He choked out a laugh. "What did I do?"

Ignoring his question, I marched straight into Silvia's office.

"Before you say a word." Silvia held up a hand, and I froze in my tracks. "What's going on with you two and this whole proposal thing?"

"Your guess is as good as mine. He hasn't proposed yet." The anger melted out of me, leaving a buildup of tears in its wake. "And it gets worse."

"Worse? How could it possibly get worse?"

Standing in her doorway nodding like a bobble-head, I tried to form the words that were right there on the tip of my tongue but refused to solidify.

"Oh, for heaven's sake, Katie." Silvia huffed. "Spit it out."

"She's here!"

Silvia peeked around me at the empty lobby, and then her eyes searched my face for some hint of what I was talking about. I apparently hadn't been clear enough.

"Vivian."

Silvia scrunched up her face in confusion. "Vivian?"

"Cooper's publicist!" I shrieked, and the dam inside me broke. All the emotions I'd kept bottled up that morning poured out of me. Once the words started to tumble out, I couldn't stop them. "She's here. And naturally, she's beautiful. Horrible, but absolutely stunning. She has these really blue eyes and all this dark curly hair and legs up to her... I really can't blame Cooper for finding her attractive. My God, *I'd* do her if I were a guy. And she does *not* like me. She practically told me she so. Did I mention how completely drop-dead gorgeous she is?"

I didn't wait for a reply. I perched on the edge of Silvia's desk, twisting my long strand of pearls around my hands like a vise, and launched into another tirade.

"She had the nerve, the unbelievable audacity, to give me icy looks behind his back. Can you believe that? I could have slapped her. I didn't, of course. I just stood there like an idiot. Do you think I should have slapped her? Don't answer that."

Silvia didn't say anything. She merely raised her eyebrows, and her lips twitched with a suppressed grin.

"I know. I know... you're right." I flopped into the chair across from Silvia. "I can't go around slapping people. But believe me, I wanted to. I can't believe I managed to leave the house with her there. Probably the hardest thing I've ever done."

Something I said seemed to light a fire under Silvia, and she jumped up from her chair. "You left him there with Vivian? At his house? Are you crazy?"

My mouth fell open with a *pop*.

"Katie, if she's the succubus you say she is, you can't leave Cooper alone with her!"

My eyes welled up with tears, and I blinked them back. "It's okay. I'm just overreacting. I know Cooper, and he's not interested in Vivian like that. He promised."

"Of course *he's* not interested in *her*. That's not the point. *She's* interested in *him*, and for more reasons than you think." Silvia planted her hands on her hips and tapped her suede pump against the low carpet. "You're going to march right back to your car, you're going to drive back to Cooper's house, and you're going to stay there until that woman is gone."

"But, what about work? Phil—" My voice came out in a strangled whisper. I'd left my boyfriend in the house with another woman, a beautiful woman with more than one motive to break us up. *I'm an idiot.*

"Don't worry about Phil. I'll take care of him. Just go." She pointed toward the door and waited for me to leave.

I snatched my purse from her desk where I'd flung it when I came in and marched—as ordered—right back out the way I came in.

# Red Roses and Little White Lies

O N THE SHORT DRIVE BACK, I thought about love... and trust... and respect... and why I should've stood up to Silvia. I should've insisted that Cooper was worth every bit of my trust and respect. I knew Cooper. He would never even think of—let alone act on—any impulse that would endanger our relationship.

But even as I tried to convince myself of Cooper's unwavering loyalty, I couldn't help envisioning Vivian slinking around the bedroom in the shadows, like a serpent taunting Cooper with her bright-red... apple. My foot came down harder on the accelerator.

After making it back to the house in record time, I let myself into the garage with the remote Cooper had given me weeks ago and hurried inside. The house was eerily quiet. Both cars were still there. I'd parked beside the BMW, and Vivian's red sports car—I'd almost expected her to pull up on a broom—was parked in the driveway, so I knew they hadn't left.

My stomach clenched as tight as a fist while I kicked off my shoes at the bottom of the stairs and dropped my purse on the floor beside them. As I took the first few steps, it did a full-on flip. By the time I reached the top, I was ready to double over and vomit.

The hallway was dead silent. Not even the sound of voices reached my ears as I approached. That terrified me. I wasn't sure if I wanted to know what they were doing. It was too awful to even think about. Standing outside the closed door to Cooper's office with my pearls wound around my hands again, I debated fleeing. What would I do if I found them in a compromising position, anyway? Vivian looked like she could totally kick my ass. My precious beads creaked under the pressure as they always did, and I knew I should let up. And I would have—eventually. But before the signal could make the short trip from my brain to my hands, something snapped. My necklace seemed to heave a sigh of relief, releasing the pressure as the entire sixty-inch length of pearls clattered to the hardwood floor, bouncing in every direction.

*Crap, crap, crap!*

With a strangled gasp, I fell to my knees, trying to capture the wayward beads before they could completely get away. While I crawled along the floor, scooping up scattered pearls, the office door flew open, and Cooper peered down at me, a deep crease forming between his eyebrows. Behind him, Vivian sat on the edge of his desk, her long legs crossed at the knee and one perfectly arched eyebrow raised in condemnation.

I fought my natural instinct to cry. I would *not* cry with *her* watching. Instead, I found myself heaving breath after shallow breath in and out like a woman in labor.

"Katie?" Cooper crouched down beside me, absently gathering pearls in his hands. "Why aren't you at work?"

*Perfect.* I knew I should've spent the drive thinking of a good lie. I knew it before he'd gotten the entire question out of his mouth. But I had nothing, not a single excuse that sounded even remotely sane or rational. So I decided to edit the truth just a smidge.

"S-Silvia told me to leave! She, uh, pointed to the door and said 'go home.' What was I supposed to do?" I looked down at the trail of pearls on the hardwood. "I was just about to knock, but my necklace broke for no reason whatsoever, and well, that's when you opened the door." Once I'd gotten the whole lie out, I dragged in a deep breath and felt the dizzying effects of hyperventilation coming over me. "I feel funny."

Since I was already on my knees, I didn't have far to fall. I shifted my weight until I'd landed on my backside, and laid my head in my hands to catch my breath.

"Katie... baby, I'm so sorry. I thought things were better at the bank?" It was a question and a statement wrapped into one, and it was a horrible misunderstanding.

Cooper thought I'd been fired.

I knew I'd eventually have to dig myself out of this one and probably in a hurry, but at the moment, I had bigger problems than my current job situation.

"We'll figure something out." Cooper sat beside me on the floor and wrapped his arm around my shoulder, tugging me against his chest. "Don't worry. They can't fire you like that without consequences. I'll move every single one of my accounts today if I have to."

As if a dirty bomb had gone off in my chest, my heart rocketed to life. "No! Oh, please don't rush into anything. I-I'll talk to Silvia. I'm sure everything will work out. Don't move your accounts just yet." *Or ever.* The absolute last thing I needed was Cooper's accounts moved. I really would get fired then.

I needed to get a message to Silvia in a hurry. But that wasn't going to happen with Cooper clinging to me like my cat had just died. Then again, I wasn't about to complain about Cooper being wrapped around me like a vine. He crushed me against him, smoothing my hair back with one hand and rubbing circles over my spine with the other.

"Poor Katie," Vivian cooed from the doorway. She positioned herself so I could see halfway up her tight skirt. And if I could see that much from where I sat, from his vantage point, Cooper could see *everything.* "It's a rough time out there for people in the financial industry. It's a wonder you kept your job this long. I could help you write a resume if you like."

Her phony smile irritated the crap out of me, mostly because Cooper seemed to find it genuine. I never thought of him as gullible, but at that moment, he was a rabbit in a snake pit.

"That's a great idea." He beamed at her, and I wanted to scream. "I can personally vouch for her skills with a resume. You should take her up on that while she's here."

*What happened to Cooper hiring me to balance his checkbook naked?* Oh sure, we both knew he was kidding when he made that offer, but under the circumstances, it seemed appropriate that he should reiterate his proposition.

He didn't. And worse than that, he actually wanted me to accept Vivian's help. My mood suffered another serious blow, and the tears I'd been fighting hit me with a fresh assault. I blinked them back as quickly as I could.

"It'll be fine," Cooper soothed. "You'll see. You'll have a new job before you know it."

Everything I thought I knew was wrong. Again. I wasn't worried about Cooper's feelings for me. Those were obvious. He spent most of the day comforting me while Vivian sat in his office, doing whatever publicists do. *Note to self: Do a Google search on publicists.*

What I *really* wanted for comfort was the damn engagement ring I'd been so certain he had at the ready. Not only that, but the tentative plans I'd finally managed for his birthday lay in tatters now that he thought I'd been fired. Keeping him away from Phil and Silvia was now a priority. I didn't dare tell him he'd misunderstood, not after I'd let him believe it for so long.

Vivian needed to leave.

After excusing myself to use the bathroom—the only place Cooper hadn't accompanied me all day—I called Silvia for advice.

"What am I supposed to do now?" I hissed.

She laughed. "I could probably get Phil to fire you for real."

"How would that help?"

"That way you could beg him to hire you back. In fact, I bet Phil would love that."

"I'm sure he would. But no thanks. I'll think of something."

Silvia cleared her throat, and I knew I was about to get a lecture. "You could always tell him the truth, you know."

"It's too late for that," I snapped. "I already cried on his shoulder. I don't want him to think I'm a big fat liar."

She chuckled. "Well, you *are* a big fat liar."

If I could have glared at her through the phone line, I would have.

"Oh, fine." She let out an audible huff. "Are you sure he doesn't already suspect? You're a terrible liar."

"No, he totally bought it. He's too distracted by the dragon lady to pick up on the usual signs."

"She's still there?" For an instant, Silvia sounded exactly like my mother.

"Yes! They've probably got their heads together, working on that stupid vampire series as we speak." The irony didn't escape me. That "stupid" vampire series had kept me company long before Cooper and I became a couple.

"If Vivian's with Cooper, what are you doing talking to me? Go find them!" She hung up without waiting for a reply.

Silvia's words rang in my ears as I made my way back to Cooper's office. I heard him arguing with Vivian through the door, and I crawled into the hallway to press my ear against the wood. This time, I had my excuse ready. I even had the forethought to plant a few loose pearls in the corners to support my lie if I was caught eavesdropping.

Cooper's voice was muffled, but I managed to pick up at least part of the conversation. "...press release with my real identity."

"Are you crazy?" Vivian snapped back. "I don't think you realize what'll happen if you tell the world who you really are."

"I've given this a lot of thought, and I'm ready."

"Well, I'm not. Things are finally exploding for you, and you're talking about walking away."

I didn't know about Cooper, but I was on to her. She didn't say so, but I could tell she hoped he'd change his mind and write another one. I cringed as I listened to her argument.

"The next book could easily find Henry mourning the loss of his one true love, only to have him on a new quest." I had to hand it to her. She didn't give up easily. I needed to take notes.

"I've told you at least a dozen times, I'm done with the vampire. I'm almost finished with *To Katie with Love*."

A thrill went through me when he said my name. I knew he was writing about me, but I had no idea he was using my name in the title. Or maybe I did. I'd found a sticky note attached to his desk the first time I'd snooped, but I had no idea what it meant.

"Oh..." Vivian purred. "I'd love to see you finally finished with *Katie*." She coughed up my name like it was fur ball.

The room went quiet, and at first, I thought they'd stopped talking. Then I picked up a low hum. I could only make out a few words, "please..." and "darling..." Just enough to make me uncomfortable. I froze with my ear crushed against the door. Vivian was pleading with him in her honeyed phone-sex voice, begging him to reconsider... *something.*

I couldn't hear what.

And then she invited him to... *dinner?* "Come on, Cooper. Just the two of us, like old times. I'd love to go to that little French place you're always raving about."

*Like old times?* Who did she think she was? And that little French place was *our* place. I had to hold myself down in my crouched position to keep from storming through the door and slapping her.

Cooper's laugh startled me, and I almost lost my careful footing, nearly banging my head against the door. I managed to regain my footing, ear still pressed firmly in place.

"Like old times? Come on, Viv... don't you think you've overestimated the sentimental value of our *relationship*?" He bit off that last word with just the right amount of sarcasm to bring a smile to my lips.

I couldn't hear her response, but the doorknob rattled slightly—as if someone had grabbed it but didn't turn—and I jerked back just enough to throw me off balance. My rear hit the floor with a *thud,* and a combination of instinct and adrenaline sent me scrambling backward in a crab crawl until my back slammed against the bedroom door.

That's where I was when Cooper stepped out of his office. He didn't notice me right away, giving me just enough time to reach into the corner.

"Found it!" I pinched the pea-sized pearl between my thumb and forefinger and held it up for inspection.

He tilted his head to the side and made a face. "Katie? What are you doing on the floor?"

I sucked in a gulp of air. "Searching for pearls, of course." I almost said, *What else would I be doing in the hallway while you're having a private conversation?*

"Don't worry about the necklace." He reached out a hand and pulled me to my feet. "I'll get you a new one."

My cheeks flamed. "You don't have to do that. Besides, I need to get this one fixed. It was a graduation present from my father."

"Oh. Right... as soon as we find the rest of the pearls, I'll take it to be restrung." He dipped his head down to brush his lips against mine. "I have a few things to finish up, then we should talk about dinner."

Cooper turned and walked off, disappearing down

the stairs. I stayed in the hall, watching the door to his office for her. I knew she was still in there, listening like a serpent slithering through the tall grass. I stalked back into the bedroom, snatched my phone off the bedside table, and hurried into the CRWAT. Once the door was shut and locked behind me, I dialed Vicky's number. She wasn't my first choice of allies, but we'd reached DEFCON 1, and Silvia was no help. Out of everyone I knew, Vicky was probably the best equipped to deal with someone like Vivian.

When it came right down to it, Vicky was my friend. Vivian was not.

She answered on the second ring. "Hello?"

"Vicky!" I whispered like the sneak I was. "I have a huge favor to ask."

"Katie?" She sounded surprised to hear from me. "Why are you calling me? And why aren't you at work today?"

"Silvia told me to go home. It's a long story. Listen, I really need your help." I climbed into the glass shower stall to further block the sound. "I didn't know who else to ask."

"Sure," Vicky chimed. "Lemme have it."

"Cooper's publicist is in town, and I'm positive she's interested in more than doing business with him, if you know what I mean. I need to create a diversion of some kind. I don't know, maybe make him jealous? I need something epic here, Vik. I have no idea what do to, but I was certain you would. Will you help me?"

The sound of her breathing was the only indication that she hadn't hung up. Then she laughed, and I could almost hear her crimson lips curl up on both sides. "Will I? You'd better believe it. I know exactly what to do."

Vicky wouldn't tell me what she had in mind, other than to say it was risky, expensive, and childish, but guaranteed to get the response I was looking for. I was immediately sold and gave her my consent—and my credit card number—to go ahead.

Two hours later, the doorbell trilled through the otherwise quiet house, making me jump out of my skin. Vicky hadn't wasted any time putting her plan into play. I had to force myself to stay where I was, hiding out in the sitting room, aimlessly flipping through Cooper's book again without reading a single word.

"What the *hell*?" Cooper's voice echoed through the house, making the windows vibrate. And then I heard my name as he roared up the stairs. "Katie!"

I slammed the book shut, frozen in my spot. Well, Vicky did say her plan would elicit a response.

The last threads of restraint in Cooper's voice snapped. "Katherine Grace James, where are you?"

*Holy crap! He full-named me.*

I jumped up from the sofa and hurried to the top of the stairs, where I stopped cold. The overpowering scent of roses hit me before I even reached the first step.

*Vicky!*

This was going to be very costly—in more ways than one.

With measured steps, I eased my way down the stairs. Even though I'd agreed to this little ruse, I wasn't prepared for the magnitude of Vicky's scheme. I told her to be subtle. Hundreds of bloodred roses definitely didn't count as subtle. It made the look on my face that much more authentic, which was a good thing, because I was going to have to lie... convincingly.

I wasn't sure where to look first. The foyer—and part of the living room—could've hosted a wedding... or a funeral. *Mine.*

Cooper's eyes were wild with anger and confusion. But Vivian wore a wide smile.

"Katie..." Cooper closed his eyes, drawing in a deep breath through his nose before composing himself enough to finish. "Do you have any idea why Dean would be sending you roses?"

*Oh, holy mother of...* "Dean?" I gasped, both hands flying up to cover my gaping mouth. I should've known putting Vicky in charge was a bad idea. Why would she send flowers from Dean? "I-I didn't know you could send flowers from jail."

Cooper clamped his lips shut and waved his arm over the sea of red clogging up his foyer.

"Apparently, you can." Vivian plucked the card from the closest arrangement and began to read. *"I haven't forgotten about you. Dean."*

Cooper's face twisted into a pained expression as he snatched the card from Vivian's fingers and ripped it into tiny pieces. I watched every encounter with Dean flit across his face, each one more painful than the one before it. "Trying to kill you wasn't enough? Now he's reaching out to you from prison?"

*Oh, Vicky...*

"I... he..." I had no words. I was stunned speechless. I suppose I should've thanked Vicky for giving me something to work with, but I really wished she hadn't gone quite so far.

"There's more." Cooper snatched another card from another arrangement and waved it in the air. "Listen to this one. *'I'll be seeing you... Soon.'* Has he contacted you?" he demanded. "Why does he think he'll see you soon? Did you tell him you'd visit or something?"

"Of course not!" Again, my horror was real.

Vivian snickered at my reaction—or Cooper's—and Cooper shot her an icy glare.

"Sorry," she mouthed, taking a step back. But I didn't think she was sorry at all.

"Shall I keep reading?" He approached another large arrangement of roses, snatching the card from the flowers.

He had me frozen like a gazelle staring down an angry

lion. I barely shook my head, struggling to remember what I was trying to achieve with this stunt.

Cooper shuddered, ripping the card into tiny pieces. Then he pressed his fingertips into his temples, closing his eyes. "I don't know what to think about this, Katie. I'm not sure if I should worry for your safety or his sanity."

"Someone should worry about Vicky's safety when I get my hands on her." I mumbled the words, unable to speak out loud for fear of a spontaneous admission of guilt.

"I'd like nothing more than to dispose of each and every one of these fucking flowers, but I keep reminding myself they don't belong to me. They're yours." His jaw ticked like a time bomb as he waited for a reply.

An array of words flashed through my thoughts, but none of them seemed remotely adequate. I felt sick. My stomach roiled and churned. My guilty conscience— apparently the only part of me that hadn't regressed to my high school years—wanted to confess before things got even further out of hand. Paralyzing fear prevented me from taking that path.

"I-I don't want them." My voice cracked. "You know I don't even like roses. And if I thought for half a second that Dean would actually come here..." A shudder ripped through me. "I wouldn't be able to sleep at night. I'd be on the next flight out of the country."

I bit my tongue to stop myself from thanking Vicky for not sending orchids and mentally tallied the cost of the extravagant flowers.

"You know..." Vivian ended the awkward silence. "I'm beginning to see what you mean about Katie and the wealth of stories to draw upon. She really is a disaster waiting to happen, isn't she? It's like you're sailing on the *Titanic*, and she's the iceberg." She snickered again and scooped up the smallest of the arrangements. "If you don't want these, I'll take them up to my room."

Cooper spun around to glare at Vivian. "Please refrain

from attacking my girlfriend, if you wouldn't mind. She may have a bit of bad luck, but she's hardly in the business of sinking ships."

"Oh, come on, Cooper. Surely you can see she's making a mockery of you? You've been one of the most successful romance writers of the past decade, and you're walking away from all of that to write a stupid diary? Your parents are diplomats, for Chrissake!" Vivian's fangs were showing.

"Drop it, Viv. You're treading on dangerous ground."

With my mouth hanging open and my eyes darting back and forth between them, I was too stunned to speak.

"Oh, whatever," she said with a roll of her eyes. "I need to make a phone call before dinner. Are we going to the French place or not?"

She was amazing. I was almost impressed. She actually believed he was taking *her* to *my* restaurant. *The bitch.*

"I've lost my appetite." He sighed, staring at the roses again.

"Suit yourself." Vivian huffed as she turned for the stairs.

Cooper waited until Vivian had disappeared into her room before turning to me. "Are you unhappy with me?"

"What? No!" I reached out, grasping his hand and lacing my fingers between his. How could he even think something like that? "I'm deliriously happy. I couldn't love you more if I tried."

"Then why keep me guessing? Is it because my birthday's in two days? Are you planning to surprise me then?" He averted his eyes from mine, staring at our intertwined fingers.

My stomach plunged, and I felt the all-too-familiar prickling on the back of my neck. I did a quick mental review of the past two weeks to somehow unearth which question I was supposed to be answering. I came up with nothing.

So I stalled.

"Birthdays are meant for surprises. You don't want me to spoil it, do you?" I prayed he didn't catch the tremor in my voice.

My answer seemed to placate him, and he smiled. "I guess not. I'll wait for the surprise. It won't be easy—I'm not patient—but I'll do my best."

I let out a breath and forced a bright smile to my lips.

"Dinner then?" he asked cheerfully.

*Fabulous. I guess I'll be dining with the enemy.*

# Maybe I Should've Read Between the Lines

I JOLTED AWAKE FROM A DEAD sleep, in a cold sweat like I'd narrowly escaped a terrible nightmare. Tiny pearls of frosty perspiration beaded up on my forehead and rolled into my hair. But under the blankets, tucked into the crook of Cooper's shoulder, my body went up in flames. The real nightmare had just begun. I was in my own personal hell. The day had finally arrived. March sixth. Cooper's birthday.

I slithered out of his arms and crawled unnoticed from the bed. I didn't bother with clothes—just one of Cooper's old sweatshirts over my underwear. My only hope was to distract him with breakfast in bed and sex, not necessarily in that order. But I was prepared to do whatever I had to. With Vivian gone and the code to disable the alarm memorized, I was all about living dangerously.

Getting rid of Vivian turned out to be far easier than I'd expected. I might have gone a little overboard by enlisting Vicky in the plot to make Cooper jealous, but it'd worked. Cooper refused to let me out of his sight for the entire day and night, putting a kink in my mission to chew Vicky out for maxing out my credit card, and sending Vivian into a tantrum worthy of a three-year-old on a candy binge. The woman had no patience and no internal monologue. Every word she thought, she said. Out loud. Not a good decision on her part, not when Cooper's mood was already dangling by a frayed thread.

"Cooper...?" Vivian tapped her French-tipped nail against the tabletop and puffed out her pillowy lips.

One after another, her random questions had come almost nonstop after Cooper moved their base of operation to the kitchen table, where he could keep an eye on me while I surfed the Internet, pretending to look for a new job.

Cooper heaved out a sigh. "What now, Viv?"

"Why is it we never dated?"

"What?" She'd caught him mid-swallow, sending him into a coughing fit. His face turned bright red as he slowly regained the ability to speak. "You mean each other?"

"Yes, I mean each other. I find you attractive, and I'm sure you find me attractive..." With her fingers dancing up Cooper's forearm, Vivian slid her eyes in my direction and smirked. "So why didn't we just throw caution to the wind and explore a relationship?"

Determined not to let her get to me, I pretended to be absorbed in what I was doing.

Cooper wasted no time shaking off her touch and shot a glance my way. "Because attractive or not, I've never been interested in you. The reasons I hired you are the same reasons I'd never date you. You're tenacious, ambitious, and unfailingly ruthless."

Vivian grumbled out some reply, but I couldn't make out the words. Then she leaned in and whispered something in Cooper's ear. Whatever she said upset him, because he jumped up from his chair, knocking it to the floor.

"No! Absolutely not." He shoved his hands into his hair as he paced the kitchen. "I, uh, I think we're done here."

"Done?" She looked stricken. "We still have to work on your ridiculous press release, unless you've changed your mind."

"No." Cooper slammed his laptop shut. "I haven't

changed my mind. But you can work on that on your own time and email me a copy when you're finished."

"Cooper, there's a lot to be done before the last book is released, and we haven't even discussed the publicity tour—"

"Email, Viv. We can do it all via email." Cooper shot another nervous glance my way before organizing his pile of loose papers. "I'll check in with you after my birthday."

He shoved the pile of papers into her hands then backed away from her like she'd bitten him. I had no idea what Vivian had said to him, but his rejection seemed to hit her hard. She collected her things and was out of the house within fifteen minutes, the longest fifteen minutes of my life.

But she was gone, and now, two days later, I had more important things to worry about—namely, the mysterious birthday present he'd supposedly asked for while I was too drunk to remember.

If Cooper hadn't stayed attached to my hip, my Silvia-imposed mini-vacation would've been the perfect time to shop. As it was, his near-constant presence forced me to enlist Vicky in another doomed-to-fail plot, this one more expensive than the last. Thanks to my excessive alcohol consumption on Valentine's Day, I had absolutely no clue what he wanted. My stomach swirled with the memory.

*Ugh, champagne.*

I, Katie James, was officially on the wagon. Not that I was an alcoholic—I could count the times I'd been drunk on one hand—but since I had the tolerance of a kitten, I needed to steer clear. Even Silvia agreed, and she thought I was too cautious most of the time, but not so much lately. Lately, I'd been reckless, and I wasn't about to stop now.

*My mission: overwhelm him with attention until he forgets his secret birthday wish.* Or until I figured it out.

After flipping the third pancake onto the plate and adding a square of butter to melt, I slathered them in warm maple syrup. The presentation was hardly impressive, but if they tasted anywhere near as good as they smelled, I was on the right track, especially if the hype was true, and the path to a man's heart was truly through his stomach. With the plate in one hand and a steaming cup of coffee in the other, I headed for the stairs.

From as far back as I could remember, my mother told me I was cursed with bad luck. She'd even given me her name, hoping to tip the odds in my favor. Grace might have been my middle name, but that's as far as it went. Halfway up the stairs, I lost my balance. I don't know what made me trip. Maybe the pressure of *not* tripping caused me to stumble and fall forward in what seemed like slow motion but actually happened in less than the time it took me to blink.

Lucky for me, the pancakes broke my fall. I landed squarely in the plate. Unfortunately, the impact sent the hot coffee rocketing from the cup like a science experiment gone wrong, and it rained down on me like molten lava.

Some time after the squish of the pancakes and the stream of obscenities flowing unfettered from my lips, I heard the pounding of footsteps as Cooper rushed to my side, wearing nothing but a frown and some rather impressive bed head.

"Jesus, Katie, are you okay?"

"Oh, I'm fine." Hot coffee dripped from my nose, and I wiped it using the sleeve of my sweatshirt. "Nothing the burn unit can't handle."

"Are you burned?" Cooper crouched beside me, inspecting my face for damage.

"Only superficially. Apparently, I'm much worse at making coffee than I thought."

"What happened?"

"Same thing as always," I groaned. Long strings of syrup formed between my body and the plate as I peeled myself from the pancakes.

Cooper shook his head, and I could tell from his expression, he was trying not to laugh. "Tripped?"

"Yeah."

He pulled a chunk of pancake from my hair and ate it. "Not bad."

"I ruined breakfast." I sniffed.

"You know, it's almost scary how clumsy you are." Cooper leaned in and licked a string of syrup from my chin. "At least you taste good."

"It's not funny." My emotions simmered somewhere between tears and a tantrum. *So much for breakfast.* This wasn't at all how I'd intended to distract him. It was an omen. That's what it was. What else could go wrong? Oh, yeah. Everything. I still had to give him the birthday present I'd sent Vicky to pick up for me—the *wrong* gift but the only one I had.

"Come on." He set the plate on the stair beside me and pulled me to standing. "Let's hit the showers."

After two rounds of shower sex and the replacement breakfast Cooper cooked for us, I'd run out of distractions. Cooper was thoroughly exhausted but far from placated. Before I could come up with another excuse to stall, Cooper dragged me to the bedroom and sat on the edge of the bed.

"Okay, I'm ready." He kept a straight face, but I could tell it wasn't without effort.

With a nervous smile perched on my lips, I pulled the hastily wrapped present from its hiding place in the nightstand and joined him on the bed. I handed him the package and exhaled a shaky, "Happy birthday."

He unwrapped the antique pocket watch with a sad smile. "This is lovely, Katie. Thank you."

"Do you really like it?" My voice cracked. I just knew he didn't like it. I'd failed at being a girlfriend. How could I possibly hope to be a wife?

"I'd love anything you gave me." Cooper's words were at odds with his totally devastated expression.

The heat of fresh tears pricked behind my eyes, and I finally lost it, dragging in one last breath before the sobs hit. "I'm sorry. I-I had no idea what I was supposed to get you. I don't even remember when you told me what you wanted. It's all my fault. I've been wracking my brain for weeks, trying to figure it out, but I'm completely clueless. Can you ever forgive me for ruining your birthday?"

"No idea?" Cooper scratched the back of his head, and his pained expression slowly melted away.

I sniffled. "None whatsoever. I'm a terrible girlfriend."

"Katie." A pair of serious blue-green eyes locked on mine. "You didn't read the book I gave you, did you?"

"I..." *Lie? Avoid? Distract? Come clean?* My dwindling options zipped through my head on fast-forward as I tried to figure out why he would ask me that now. "Not exactly." I came clean, reluctantly meeting his steely gaze. A little voice in the back of my head told me I'd made a grave error by not reading that book.

"Not exactly," he repeated flatly. He ran a finger over his bottom lip as the whisper of a smile played along the edges. "What *exactly* does 'not exactly' mean?"

"I-I did read it. Well, most of it. I mean, you know I love your books, right? I'm totally your biggest fan. While you were doing your edits on *An Immortal Heart*, I snuck a few pages here and there."

"Here and there, huh?" Somehow, Cooper managed to look disappointed and delighted all at once. "What about the copy I gave you? Do you still have it?"

I nodded frantically, terrified I'd suddenly blurt out how I almost gave it to Vicky because I was so disappointed to get a *book* for Valentine's Day. "Of course I kept it."

"But you didn't read it."

"I may have skimmed the first two chapters. But I read the dedication so many times I memorized every word.

I honestly thought that's why you wanted me to read it again. If I'd known..." *If I'd known?* I still had no idea why reading the book was so important to him.

He stared off into space for a moment, as though working through a puzzle, then gave a single nod as if satisfied with the result. "Where's the book now?"

I gaped at him. "Do you want it back, because I didn't read it?"

"Just tell me where it is." He waited quietly while I deliberated, his expression still inexplicably satisfied.

"Uh..." I started to stand, but Cooper beat me to it.

"You stay here. I'll get it."

"No! I'll go." The last thing I needed was for Cooper to find out I'd left the book open to a particularly steamy scene in chapter two.

He raised his eyebrows and nodded for me to go ahead. I quickly retrieved the book, pulling out the bright-yellow Post-It that marked my page before slamming the book shut. I hurried back to where Cooper waited and crawled into bed beside him.

Cooper set the book between us and took both of my hands in his. He seemed to struggle for the right words before flashing his trademark grin. "Why don't you start by telling me why you were disappointed to get a book for Valentine's Day?"

"I never said—" I blinked at his growing smile and found myself on the verge of tears again.

"Katie, please. The truth this time." His eyes pleaded with mine, and I felt his frustration pass through me.

Wringing my hands together, I stared at my lap. I had no idea how to say it without sounding stupid, so I just spit out the words. "I-I thought you were going to propose."

All the tension I'd felt moments before drained from Cooper, and he started to laugh.

My eyes snapped back to his as a spark of anger flared

in me. "You think that's funny? Is this just some great big joke to you? Because I don't find it at all amusing."

His laughter cut off abruptly, but I could tell it took effort. "Sometimes, I don't know what to do with you." With a quick peck on my lips, he opened the book and flipped through the pages, stopping somewhere near the middle. "Read this." He pointed to a specific paragraph near the bottom of what looked like a random page.

*This woman—the embodiment of everything I'd ever hoped to love—had become...*

"Out loud," he demanded.

My focus shifted from the page to his face. His expression was a mixture of amused and serious, so I looked back to the page and began reading the paragraph out loud.

"*This woman—the embodiment of everything I'd ever hoped to find—had become the bright spot in my darkest night. She illuminated my path like a beacon of hope. She burned like a fire in my coldest winter, wrapping my icy soul in warmth I'd never known.*" I stopped to study his face again. "I don't remember this part."

"Keep reading."

Quickly finding my place again, I continued. "*From the first moment she stepped into my world, she lifted me up, giving me strength I'd so sorely lacked. Before we crossed paths, I'd suffered from a dark soul, but her love for me filled me with light. I'd never experienced hope until she awakened it in me. To her, I declare my love, crying out in the night, begging her to indulge me this one selfish wish. Should she agree, I will be truly immortal, for I will have the everlasting promise of her love. And so, my darling Katie...*" A sob broke free. "I'm such an idiot."

"Keep reading." He took my left hand in his and caressed my fingers.

"No, Cooper, seriously." I used my shirtsleeve to wipe tears from my chin. "How can you even begin to forgive me—"

He dipped his head down and gazed straight into my eyes. "Read."

"*My...my...*" My voice slipped into a faint whisper. "I-I can't."

"My darling Katie..." Without relinquishing my hand, Cooper slid from the bed to kneel on the floor in front of me and recited the words from memory. "Consider me falling to my knees before you, proclaiming my love for all the world to hear. I would sooner tear out my heart than to hear it beat without you."

My heart jumped to life as if I'd been shocked. My legs shook, and my mouth went as dry as the Sahara. I couldn't tear my eyes from the next words on the page. *Marry me.* He hadn't spoken them, but simply seeing them in print left me in a stunned silence. I wasn't even sure I was still breathing.

"Marry me."

My eyes snapped up from the page to see his lips moving, but I couldn't be sure I'd actually heard the words. Then I felt the cool circle as it slid into place on the fourth finger of my left hand, and the fog around me lifted as he repeated the words I'd been waiting to hear.

"Marry. Me." His face was a mask of grim determination.

I'd yet to take a breath, and I couldn't find my voice to speak, so I nodded, letting the tears fall freely.

Before I'd realized he'd moved, his lips were on mine—hot, demanding—*elated.* "I love you," he murmured, pressing my body back against the cool sheets. His heart slammed against his chest.

"I love you more," I whispered back.

"Impossible."

"We're getting married." I marveled as he kissed his way across my shoulders.

He chuckled as he lifted his head to look into my eyes. "We're getting married."

# Congratulations to the Happy Couple

I CAUGHT MYSELF STARING AT MY ring again while Cooper slept. I had no idea how much time I'd spent staring at the enormous pillow-shaped stone, turning my hand until the light danced in the facets. The large diamond was flanked by several smaller round stones set across the platinum band. It was unique, and I couldn't have picked anything better if I had picked it myself. As usual, Cooper had impeccable taste.

I sat up and stretched, stiff from spending so much time in bed, not that I was complaining. I was beyond satisfied.

*And engaged.*

I could barely contain my excitement, and I itched to make the announcement to my friends. I was going to the bank this morning. I had to work myself back into my job after several days of self-imposed exile. I managed to convince Cooper that Phil had begged me to come back. He liked the idea of Phil begging, so he was almost satisfied with my decision to go back. He had no idea that I'd never left. But since I still had a job, I needed to get to it.

Besides, I needed to make an announcement.

"What are you doing?" His sleepy voice interrupted my thoughts, and I smiled.

"I have to get ready for work." I curled back into his arms.

"No, you don't. Stay home with me," he murmured into my hair.

I groaned. "I can't."

"You want to."

"Of course I want to. But I'm lucky to have a job, you know."

"You could work for me."

"And what would I do? Naked checkbook balancing? How can I show off my ring if I stay here, naked, all day?" I teased.

"I think you would look wonderful if you wore nothing but your ring. I would stare at it all day." He leaned in to capture my lips in his.

I raised my eyebrows. "You'd stare at the ring? If I was naked? Hmmm." My mouth curved into a smile.

His lips trailed along my jaw to my ear. "Well, I'm sure I would notice a diamond that big," he whispered.

I held my hand up between us and wiggled my fingers. "It is enormous. It's a wonder I can lift it."

"You need to be careful, you know. The weight could completely throw off your balance. Stay away from cliffs and chasms."

"Oh, absolutely. I avoid them most of the time as is. No sense taking chances."

"My thoughts exactly. You can't afford to take chances." He continued to kiss his way to my neck, messing with my ability to think rationally. "Should I send flowers to the bank? Now that we're engaged, that is?"

"That might send *Phil* over the edge of a cliff or a chasm, especially if you send orchids."

After Phil's revelation, even *I* thought of tiny vaginas when I saw them.

Cooper laughed quietly as his lips worked their way back to mine. "We wouldn't want to send Phil over the edge."

"No... we wouldn't." But I didn't really care about Phil or whether Phil fell. I was dangling over an edge myself, and I was about to fall over. But it would be a wonderful trip. I was looking forward to it.

"Don't you have to go to work?" Cooper interrupted my bliss with a harsh reminder.

My bottom lip poked out on its own. "Yes. I guess I need to shower first. You stay here."

"Why?"

"Because if you don't, I'll never get to work on time."

With one last wave at Cooper, I ran from the car to the door. As usual, I was late. *Seven minutes late.* Despite Cooper's insistence, I refused to allow him to walk me in to "have a word with Phil." That was one conversation I couldn't allow to happen, definitely not until I'd had a chance to brief everyone.

I promised myself this would be my absolute last foray into lying. Cooper and I were getting married soon. Honesty would probably be a good idea going forward. As they say, I was turning over a new leaf. No more games. No more little white lies. And especially, no more alcohol.

Starting today.

With my left hand leading the way, I took several long strides across the lobby, wiggling my fingers dramatically. No one noticed, not Silvia with her marriage radar, not June with her uncanny ability to say the right thing for every occasion, and not Vicky and her uncanny ability to smoke out gossip, not to mention her attraction to shiny things. Disheartened, I threw my bag and my coat into my office and turned back to the lobby. The place was deserted. Voices carried from the back, Vicky's louder than all the others, so I followed the sound.

I found them all lounging in the break room. No one paid a moment's attention to me. They were all too interested in a large box of donuts.

"Phil! You took the last jelly," Silvia grumbled. "I wanted that."

He bit into the donut and flashed a red-jelly smile. "You should've said something."

"I did say something." She picked a chocolate frosted from the box.

"Ahem." I cleared my throat loudly. "Hi, everyone."

"James, you're back." Phil stuffed the rest of his donut into his mouth, white powder falling like snow on his blue sweater-vest.

"Welcome back, Katie," Silvia said.

"Katie!" June exclaimed, wrapping her arms around me for a bear hug. "I thought you quit."

"Who said—"

In the corner, Vicky smirked, licking glaze from her fingers.

I tried to glare at her but couldn't muster any real anger. Despite my better judgment, Vicky and I had forged a new bond—often awkward and strange but definitely uncharted territory—thanks to vajazzled nether regions and covert ops.

"I *may* have said something to that effect." Vicky shrugged.

"Well, I didn't quit. I took some well-deserved time off." I slid my hand into my hair, pushing it back from my face, making sure the rock on my finger faced my audience.

No one noticed.

"So... what's everyone been up to while I was gone?" I was dying inside. How could my coworkers—my *friends*— be so unobservant when I was trying so hard to be noticed?

"Not much," June offered as she dug into the donut box.

"Oh, you know. Work, work, and more work," Silvia said with a flourish of her hand.

"It was pretty boring around here without you to spice things up," Vicky added with a wink.

"Gee, thanks." I dropped into a chair with a loud sigh and held my ringed hand over the donuts as if I was about to pluck one from the box. "Nothing at all exciting? That's too bad."

Inside, I was screaming. How was it no one—not any of them—noticed my engagement ring?

"I've actually had something exciting happen." I threw out the bait and waited for someone to latch on.

"That's nice, sweetie." Silvia patted my head like I was one of her little dogs. "You need some excitement in your life."

That was the last straw.

"Are none of you going to ask me what happened that was so exciting? Has no one even noticed the sparkling rock on my finger?" I wiggled my fingers in the air a little more vigorously than necessary. Absolutely no one seemed the least bit impressed. In fact, they seemed amused. All of them bit back smiles and avoided eye contact with me.

I groaned. "Okay, how did you know?"

That time, Vicky squealed. "Silvia saw you get out of the car, and the sun caught your ring, just about blinding the old girl."

Silvia chuckled. "It wasn't quite that bad."

"Way to steal my thunder, Sil." I grabbed a plain donut—the only kind left—and took a big bite. Every drop of excitement drained out of me like a flaccid balloon.

"For the record, I found it nearly impossible not to pounce on you when you came in." Vicky plopped down at the table across from me.

"Silvia made us do it," June blurted then covered her mouth with both hands.

The donut turned to dust in my mouth. How did people eat these things without benefit of frosting or glaze? I choked it down and glared at Silvia. "Of course she did."

"Oh, come on now, sweetie, don't be mad. Now, let's

see that ring up close and personal." Silvia tugged on my sleeve.

I reluctantly surrendered my hand from under my arm, where I'd tucked it out of sight.

"How do you walk with this thing on your hand?" Silvia teased.

"Same as always, very carefully." My lips twitched, but I wouldn't give her the satisfaction of smiling quite yet.

"My turn." Vicky snatched my hand from Silvia and turned it from side to side in her hands, marveling at how it caught the light. "That boy doesn't mess around, does he?"

"It's very pretty," June added from over my shoulder.

"Pretty?" Vicky scoffed, rolling her eyes. "June, anything over three carats is automatically stunning. This stone is easily four."

I tried to free my hand, but Vicky wouldn't let go.

"Check out the setting." She wrenched my wrist to the side to get a better angle, nearly breaking it. "Platinum. And look at all the side stones. Color me impressed."

*Finally.*

With my left hand still gripped tightly in both of Vicky's, I pressed my right to my chest. Vicky blurred behind a sheen of tears. "Thank you."

"You must be pretty good in bed to warrant this." Vicky shook my wounded hand in the air. "I would've never guessed."

"I'm sure you're right." I wanted to be irritated, but I was too happy. Everything was finally right with the world. "Now can I have my hand back so I can ice it?"

The rest of my morning went smoothly. Phil stayed in his office to avoid all the girl talk, which suited me just fine. Throughout the day, June, Silvia, and Vicky quizzed me on the wedding plans, which were, as of yet, nonexistent. They all wanted to know where and when we were getting married, whether we were going formal or casual, and if I'd chosen bridesmaids. Phil even popped his head out of his office long enough to ask if we were having an open bar.

After all the drama of our engagement, Cooper and I hadn't even discussed the actual wedding. With Vivian's visit, Cooper's jealous streak, and the confusion over the proposal itself, we were too exhausted to broach the subject.

After making me promise to bring up the topic at dinner, Silvia moved on to the matter of the dress. She insisted on dress shopping with me—something that would undoubtedly spell disaster once my mother got wind of it. One thing I was sure of: Grace James wouldn't take kindly to being left out of the loop when it came to her daughter's wedding.

My sister's wedding had been a three-ring circus, something I was desperate to avoid. Even my imagination couldn't reconcile Cooper's diplomat parents being involved in the colossal train wreck that was the last James family wedding.

"Have you decided on a color scheme yet?" Silvia's pen hovered over a slip of lined paper. "Will you wear white or ivory? I think either would be lovely with your skin. Oh, I saw the most beautiful dress in a magazine while I was at the hairdresser's recently, and my goodness, it was breathtaking. We should really find time to look. It takes a long time to have a dress made." Silvia went on and on, adding to her growing list without waiting for a response. As usual, she was talking more to herself than she was to me.

"We only got engaged on Friday."

Silvia ignored me. She was too busy searching for wedding gowns on the Internet.

"And with everything else going on, I haven't thought about churches, dresses, or flowers."

Silvia finally stopped what she was doing and gaped at me as if I had horns growing out of the side of my head. "Katie James, you've been convinced that boy would propose for almost a month, and you're telling me you didn't at least daydream about the wedding?"

I took a quick step back in case Silvia tried to tackle me in her office. "I-I was too preoccupied with the stupid birthday present I thought I was supposed to get him. And he was so moody. I almost believed he was about to break up with me. And then the dragon lady showed up."

Her eyes popped wide. Both of her eyebrows shot up her forehead at the same time her glasses slid down her nose. "Have you learned nothing from me?"

I forced a look of righteous indignation I didn't actually feel. Silvia scared me when she was on a mission. "Why else would I be looking at dresses with you when I should be working?"

Silvia scowled. "Don't patronize me. I know why you're here, and it has nothing to do with dresses. But..." Before I had a chance to feel guilty, her frown flipped up into a grin. "As long as you're here, we may as well start. What do you think of this?"

She turned her monitor around to show me a strapless silvery-white gown. Shimmering glass beads dotted up and down the form-fitting bodice and disappeared into the cathedral train. The dress was stunning but certainly not simple.

"Isn't it a bit much?"

"You mean the cost? Please, if your mother won't pay for it, Cooper will."

The idea of my mother forking out the money for my wedding gown made me sick to my stomach. "No, I mean... well, that too, but it's awfully ornate, don't you think?"

"Nonsense. It's perfect for you."

I twisted my lips to the side and gave a second look. "I don't know. Maybe if I saw it on..."

"Oh!" Silvia's face lit up. "Why don't we go dress shopping one night this week?"

"Really? That might be—"

"We can take Vicky and June!"

"That sounds like... fun. We can go to dinner and then try on dresses. Oh! You three should be my bridesmaids." I blurted out the invitation before thinking it through. I hadn't even talked to Cooper about the wedding, and suddenly, I had bridesmaids.

*Fabulous.*

Tears formed in Silvia's eyes. "I haven't been a bridesmaid in years. But you should know, I look terrible in pink... or blue."

"Got it. No pink or blue."

"And yellow washes me out. What about red? That would make for a nice modern take on a bridesmaid's gown." Silvia disappeared into her own little world again, spinning the monitor around to search for bridesmaid's gowns, no doubt.

"I'm going to tell Vicky and June about the shopping trip. I'll talk to you later." I took my chance to escape, scurrying out before she could call me back.

On my quest to find Vicky and June, I wandered into the break room, where Phil was prepping his lunch.

"Did you miss me?" I sat at the table, picking at the remaining donuts.

He had his back to me while he assembled his sandwich, but he turned around and smiled. "Actually, it's been a bit boring with you gone."

He stuck his sandwich in the toaster oven and shut the door before sitting across from me at the table.

"Boring? Come on, you and June are like the Fourth of July with your fireworks displays." I snickered. Watching June and Phil go at it was far more entertaining than watching my imaginary cat catch imaginary mice.

"Well, after my exciting turn as a drag queen, I've been on my best behavior, so June's had nothing to get upset about."

"Nothing?"

"*Nada*. No one's tripped over anything or fallen out of their chair. No bomb threats, jealous boyfriends, crazy mothers, or anything even remotely entertaining has happened in over a week. I figure we need to put emergency services on speed dial because we're definitely due for some kind of disaster. Hell, we haven't even had a flower delivery in days."

I remembered Cooper's offer to send flowers to the bank and giggled. "I'll see what I can do."

"No, please. I'm getting used to the quiet." The words had barely left his mouth when the first plume of smoke billowed from behind him.

"Uh, Phil?" I kept my eyes riveted on the toaster oven while Phil scrolled through his phone. "I think your sandwich is burning..."

"Can't be." Phil scoffed. "I just put it in."

"No, I'm serious, I think it's—"

The sandwich ignited like an exploding supernova, orange flames licking the sides of the toaster oven as dark smoke poured through the door seams.

"Fire!" I jumped up. "It's on fire!"

Phil shot out of his chair, tripping over it in his attempt to reach the fiery sandwich. "Shit!" He yanked the oven door open and blew on the flames like a child struggling to extinguish birthday candles.

"Damn it!" He slammed the oven door, trapping the charred sandwich in a cloud of dark smoke, and stared at the ceiling. "I was really looking forward to that. Now what do I eat?"

While Phil continued to mourn his lost lunch, a fresh spark caught my eye as the blackened brick in the oven reignited.

I waved my hands through the air, frantically trying to get the words out before I found my voice. "Still on fire! It's still on fire!"

Phil snapped to action again, huffing and puffing on the flames to no avail.

"The sink!" I squealed, watching in horror as the inferno threatened the tiny kitchen. "Get it to the sink!"

Phil grabbed a knife from the counter and staked his lunch before flinging it into the sink, where he promptly drowned it. Smoke engulfed the entire room. I couldn't breathe, and my eyes burned, but I was too stunned to move. With one hand over my mouth to stifle the coughing, I fanned the air with the other.

"So much for peace and quiet." Phil choked out a laugh. "Welcome back, James."

Cooper picked me up at five o'clock on the dot.

"Why do you smell like burnt toast?" He sniffed my hair as I climbed into the passenger seat of his car.

All it took was one look at his perplexed expression, and I lost it.

"What's so funny?"

"It's a long story."

"I don't have anywhere I have to be."

"Well..." I gave him the short version of my day, including the topic of dress shopping with Silvia and asking her, Vicky, and June to be my bridesmaids. I expected at least some pushback, but he actually seemed excited about the prospect of planning a wedding. Then he had to go and ruin my mood.

"Have you told your mother yet?"

"You know my mother. She's horrible. She'll try to take over the whole thing. You haven't seen her in wedding mode. It's terrifying. When my sister got married, Mom insisted on having a hundred white doves released at the end of the ceremony. Thirty minutes before Lauren was set to walk down the aisle, my mother checked on the birds and discovered that instead of being white, several of the doves were a light gray.

"The woman had a complete meltdown. She refused to continue until the bird wrangler replaced the gray doves. An hour later, after the odor from the carriage horses had permeated every inch of the church, the ice sculpture had melted, and the organist had passed out from heat exhaustion, Mom finally agreed to go ahead with the gray doves. Then, afterward, she refused to pay for the birds. And she demanded a discount from the carriage driver for allowing the horses to relieve themselves in front of the church. And that's only what happened *before* the reception." I blocked the images from my brain and shuddered. "I'm pretty sure my sister's still in therapy."

"Katie." Cooper kept his attention focused on the road, but I could see the disappointment shining in his eyes. "I understand how you feel. But unless you're planning on keeping our engagement a secret until the birth of our first child, you need to call your parents."

"Have you told your parents?" I snapped back.

He glanced over at me. "I called them the minute you said yes."

"Liar," I teased. "The minute I said yes, your lips were otherwise engaged."

"Well, it wasn't that minute..." He smirked. "But the point is, I *did* tell them. You shouldn't wait with news like that, no matter what your mother's reaction may be. You need to tell her."

He had no idea what he was in for.

# Daddy's Little Girl

*What's the big deal? Just tell her.*

That had sounded easy enough when Cooper suggested it, but when it came right down to it, he had no idea what my mother was like. His limited experience, as colorful as it may have been, was still brief. I'd spent my entire life finding ways to survive her emotional blackmail, and I had the scars to prove it. To her, a wedding was an epic event, an opportunity for her to show off for the entire world. And to hell with what the bride wanted.

So maybe Cooper could simply call his parents and spill the beans, but I couldn't make an announcement like that over the phone. I needed backup. I needed my dad in my corner. As far as I knew, my mother still had it in her head that Cooper killed people for a living, and my father hadn't even met him yet.

This was why we were about to take our third detour on the New York leg of our journey to Greenwich, Connecticut.

"Tell me again why we're driving when we could have flown?" Cooper laid on the horn, narrowly avoiding a collision on I-95. He'd asked the same question roughly a hundred times since we'd left home that morning.

"I like the scenery," I lied, staring out the window at the lines on the black road ahead. I couldn't see much more than that—it was after eleven—but barring any more detours, we'd be there soon.

He raised his eyebrows and glanced at me before letting

out a deep sigh and shifting his eyes back to the dark road. "Why don't I believe you?"

"It's complicated." I turned my attention to the navigation system. In less than an hour, I'd be back in my childhood home. With Cooper. That was, if I didn't die of anxiety first.

"Complicated?" Cooper groaned, shifting his weight in the seat. "Katie, we've been in the car for almost two days."

I scoffed. "It hasn't been two days."

"It's been fifteen hours."

"It's been barely fourteen."

Cooper flipped on the blinker to change lanes. "We could have flown to Hawaii, checked into a hotel, and gotten naked in less than fourteen hours."

A shudder cut through me at the idea of being in an airplane for that long. "Stop complaining. You're the one who wanted me to tell my parents. Besides, we're almost there."

"You realize you're going to have to come clean at some point, right?"

"Yeah..." *Maybe.* I turned to watch the trees fly past the window.

Forty-five silent minutes later, we pulled into my parents' driveway.

"This is nice." Cooper cut the engine and got out of the car.

A pang of nostalgia riveted me to my seat as I stared up at the house I'd grown up in. Unlike me, the old colonial hadn't changed much since the last time I'd been home. But in my head, I saw every passing year reflected in the aging facade. I'd been ten the summer my mother had the redbrick siding redone in a creamy white then demanded the painters sandblast the painted brick to create a time-weathered patina. Several years later, my parents changed the shutters from inky black to the current muted gray and added the tumbled-brick walkway. Every change marked a milestone in my life.

Cooper opened my door and took my hands in his. "Breathe, Katie." He had no idea how hard it was to breathe with all the memories pressing down on me.

"Hey." Cooper tipped my chin to meet his gaze. "Are you okay? It's not too late to find a hotel."

"No, I'm fine." I forced a smile to hide my fear. I wasn't fine. I was terrified. I'd never contemplated getting Mom and Cooper in the same room again, let alone telling my parents I was getting married. "Besides, my mother already shot down the idea of a hotel, remember?"

Cooper nodded, sliding his fingers between mine and giving my hand a squeeze. "Everything'll be fine. You'll see. Your mom loves me."

My jealousy radar went off again. That was what I was afraid of. I was pretty sure she liked him better than she liked me.

Gnarled rose bushes wrapped the white picket fence surrounding the property. In a few months, those tangled vines would host an explosion of yellow and red blooms— my mother's pride and joy. I could almost smell the sweet fragrance.

Cooper held the gate open for me, and I walked up to the side entrance. I'd barely raised my hand to knock when the door flew open, scaring a gasp out of me. My dad stood in the doorway, beaming as if he hadn't seen me in years instead of a few months. He towered over me, tall, lean, and in amazing shape for a man his age. His dark-brown hair had long since turned gray, and he had lines where his skin used to be taut, but he hadn't lost that mischievous twinkle in his eyes. He flashed two rows of perfectly white teeth—his only cosmetic alteration to my knowledge—and I could easily see why my mother fell for him all those years ago.

"Hi, Daddy."

"Hey, pumpkin!" Dad grabbed me around the shoulders and yanked me inside to crush me in a bear hug. Before I could take a breath to object, my feet left the ground, and he had me dangling from his arms like a rag doll.

"Come on, put me down." I groaned.

"You're too thin. You should eat more." Dad dropped me to my feet. He smiled again, and the skin around his green eyes crinkled.

"I eat—more than you, by the looks of you."

"We should sneak out to the bakery tomorrow morning. Just the two of us. Mrs. Cohen promised to make her cardamom fig baklava next time you came home."

"It's a date." I had a feeling he overcompensated to counter Mom's attacks on my weight. But I didn't mind. I loved Mrs. Cohen's baklava. I brushed the zigzag scar across his chin with my index finger. I couldn't remember a time when it wasn't there. "Mom hasn't convinced you to have this removed yet, I see."

Dad chuckled. "No, but she hasn't stopped trying, either."

"Speaking of Mom, where is she?" I hadn't noticed her absence until then.

"I slipped her some Benadryl and sent her to bed about an hour ago."

"Dad!" His admission had me torn. On one hand, I was delighted to find Mom already in bed, but on the other, knowing my dad had drugged her didn't sit well with me.

"Don't give me that look. After complaining about her allergies all damn evening, she needed it."

*Thank God for Mom's allergies.*

"So is this the guy?" Dad finally acknowledged Cooper standing patiently just outside the door.

"Oh my God, Cooper!" My face went up in flames as I waved Cooper inside and slid my fingers between his. "Daddy, this is Cooper. Cooper, meet my dad, Henry James."

Cooper extended his free hand. "It's wonderful to finally meet you, Mr. James."

Dad grasped Cooper's outstretched hand. "Call me Hank. Everyone does. It's nice to finally meet you. Grace has told me a lot about you. But don't worry." He lowered his voice to a whisper and winked. "I don't pay attention to half the things she tells me."

Cooper threw his head back and laughed. "I'm sure Grace had nothing but nice things to say. We had such an interesting time when she visited."

My two favorite men laughed together, washing away all my pent-up dread and worry. Maybe this trip wouldn't be so bad after all. The thought hadn't even fully formed in my head when I heard her voice.

"Katherine Grace James, is that you?"

"Hi, Mom." I choked out her name, my nerves back on edge.

"Why didn't someone tell me you'd arrived?" She flipped the switch as she entered the room, bathing us in incandescent light. She'd pulled an expensive fleece robe over her pajamas, making her look like a wealthy polar bear. "I expected you hours ago. Don't tell me you got lost again. How many times do I have to tell you not to take—"

"Now, Grace." Dad put his arm around her shoulder. "Let's wait until morning to give Katie a hard time. She and Cooper drove all day to get here. I'm sure the kids are tired."

"I tried to convince Katie to fly, but for reasons I've yet to figure out, she preferred to drive." Cooper dropped the line and waited for someone to bite.

My parents shared a knowing glance, then both gave me an awkward smile. I knew the look well. It said, "Poor Katie... not very brave... such a shame... never travels." I'd heard the speech enough times to play it in my head from memory. It was as if I'd been born with some horrible birth defect: the fear-of-flying disease or something. But to their credit, they said nothing.

The awkward silence stretched on for too long, and I cleared my throat. "It's a pretty drive. Beautiful scenery."

Thankfully, Dad took my cue and changed the subject. "So do you have bags?"

"Uh, yes. Bags." I stammered out the words. "I can—"

"Why doesn't Cooper get the bags, then you can head up to your room and get some sleep." Dad patted Cooper on the back, leading him toward the door we'd come in.

"*Rooms,*" Mom added with a strong emphasis on the word. "As in plural."

"Mom..." I groaned.

"Don't even start with me, Katie. You're an unmarried couple staying in my house." She said *unmarried* like it was a dirty word.

I glanced at Cooper's carefully composed face and recognized the shock hiding below the surface. I looked over at my father, and he shrugged. I knew what that meant. He wasn't willing to fight this battle for me. Or he agreed with her. Not as likely, but entirely possible. I wanted to flash my fancy new engagement ring under her nose and argue my position as a *soon-to-be-married* woman, but I'd safely tucked my ring in my pocket until we could make the announcement. That would have to wait until the morning.

So *rooms* it was.

"I'll help you with the bags," I called after Cooper as he exited the house like his hair was on fire.

Once we were alone, leaning over the trunk of the BMW, I whispered in his ear, "I'm sorry."

"This should be interesting." He chuckled. "Your father seems nice. He loves you." He kissed me quickly then swung my overnight bag over his shoulder.

"Daddy's little girl."

"Absolutely." He flashed his lopsided grin at me. "I guess we'd better get back in there."

I grabbed the only bag he wasn't carrying. "Do we have to?"

In retrospect, having separate rooms wasn't such a bad thing after all. It made the sneaking around so much more exciting. My mom put Cooper in my old bedroom—she'd converted it to a guest room several years ago—and I was relegated to the old guest room. I'm certain the reason for this was the en suite bathroom in the new guest room. She'd assigned Cooper the bedroom that didn't require him to step into the hall to use the bath—a tactical error on her part. I knew the house better than Cooper, and I could sneak around in the dark without losing my way. I made sufficient noise going into and out of the hall bath to distract from the fact that I didn't go back to my assigned room. Instead, I snuck into Cooper's. I had no idea how we managed to keep the giggles down, but we did. Right before sunrise, I snuck back to my own room.

That was where my mom found me the next morning—curled up on top of the covers, pretending to be asleep.

"Katie?" She used the sweet tone I knew she possessed but rarely used. "Dad made breakfast. Are you hungry?"

"G'morning." I fluttered my eyelids and made a few groaning sounds before focusing on her slender figure in the doorway. "Breakfast sounds great. I'll go wake Cooper and be right down."

Elegant, as usual, in some designer or another, Mom flashed what appeared to be a genuine smile. "He's already down there, talking with your father."

"He's what?" I sat bolt upright in bed and was on my feet in an instant.

"They've been down there for nearly an hour." She sat on the side of the bed and looked up at me, all sunshine and happiness, like some Stepford version of herself.

"What are they talking about?" I watched her out of the

corner of my eye as I grabbed a clean pair of jeans and a fresh sweater from my bag. I tossed them on the bed and went back in for underwear. I purposely searched for the unflattering pair I knew I'd tucked somewhere near the bottom of the bag. When I finally found them, I pulled them out with a triumphant look on my face.

"Katie, really," Mom huffed. *That* was the woman I remembered. "Would it kill you to have a little style?"

"What are you talking about?"

She snatched the plain white panties from my hand. "Even I have sexier underwear than this."

"I-I have sexy underwear."

She raised a single arched eyebrow.

"I do! I'll show you." I went back to digging, to prove my point.

"I don't need to see your underwear." She stood, dismissing me with a wave. "Hurry and get ready before the food gets cold."

As soon as the door shut behind her, I tossed the boring panties back into the bag and pulled out the ones I actually intended to wear. With my clothes in hand, I hurried to the hall bath and showered in record time. I finger-styled my hair, slicked a light coating of gloss across my lips, and dressed—all in less than five minutes.

I heard them laughing before I reached the kitchen, setting off an entire village of butterflies swarming in my stomach. Without a word, Cooper set down his fork and crossed the kitchen, greeting me with a chaste kiss.

"You look well rested." I batted my eyelashes at him and bit back a grin.

"I slept like the undead." Cooper blushed, keeping his back to my parents. "Hungry?"

"Famished."

"Come on." Cooper took my hand. "Your mom already made you a plate."

"Sit by me. I've missed you." Dad patted the chair beside

him at the round breakfast table. "So Cooper's been telling us about how you two met—fascinating story."

"Oh, really?" I sank into my chair and attempted a covert glance at Cooper, trying to read his expression without much luck.

"Mmm." Dad nodded. "Sounds like you're doing quite well for yourself down there in Atlanta."

"I-I do all right..." I darted my eyes to Cooper, trying to figure out what he'd actually told my father.

"Oh, come on. According to Cooper, you're a topnotch banker."

"She is." Cooper beamed.

"I, uh..." I stabbed a potato chunk with my fork. "I've been struggling a little lately."

"Who hasn't?" Dad rested his elbows on the table and leaned in. "I saw a huge drop in my clientele this winter. But hey, that's what happens in a tough economy—the boobs are the first thing to go."

Everyone laughed. Even Mom.

Desperate to shift the focus away from me, I changed the subject. "Did Cooper tell you about *his* exciting career?"

"He did." Mom and Dad answered simultaneously.

"He did?" My mouth fell open. I wasn't prepared for Cooper to be so forthcoming about his career. It'd taken me a year to finally drag that information out of him. I almost wondered if he'd made up something else to tell them. "He told you he's a...?"

"A best-selling author? Yes. It's quite impressive actually," Mom added sweetly. She looked at Cooper with the same dreamy gaze she'd had when she first met him.

Cooper flushed, but I could see the satisfaction peeking through.

"Can you believe, I've actually read a few of his books?" Mom added with an almost insulting degree of surprise in her voice.

"I always knew he was talented." I beamed.

Mom made a choking sound and tried to pass it off as a laugh. "You thought he was an assassin."

I glared at her, but she only laughed louder.

"You're the one who put that stupid idea into my head!" I pointed my fork at her like a weapon.

"I did not." She picked at her eggs, averting her eyes from mine. "I simply wanted to make sure he was gainfully employed."

"That's enough of that." Dad chuckled.

Mom patted his hand. "Yes, dear."

*Yes, dear?* My eyes stretched so wide, I felt as if they might fall out of their sockets, and my mouth dropped open. My mother never gave up an argument. *Never.*

Cooper noticed too, and his eyes flashed to mine. Then slowly, one side of his mouth tipped up in a lopsided grin.

Dad took that moment to change the subject yet again. "So, Katie, how was the guest room? Did you have enough blankets? I know how much you miss your old room. I was almost afraid you might end up sleepwalking your way into your old bed."

With a forkful of scrambled eggs mere inches from my mouth, I studied my dad's blank expression. *Did he know?* "The guest room was just fine, thanks. And I don't sleepwalk anymore."

"Oh, Hank, do you remember when Katie was five—or was it six—" A rare burst of excitement overtook my mother, and she seemed lost in her memories for a moment. "She'd managed to sleepwalk her way into the side garden."

"Mom, please don't tell this story." I hung my head, staring into my half-eaten eggs.

"Thankfully, we were still awake, because the child was stark naked! She could have frozen to death out there if we hadn't found her." Mom fanned herself with a linen napkin. "We were terrified we'd wake up one morning, and she'd be floating facedown in the pool."

"You did." I let my fork clatter to my plate. "You told it."

"Katie doesn't sleepwalk anymore." Cooper reiterated my earlier statement, and both of my parents turned toward him with raised eyebrows. "I, uh, I don't think so, anyway." Cooper's face all but went up in flames.

"No." I let out a breath. "I don't sleepwalk anymore."

"Well, that's a relief!" Dad went back to his egg-white omelet. "But if I'm not mistaken, she definitely prays in her sleep." Dad tossed out the statement like a live grenade. "I'm almost positive I heard her calling out to God last night."

*And boom!*

With my ears ringing and my skin on fire, I didn't think. I didn't plan. I just blurted it out. "I'm getting married!"

"What!" My mother shrieked in a decidedly unladylike fashion. "You're getting married? Why didn't you say so?"

"Well, *we're* getting married." Cooper smiled at me from across the table.

"Yes." I nodded. "We."

Before I registered the movement, my dad was on his feet, pulling me into a hug. He crushed me to his chest the way he did when I was a little girl. And while my father squeezed the life out of me, my stoic mother jumped up and down like a teenager at a Justin Timberlake concert.

"Katie, that's simply wonderful!" Mom gushed. "I just knew you two would get married. You'll be delighted to know I already talked to the country club to see if they could squeeze you in this June. You always said you wanted a June wedding, and well, I didn't want to miss out, just in case. But if that's too soon, we can always shoot for August. Mrs. Shilling's daughter was supposed to get married this August, but she found her fiancé in bed with another man, if you can believe it. I'm sure their date is still available." She rattled everything so quickly, I could barely make out the words.

"Whoa, Mom..." I broke free of Dad's grasp and held my

hands out in front of me. "We aren't getting married at the country club."

Like a huge vacuum had sucked the joy right out of her, my mother's face morphed into righteous indignation. "What's wrong with the country club? We've been members there since before you were born. You might recall your sister's reception was held there. Furthermore, your father and I had *our* reception there over thirty-five years ago!"

Cooper stepped in to rescue me. "Grace, I'm sure the country club would be lovely. But my parents have invited us to get married in London, and they've graciously offered to reserve the same church our family's used for centuries."

I couldn't see my own face, but I could see my parents' faces, and I had to believe mine was no less stunned.

"Well, how kind of them." Mom smoothed back her platinum bob, sounding as if she'd had the wind knocked out of her. "We wouldn't want to turn down such a gracious offer. *Centuries*, you say?" She whispered the word as if it held some mystical power.

Cooper nodded.

"Of course." Mom nodded. "London would be a beautiful place for a wedding."

"That's settled!" Dad exclaimed, smacking Cooper across the back with gusto. "I haven't been to Europe in years. Do we have a date set?"

"What about the ring?" Mom *would* have to ask about the ring.

I'd almost forgotten about the four-carat diamond in my pocket. I fished into my jeans and pulled out the ring, sliding it onto my finger where it belonged.

"Here." I held out my hand for inspection. It took a lot to shut my mother up, but as expected, my engagement ring stunned her into silence.

"Oh my... heavens." Her voice evaporated into a tiny whisper as she cupped my hand in hers, turning it ever so slightly to catch the light. "Katie, this is exquisite. I can't even imagine..." She didn't finish, but I knew she was trying to calculate the cost in her head.

I was already half afraid to wear the damn thing *without* knowing how much Cooper had spent. Cooper slid his arm around my waist, nuzzling his nose in my hair.

"So, London?" I whispered, when I was sure he would be the only one to hear.

He shrugged as if it weren't a big deal, but I had a feeling he'd been planning this for a very long time.

This meant I was going to have to come clean about my fear of flying. And soon.

# Colette Bridal Couture

IN THE WEEKS AFTER SHARING the happy news with my parents, I did my best to avoid all things wedding. I would've married Cooper tomorrow if he'd have let me. I just couldn't wrap my head around the idea of traveling to London. *As in England. As in the other side of the ocean. And the inescapable fact that I'd have to get on an airplane to get there.*

We'd decided on a June wedding, and I'd yet to tell Cooper about my insurmountable fear of flying, an eensie-weensie detail that left me less than three months to either discover the secrets of teleportation or overcome a lifelong phobia.

At least I had realistic expectations.

"I haven't looked through a *Brides* magazine in over twenty years." Silvia let out a girlish sigh as she perused the thick spring issue.

The glossy pages called out to the teenage girl in me, and I snatched the magazine from Silvia's hands, hugging it to my chest.

"Hey!"

I hopped onto her desk and flipped to the first page. "My wedding. My book." I tried to act mature about the whole thing. I really did, but even the smell of the crisp new magazine gave me a strange kind of high.

Silvia planted her hands on her hips and narrowed her eyes at me. "You aren't about to go all Bridezilla on us, are you?"

"No." I laughed as I thumbed through the pages, stealthily huffing the inky scent. "No Bridezillas here."

"Wait! What about that one?" Vicky stood over my shoulder, shoving her finger between two pages as she pointed to a frothy confection of a gown.

"Eww. No. I can feel the type-two diabetes coming on just looking at the picture." I resumed my flipping until I landed on something simpler. The milky-white sheath hugged the model's curves just enough to be sexy without being scandalous. "Now this is me: simple yet classy."

"Are you kidding?" Silvia popped her head into the conversation. "I suppose it's a pretty dress, but you're never gonna walk down the aisle in that."

"Why?" I had no idea if she was insulting me or daring me.

"First of all, it's too clingy for underwear." Silvia eyed me over her reading glasses. There was no mistaking the challenge in her stare.

Vicky mouthed, "Panty lines."

"Looks to me like she's wearing a thong." June leaned over the page, pointing to a barely visible flaw in the image.

Silvia slid her glasses to the end of her nose and clucked her tongue. "Nope. That's a crease in the page."

I squinted to get a better look.

"Oh, yep, look at that. A wrinkle in the paper." June nodded, and I had to agree.

"And here..." Silvia ran her finger over the bodice. "You can almost see her nipples through the crepe."

"Okay, fine." I closed the magazine and tossed it onto the desk. "No see-through nighty-dresses, but I'm not wearing one of those whipped cream parfait jobs either."

"Don't worry. We'll find something." Silvia patted my shoulder.

Phil poked his head into the office. "I don't suppose I could get you ladies to do a little work today. I mean, you do still work here, right?"

"Yeah, yeah." Vicky scooped up my discarded magazine and ducked under Phil's outstretched arm. "Keep your boxers on."

June and I followed behind her, splitting off in the lobby to head to our individual offices.

Vicky caught up to me in my open doorway. "Cooper isn't going to give you crap about meeting us Saturday morning to go dress shopping, is he?"

"No, he's so deep in the trenches on his new project, I doubt he'll even notice I'm gone."

Aside from the occasional comment about how wonderful the wedding would be or how excited he was to introduce me to London, Cooper spent every spare moment working on his new book. And other than telling me I'd inspired the story, he kept mum on the details—something that would've ordinarily set off my curiosity radar. Luckily for him, I had far more important things to worry about.

Bright and early Saturday morning, Silvia picked me up in her magenta minivan and headed to the most exclusive dress shop in all of Atlanta: Colette Bridal Couture. June and Vicky waited for us on the sidewalk. Then with Silvia and her spiky caramel hair in the lead, the four of us strutted through the plate glass front doors as if we were part of Ziggy Stardust's entourage.

"Excuse me." Silvia cleared her throat, but when the skinny blonde behind the receptionist desk didn't bother to respond, Silvia repeatedly slapped the shiny silver call bell until I jumped in and took it away from her.

Finally, the girl looked up from her cell phone with a bored sigh. "*Oui?*"

"We have a nine o'clock with Genevieve," Silvia said.

"*Genevieve...*" The girl corrected Silvia's pronunciation, saying the name like *Zshaun-vee-AHVE*. "Is in *zee Aubergine Salon*."

"Where exactly is *zee*, I mean *the* Aubergine Salon?" Silvia asked.

The blonde raised a bloodred fingernail and pointed to a mahogany door to our right. "Zat is zee *Aubergine Salon*, and Genevieve is expecting you."

"Your accent is slipping," Vicky snarked as we lined up in front of the door.

Like Alice stepping through the looking glass, the moment I crossed the threshold, I knew I'd entered a magical world. From the black-lacquered ceiling to the gleaming mahogany floor, the place screamed expensive. Glossy eggplant walls and sparkling crystal chandeliers only added to the fantasy. Fairy lights seemed to dance off every surface like mirrors.

Dark-purple velvet curtains framed rows of satin and lace. In fact, gowns in every shade of white imaginable lined the entire perimeter of the room. A glass display case filled with sparkling crowns and veils sat just off to the side, and a long button-tufted sofa upholstered in the same velvet as the curtains anchored the center of the room.

Vicky plopped onto the couch. "Well, this place'll set you back a few pennies, won't it?"

Like she'd sucker punched me in the gut, I flinched, almost doubling over from the shock of it. I'd already wrestled with the cost of everything, but between my parents and Cooper, I'd been told to go with the flow. My mother insisted on paying for the dress, and I was told to "spare no expense." The lack of a budget should've thrilled me, but instead, it made me nervous.

A short, curvy brunette in a bright-yellow dress bounded into the room, pushing a serving cart in front of her. Empty champagne glasses continued to rattle and clank against each other long after she came to a stop. "Welcome to Colette Bridal Couture. My name is Genevieve." Her French accent was less pronounced than that of the receptionist, but I suspected it was equally fake. She filled a tall flute with champagne. "A toast to the bride?"

"To the bride!" Vicky took the first glass. She quickly drained it then held it out for a refill.

Genevieve poured, keeping me in her peripheral vision. Before I had a chance to protest, she shoved a bubbling flute into my hand.

"I, uh, I'm not... I don't drink." I tried to give it back, but Genevieve jerked her hand away, refusing to take it. *What is this? Hot Potato?* "Silvia, tell her."

With a wave of her hand, Silvia took a fresh glass from the bridal assistant. "Don't be ridiculous. You only shop for a wedding gown once."

"Sil, you've been married three times," I reminded her.

"Well..." Silvia recovered quickly. "You only get married for the *first* time once. So live a little, and drink up!"

"No, really." I tried to pass my champagne to June, but she dodged me with far more grace than I would've expected from a woman of her size, and accepted a glass from Genevieve. I resisted stomping my foot like a five-year-old, but I might have whined a little. "I gave up alcohol!"

"Are you knocked up?" Vicky blurted, and the entire room went silent.

Four pairs of eyes locked on me like a pack of wolves eyeing a wounded deer. The air crackled with tension, and I had to take a step back to avoid the intense scrutiny.

"N-No, I'm n-not—" My throat tightened, and my mouth went dry. I had no idea why I was so nervous. I hadn't done anything wrong. It wasn't as if we lived in 1953. So why did I feel as if I were about to be burned at the stake?

Silvia ran her tongue over her bottom lip as she contemplated the situation. "Is *that* why you're pushing for a June wedding?"

Vicky gasped, pointing to my flat stomach. I could almost hear the *Ah ha!* in her eyes. "You're afraid you'll be showing when you walk down the aisle."

"I'm *not* pregnant!" I squealed. "It's just... well, alcohol does bad things to me. And after what happened on Valentine's Day, I'm not taking any chances."

Our bridal consultant's eyebrows shot up. She didn't say a word, but I could tell she was dying for details.

"Oh, Katie." Silvia nudged my elbow, making champagne slosh over the side and down my hand. "Sweetie, one drink won't kill you."

"See... that's where you're wrong." I set the glass down and backed away slowly. Thoughts of champagne volcanoes and waxing gone wrong flipped through my head. "With my luck, one drink could very well kill me." *And if the champagne doesn't, Cooper just might if I come home drunk again.*

Vicky eyed me with renewed interest. She didn't have her clipboard with her, but she obviously checked off imaginary boxes in her head. "You *are* pregnant!"

I groaned. "How many times do I have to tell you—"

"Prove it." Vicky snatched up my glass and held it out to me.

Between Vicky and Silvia, I'd been talked into slutty outfits, drunken karaoke, and a vajazzled crotch—among other things. This time, I wouldn't be bullied. "Think what you like, but I'm not drinking that."

"Fine." Vicky drained the contents and slammed the glass onto the table. "Let's find this woman a dress before she gives birth!"

The four of them tag-teamed me like a group of savage six-year-olds dressing a life-size Barbie doll. If Silvia was the ringmaster of our little circus, Genevieve was the head juggler. Vicky and June picked out dress after dress, and Genevieve stuffed me into each one with relentless zeal, while Silvia used her iPhone to snap pictures of me in each one, "capturing every moment for all eternity" from the comfort of the purple velvet sofa.

After two hours, I'd gone half-blind from staring into a blizzard of white, and I was beginning to wish I hadn't passed on that champagne.

"What about this one?" Vicky asked for the umpteenth time in the past hour.

I shrugged at the old-fashioned A-line dress in the mirror. The simple lace overlay on the bateau neckline managed to highlight my perfectly average cleavage and adequate collarbones. It reminded me of Jackie Kennedy's wedding gown. My mother would've loved it. "It's nice."

Silvia sighed. "You really need to take this more seriously. Unless you're fine with ordering off the rack, we're running out of time." She said *off the rack* the way my mother might say *boxed wine,* as if it were the epitome of déclassé.

I shuddered. My mother would kill me if I ordered an off-the-rack gown, and Silvia knew it. "I know. I'm trying. I really am." I forced a smile and marched back into the dressing room.

Genevieve snapped her fingers, and I turned for her to unbutton me. She helped me step out of the bell-shaped gown, and I waited in nothing but my best pair of lace panties while she fetched the next dress.

Genevieve peeked her head back in. "Are you set on white?"

"Why?" I eyed her suspiciously. Was she making some comment on my so-called pregnancy?

"Well, I have a simply beautiful gown in a color that would look lovely with your skin tone. It's not quite champagne, not quite pink. Almost a pink champagne."

Her description intrigued me. "Show me?"

Genevieve flashed a smile then pulled the dress from where she'd kept it hidden. She held the strapless gown out for me to step into. She tugged the gauzy fabric up my body, positioning the silk folds across my bust line before fastening the sweetheart neckline in the back. The full, embroidered skirt fell like delicate tissue roses from my waist to where it puddled at my feet.

"Stunning," I murmured, fixated on my own reflection. The gown was the first to bring a genuine smile to my lips.

Genevieve held the cathedral train for me as I staggered out to the three-way mirror where Silvia and the girls waited for me.

"Hot damn, Katie. That dress is gorgeous." Vicky blurted as I took a cautious step up to the platform. "And the color... well, at least you won't have to worry about wearing white, am I right?"

"Shut up, Vicky." Silvia clucked her tongue loudly and beamed from ear to ear as she clicked away with her phone. I guessed by her silence that she was too awed to comment.

"I love it. I absolutely love it," June gushed with out-of-character enthusiasm.

"It's beautiful, Katie. It really is." Silvia finally stood and lowered her phone to walk around me. "The train is delicate but quite substantial. I love the fabric roses. Is this silk?" She turned to Genevieve, who nodded. "And the way the fabric gathers like..."

I nodded. "Tissue roses."

"Hmm..." Silvia made another pass around the back of me. "Did you see the pearl buttons? Just precious." She finished her circuit, stopping directly in front of me. With her hand resting on her chin and a smile spreading across her lips, she stared at me. "I absolutely love the color. I would've never thought. It's old-fashioned yet trendy. And very sexy. I can imagine you wearing a triple-strand choker of pearls and simple pearl earrings. You wouldn't need anything more than that."

"What about her hair?" June asked.

"I'm not sure if it's long enough for a French twist, but that would be gorgeous." Silvia continued to work out the details in her own head.

"Did you pick out a..." Vicky drew an invisible circle around her head.

Silvia raised her eyebrows. "A veil?"

"Yeah, whatever." Vicky scoffed.

"Not yet." Genevieve fluffed my skirt. "But I think something simple is in order. The dress is too beautiful. You don't want to overpower it. We have a beautiful pearl hair clip with a blush tulle—"

I cleared my throat, and all four pairs of eyes lasered in on me. "I think I've been patient. I've certainly played my part. I've easily tried enough dresses to be bruised in the morning. And I really appreciate all your help, but I'm done."

Each of their mouths silently dropped open.

"I mean, why keep looking when I've found the perfect dress?" I beamed, unable to force the smile from my face.

My friends let out a deafening chorus of squeals that quickly morphed into a pulsating wail. Or rather, it would seem *they* weren't making the sound, but I still couldn't hear a thing over the high-pitched siren piercing the air.

"What's going on?" With my hands pressed firmly over my ears, I screamed over the deafening howl.

"Back up!" Genevieve shrieked, shoving me out of the way just before series of heavy steel doors dropped from the ceiling, trapping the gowns as if they were priceless art.

About two point five seconds later, the sprinklers came on, dousing us with an icy downpour.

"What the hell?" Vicky mouthed the words, and since I had to read her lips, I conveniently ignored the streak of obscenities that followed her actual question.

While Vicky and I scurried around like a pair of confused rats, desperate to abandon the sinking ship, Silvia held up the ends of a velvet curtain, using it like an umbrella, while June stood as still as stone, as if she hadn't yet processed the situation.

Time seemed to stand still. I had no idea how long we stood under the spray before a mature woman in a purple pantsuit burst into the room.

She flailed her arms through the air as she shouted words I only barely made out. "Why are you still here? Out! Out! Out!" She shooed us from the building, where we lined up on the sidewalk, waiting for the fire trucks to pull alongside the curb.

I must've looked worse than I felt, because one of the brawny firemen approached me with concern etched across his rugged face.

"Are you hurt?"

I pressed a frozen hand to my chest. "Who? Me?"

Eyeing my exposed cleavage, he stripped off his heavy coat and draped it over my shoulders. "You're probably in shock."

Silvia huffed her way over just in time to rescue me from my would-be savior. She freed me from the smoke-scented jacket and wasted no time returning it to him. "She's not in shock. She's just wet."

The fireman nodded, slightly dejected, and moved on to his next victim.

"I can't leave you alone for a minute!" Silvia took a good look at me and choked back a laugh. "Oh, Katie...you look like a drowned poodle in that dress."

"Did someone say poodle?" The purple lady stomped her way toward us, water streaming from her drenched beehive hairdo. "We don't allow dogs at Colette Bridal Couture!"

"No dogs here unless you count Hottie McFirefighter over there." Vicky nodded toward the fireman draping his dirty coat over another wet bridal patron. Then she smirked and saluted Purple Lady. "Carry on, Professor Umbridge."

The woman rolled her eyes then blanched as they settled on me. "You've ruined that dress!"

"Hey, *we* didn't turn the water on," Vicky spat back.

"No, of course not. For that, we can thank..." Purple lady set her sights on another waterlogged bride dripping her way out of the building. "The witch from the *Chocolat Salon!*"

Without another word, the woman spun on her heel, preparing to march off again.

"Wait!" Silvia blocked her exit, shoving me forward until I was trapped between them. "Who do I speak to about ordering a dry version of this dress?"

# You Can't Argue With Tradition

WITH MY DRESS ORDERED AND a tentative agreement in place for matching platinum-gray bridesmaids dresses, Silvia, June, and Vicky shifted their focus to the pre-wedding festivities. Monday afternoon, we'd all gathered in Silvia's office under the guise of learning a new procedure.

June practically vibrated with excitement. "What about a Las Vegas getaway? We could get Céline Dion tickets!"

"Not a fan of Sin City, sorry." *Or airplanes.* I tamped down the panic, taking a deep cleansing breath. I really needed to get my emotions in check—and maybe a prescription for Valium. "And I'm not drinking, remember?"

"Fine, no road trip. But no liquor? Really? I get that you're worried about booze hurting the baby, but the rest of us—"

The glare I shot her could've melted the steel beams in the Chrysler Building.

"Fine. Geez." Vicky drew a line through the first two items on her list. "At least let me hire a few male strippers."

"Forget it." I shook my head until my teeth rattled. "We agreed. No booze and no boys."

"Jesus, Katie, did you go to Catholic school?" Vicky jotted something down in her chicken scratch.

"No," I said. "But I've seen *Bridesmaids*, and I'm not taking any chances. Personally, I'd rather not even have a party. It's just so... cliché." Or scary. Same thing.

"Oh, mark my words, we *are* having a bachelorette

party." Vicky huffed, writing furiously in her notebook. "And for the record, *I* agreed to nothing. You made demands. I ignored them as usual."

Apparently, she wasn't going to take no for an answer. "I'll give you three reasons why a bachelorette party isn't a good idea. First of all—"

"You only get married once." Vicky countered, cutting off my argument before I'd even gotten started.

"Silvia's on her third husband," I pointed out, nodding toward Silvia, who didn't bother to look up from her fake spreadsheet. Two could play this game.

"Yeah, well..." Vicky regrouped like a champion. She tossed her red hair over her shoulder, barely pausing to think, as if she'd already anticipated my every response. "Like she said the other day, you only get married for the first time once."

"I did say that." Silvia finally joined the conversation.

"And besides," June added, "*Katie* will only be getting married once."

"Exactly!" Vicky high-fived June, and the two of them beamed at me like a pair of kittens that'd just gorged themselves on cream. "It's practically required for every new bride to have a bachelorette party to usher out her single days. And really, if you think about it, the party isn't even for you. It's for your friends. Once you're married, you're not going to want to hang out with us anymore. Think about it. It's already happening. You spend nearly every waking moment with Mr. Romance, and after the wedding, that's only going to get worse. I can't begin to imagine how infrequently we'll see you after the baby comes..."

"Nice argument." Silvia looked impressed, and I had to begrudgingly agree. Vicky had put up a valiant fight, though I wished she'd drop the whole baby thing already.

"Thank you, Silvia." If she could've folded her elbow that far, I suspected Vicky would've patted herself on the back.

"I'm still here," I reminded them with a frustrated sigh. "I'm still *not* pregnant. And I still don't want a bachelorette party."

Flames danced in Vicky's eyes as she prepared her counterattack.

"Katie, you don't want to deny your friends the opportunity to throw you a party, do you?" June pouted. She went for the low blow, hitting me square in the feels. "At the very least, let us throw you a shower."

All the fight drained out of me. Her argument was little more than blatant extortion, using guilt to win. But it worked. "Fine. You can throw me a shower—something nice and quiet with finger sandwiches and iced tea. But I draw the line at alcohol and strange men dancing naked!" I pointed a finger at Vicky.

"Whatever. You're absolutely no fun, Katie James." Vicky huffed on her way out of Silvia's office.

"We can have it here after work one day." I heard the gears spinning as June mentally planned my quiet little shower.

"That's a wonderful idea." I smiled, imagining cucumber sandwiches and lemonade—the sort of party my mother might throw with the ladies at the country club: boring, but entirely safe. *Just what I need.*

Silvia smirked. "Can't wait. Sounds like a real barn burner."

She could spread the sarcasm as thick as she wanted. I didn't care. I'd miraculously managed to dodge a bullet. I didn't need to be clairvoyant to know the sort of shindig Vicky would've orchestrated, and frankly, the mere thought horrified me.

Without giving Silvia a backward glance, I vacated her office and headed to my own to pack up for the day. I'd barely made it halfway across the lobby when I noticed Cooper and Vicky having an animated conversation in my office. My overactive imagination wrestled for control of my emotions, but I beat it back. I wouldn't let the green-eyed monster get the best of me. Not today. "Hey, you two."

They jumped apart at the sound of my voice. Cooper looked like a kid caught stashing peas in a napkin. Vicky looked... smug.

"What's going on over here?" I glared at Vicky and lifted my cheek to meet Cooper's warm lips.

"Nothing for you to worry about." Cooper's smile wavered slightly. "Vicky and I just agreed to a temporary truce. For the sake of the wedding."

"But don't expect it to last a minute longer than the I-do's." Vicky pointed at Cooper, but the hint of a grin sucked all the venom from the threat. She backed out of my office. "Okay, well, you kids behave yourself. I mean it. Keep it PG. These walls have seen about all the action they can withstand."

She had me shaking my head as I watched until she disappeared around the corner. "That's an odd truce."

"I'd do anything for you, my love." Cooper leaned down and kissed the crease forming between my eyebrows.

I studied him through narrow slits while shoving files into drawers. I'd have to sort through them tomorrow, but I didn't care. "You're up to something."

"Now, why would you say that?" Without missing a beat, he switched off my computer and tucked my phone into my purse then took my coat off the hook and held it out for me.

Staring daggers at my black wool jacket as if it were the guilty party, I worked my way through the puzzle. Then it hit me, and my eyes snapped up to meet his. "Because Vicky's clearly up to something, and since you aren't the least bit suspicious, you must be in on it."

Cooper laughed, but something uncomfortable flashed in his blue-green eyes. "Come on, Nancy Drew. Let's get out of here before the traffic gets bad."

"You know, I'm not as bad a detective as the rest of

you'd like to believe." I shoved my arms into my waiting coat sleeves.

"Of course you aren't." Cooper hooked my purse strap over my shoulder then clasped my hand in his, leading me toward the exit. "But maybe this time, you should let it go. I have something I need to discuss with you, and I'm afraid you won't like it."

My feet froze in place right outside the bank's main door. "Oh my God, what's wrong? Is there something wrong with the wedding venue? Did they have to cancel? And with only a few months to plan something else? That's *horrible*! Well, we'll just have to get married right here in Atlanta, won't we?" Torn between horror and elation, my words all ran together as the very real possibilities ricocheted through my brain.

"Katie, calm down." Cooper squeezed my hand. "The wedding venue is fine. Everything's going ahead as scheduled."

"Oh. Well..." I heaved out a shaky breath. "That's... that's good. Whew. You scared me for a minute."

Cooper pressed the remote unlock button for the car and opened my door for me. "Why do I get the feeling you're not at all relieved?"

"I, uh... I have no idea what you're talking about." I quickly climbed in and shut the door before I said anything else. I was running out of time to tell him the truth.

Three weeks later, I still hadn't come clean about my fear of flying. After Cooper divulged *his* not-so-pleasant news, I had other things to worry about, like a two-week-long press tour with Vivian and a transatlantic trip to visit his parents. When he'd asked me to join him, I knew my refusal sounded irrational—maybe even a little paranoid— but I couldn't do it.

"Does she really have to come here?" I hated arguing

with him over the phone, but I hadn't seen him in over a week, and the last thing I wanted was for Vivian to spoil our reunion.

Cooper let out a long breath. "You'd rather I stay here in New York?"

"No!" I knew I was acting like a spoiled child, but I didn't care. Just when I thought we were about to get some time to ourselves, Vivian had to ruin it.

I decided to lay it all out there. "I just wanted some alone time with my fiancé."

"We will," he cooed. "I promise."

"I don't understand why she needs to be in the same room as you at all. We live in the Internet age with access to email, FaceTime, and Skype, not to mention all the other assorted modes of communication. Surely, one of those should be sufficient." As much as I complained, I really did understand. A big part of his job included promoting the book. And as much as I hated to admit it, Vivian was a good publicist. *A horrible human being, perhaps. But a great publicist.*

"Don't pout."

"How did you—"

"Because I know you better than you know yourself."

I snuggled into the pillow, hugging my phone to my ear. "I wish you were home."

"With any luck, I'll be home before you fall asleep Friday night."

"I miss you." I tugged on my bottom lip with my teeth.

"You know, we could solve this whole thing if you'd just come work for me." He'd said the same thing a dozen times before, but it never failed to set off a thousand butterflies in my stomach.

"Let me guess." I giggled. "Balancing your checkbook naked?"

Cooper chuckled. "I suppose there's always that, but no. I was thinking maybe..."

I waited, but he didn't continue. The dead air between us drove me crazy. "What?"

"Never mind." He exhaled sharply. "It's a stupid idea."

"No, tell me."

He groaned, and I imagined him raking a hand through his hair. "What if I gradually phased Vivian out and hired *you* to be my publicist?"

I untangled my legs from the blankets and sat up straight as the warmth drained from my face. The idea both excited and terrified me. "You're joking, right? I-I don't know anything about being a publicist."

"I could teach you." He became more animated as he rattled off his ideas. "Hell, you could shadow Vivian. You have more experience in the business world than Vivian did before taking the job, and I'd certainly trust you to put my interests above your own, especially when your interests *are* my own." His voice dropped to a low rumble. "And I'd very much like seeing you every day."

It took a moment, but I finally came back to my senses. "It's a big decision. Can I... can I have time to think about it?"

"Take all the time you need."

*Friday.* I'd somehow struggled through the entire workweek without incident, and in a few hours, I'd finally be reunited with the love of my life. How had I ever managed to survive the first twenty-nine years of my life without him, when I could barely manage a week or two alone since we'd met?

Our time apart made me realize how important Cooper had become to me—to my life. According to Vicky, I should've celebrated every moment of my independence before I vowed to love, honor, and obey. Not that anyone had said *anything* about obeying...

Instead, I moped around the bank as if my imaginary cat had died. But damn it, if I wanted to pine for Cooper while he was gone, that was my prerogative. And besides, who said modern women can't pine? Who was I kidding? As a 1950s housewife, I had real potential. But as a feminist, I was a complete failure.

At 6:01, Vicky strolled into my office and hopped onto my desk, crossing her legs at the knee.

Leaning just far enough to the left that I didn't fall out of my chair, I peeked around her to the empty lobby. "What are you doing here?" When Phil insisted I stay late to finish a last-minute project, I'd assumed it was because everyone else had already left for the day.

Vicky snatched the paperwork I'd been working on from my hands, but before I could get my mouth open to ask her what the hell she thought she was doing, she ripped the page in half. "Okay, so it's like this... Silvia, June, and I are kidnapping you for your bachelorette party. And before you try to stop me, don't bother. This project is bogus. Phil gave it to you to help stall until we were ready. And I already got Cooper's permission, your mother's blessing, and enough food to feed an army, so you may as well surrender to the merriment."

An exasperated sigh escaped my throat. "Vicky—"

"*Tsk, tsk.*" Vicky leaned over and squinted down at me. "What did I say?"

*Now would be a good time to drag out that shiny new backbone of mine.* "But—"

"No buts." She reached across my desk and pushed the power button on my monitor then hopped off the desk again. With her hands planted firmly on her hips, Vicky jutted her chin out at me in some sort of challenge. "Well, what are you waiting for? Grab your shit. We're leaving."

I collected my things in a stunned silence. The blood must have rushed from my head, because I couldn't come up with a single rational argument as to why I shouldn't run the other way. And frankly, I wasn't sure whether to be flattered or frightened at the prospect of a party in my honor. It took me a minute, but I finally found my nerve and my voice. "And you really expect me to believe Cooper gave his blessing for this train wreck?"

Vicky huffed. "Begrudgingly, perhaps, but yes. He did. It's part of our truce, if you must know. And don't look at me like I just peed in your perfume. Twenty years from now, you'll look back on this day and thank me."

I seriously doubted it.

Vicky nudged me toward the exit. "Let's go! We're on a schedule."

As we crossed the dark lobby, the hair on the back of my neck prickled and stood at attention. "So if Silvia and June are part of this poorly planned kidnapping, where are they?"

With her keys in her hand, Vicky set the alarm and opened the front door for me. "You seriously worry too much."

With my feet planted firmly inside the bank, I gave her my best bitch brow, something I'd learned from Vicky herself.

"Geez, must you spoil every surprise?" She rolled her eyes. "Someone had to get everything set up for the party while I kept you busy. I can't be in two places at once, you know."

Only slightly comforted by her relatively reasonable response, I unfolded my arms and nodded. "Fine. I'll go with you."

Vicky led me to my own car and waited while I unlocked the doors.

"I'm driving." She slid into the driver's seat while I watched in horror. "Oh, close your mouth, and get in. It's a Prius, not a Porsche."

With my mouth still hanging open, I climbed into the passenger seat of my car and buckled myself in.

"Come on, Katie." Vicky laughed. "I'm taking you to a

party, so why do you look like I'm dragging you to your own execution?"

I eyed her cautiously from my side of the car. "I know your idea of a party, and I've got to tell you, I'm terrified."

"Then allow me to put you out of your misery. I'm not taking you to a strip club, a bar, or even a swanky restaurant." Vicky pulled out of the bank parking lot and took the first right—the same route I took every night on my way home.

"Then where *are* you taking me?"

"Cooper's house."

# It's Raining Men

After making multiple stops at several convenience stores and driving around the neighborhood three times, Vicky pulled into the driveway just before seven.

Her strange behavior made me antsy to get out of the car. "What the hell was all that? Are we on a secret scavenger hunt that you forgot to tell me about?"

As if she knew where she was going, Vicky clicked the remote for the garage door and pulled into the open bay. "Well, if it was a secret, I certainly wouldn't tell you, now would I?"

With a deep growl in the back of my throat, I unbuckled my seat belt and climbed out. My agitation wasn't entirely Vicky's fault. While she dragged me on her wild-goose chase, the Google Alert I'd set up for Cooper sent me an email link to a popular gossip site with pictures of my fiancé and his publicist looking far cozier than they should have been.

Not that I was jealous or anything.

I trusted Cooper with every fiber of my being. But Vivian was an evil harpy with a mission to steal my fiancé. And I couldn't exactly stop her if I was stuck in Atlanta while Cooper was with her in New York. "I'm really not in the mood for games tonight."

"Well, that's too damn bad." Vicky got out of the car and slammed the door. "Because I planned this shindig, and you're gonna play games until you puke if I have to stick my finger down your throat."

"What are you, twelve? That's gross." I stepped into the mudroom and kicked off my shoes. After hanging my jacket and my keys on separate hooks, I wandered into the dark kitchen, leaving Vicky to find her own way. "Why are we here, anyway? Are we meeting Silvia and June before heading to the party?"

"Not exactly," Vicky said from behind me.

My eyes had just begun to adjust to the dark when the lights snapped on, and my heart came to a sudden stop.

"Surprise!" Voices came at me from all directions.

Vicky somehow managed to get around me to take her spot at the front of the mob, red hair fanning out around her like a lion's mane. Behind her, June and Silvia grinned like a pair of idiots. I only recognized a few of the other faces in the crowd, most of whom I assumed were Vicky's friends.

Sparkling white and silver wedding bells hung from shiny silver streamers stretched from one side of the room to the other. Big white bows adorned the fronts of the distressed walnut cabinets, and matching satin ribbon lined the edge of the granite counters. On the left, several bottles of sparkling grape juice and a pyramid of stacked wine glasses caught my eye. On the right, several tiers of decadently decorated cupcakes reminded me of a bakery window. A display of powder-blue ring boxes topped with what I could only assume were cheap imitation engagement rings surrounded a centerpiece of white roses on the breakfast table. True to her word, Vicky had enough food to feed an army set up on the large center island.

I spun around to take everything in. The festive decor appeared to carry over into the surrounding rooms as well. Glittery confetti covered every flat surface, making Cooper's house almost unrecognizable. "H-How did you...?"

"Lots of planning, lying, and distraction," Silvia answered with a grin.

"I-I don't know what to say."

"Don't say anything, sweetie." Silvia pulled me in for a hug. "Just enjoy your party."

With one last squeeze, I stepped out of her embrace. "Thank you."

She tilted her head to the side as if to ask, "Why?"

"For not listening to me. For the party. I really needed this tonight."

"Oh pish." She swatted the air in front of me, and I could've sworn her eyes glistened with unshed tears. "You're the daughter I never had. You didn't really think I'd let you get married without a party, did you?"

"You're the best non-mom a girl could have." I tried to hug her again, but she sidestepped my attempt.

"Go on, now." Silvia nudged me toward the drinks. "Before you make my mascara run."

With a laugh, I grabbed a glass and filled it with white grape juice.

An hour later, after stuffing myself with pimento cheese dip, shellfish, and cupcakes, and opening an assortment of lotions, sexy lingerie, and one horribly embarrassing hot-pink dildo, I had to admit Vicky threw an amazing party. I'd almost forgotten about Cooper's whirlwind publicity tour with the ice queen.

"Your phone keeps vibrating." Vicky handed me my phone with an exaggerated eye-roll. *Three missed calls and four messages from Cooper.* "Tell him he can relax. I've stuck to our agreement."

Without checking the messages, I hit the call back button. "I'm sure he's not worried."

His phone went straight to voice mail.

"That's weird." I pulled up the most recent message and had to sit down before my legs gave out.

*Cooper: Hey babe. Hope you're having fun at your party.*

*:) Lost track of time in NYC and missed our flight to Atlanta. Catching the first one out in the morning. Love you.*

"What the hell?"

"What's up?" Vicky tried to read over my shoulder.

I shook her off. "Nothing. Just... Cooper's not going to make it home tonight."

"Oh, well. Cool." A wide smile split Vicky's face. "That gives us more time for fun, right? Maybe we can even stick a toe over that imaginary line Cooper drew in the sand."

With a forced smile, I nodded. I didn't bother to tell her about the images I'd seen on *TMZ* or that Cooper didn't bother to say where he was staying in New York. *I trust him. I trust him. I trust him.* And with anyone else, I really would have. But he was with Vivian.

Another quick Google search brought up even more pictures of Cooper laughing with Vivian at some swanky nightclub. I rapidly clicked through the photos until I reached one that froze me in place: Vivian, on her knees at Cooper's feet, staring up at his stunned expression while her bony claws disappeared somewhere in the vicinity of his lap.

*That bitch!*

Rationally, I knew I was overreacting. I knew Cooper loved me. There had to be an explanation for what stared me in the face, and yet at that particular moment, I didn't want to hear it. Despite listening to my serious concerns about Vivian, Cooper continued to allow her into his inner circle. And for all I knew, she was inviting him into *her* inner circle at this very minute. I needed a distraction. And fast.

"I changed my mind," I blurted to no one in particular.

"About?" Vicky's eyebrows ticked up her forehead.

"Strippers. Booze. The whole shebang." Every word out of my mouth was a metaphorical slap in the face to my own overactive imagination. "I'm only getting married once. I should totally have a bash to remember, right?"

"I thought you'd never ask." Vicky let out a huge sigh of relief and led me to Cooper's stainless steel commercial refrigerator. She opened the door and shoved an icy bottle of vodka into my hands. "Here. There's plenty more where this came from. I need to let the guys in. They've been sitting in a van outside for over an hour, waiting for you to come to your senses."

After cuing up the music, Vicky swung open the front door, and four of the hottest guys I'd ever seen filed into Cooper's enormous living room to the tune of "It's Raining Men."

The last of the dancers—a gorgeous blond in a black cape and top hat—gyrated to Heart's "Magic Man" in the center of the room while I drowned my sorrows in another lemontini. My Google alerts hadn't shut up all night, and neither had my mother since one of her country club friends sent her a picture of Cooper signing autographs in Manhattan.

Once Cooper'd finally made the announcement, outing himself as the author of the Immortal Blood series, his female fan base went completely insane. At least once a week, some sex-crazed woman would approach him, asking him to bite her. Vivian ate it up. She seemed to thrive on my discomfort. Rationally, I knew I should ignore the whole thing. But I couldn't.

Vicky was right. I needed to assert myself more, to stand up for myself against the tyranny of... of... I couldn't remember what I was supposed to be protesting. *Oh yeah... Vivian.*

I couldn't stop her from monopolizing Cooper's time tonight, but starting tomorrow, he was all mine. After careful thought and consideration—or more specifically, after having my fill of Vivian's crap—I'd decided to take

Cooper up on his offer to be his publicist. *Right after I punch Vivian in her big, stupid mouth.*

After kicking off my toe-pinching heels somewhere in the vicinity of the sofa, I wandered over to where Magic Mike waved his wand at an eager June. While the dancing magician peeled off his costume, Vicky and her friends screamed over the music.

"Come on, Magic Mike. Take it off!"

*Why's it so hot in here?*

My head spun as I joined in the strip tease, shedding my claustrophobic blouse—leaving me in nothing but a flimsy off-white camisole and black pencil skirt. "Do you come here often?" I asked him just before tripping over my own feet.

Silvia grabbed my arm to steady me. "Are you drunk?"

"No," I lied.

Vicky leaned in and smelled my breath. "You smell like Lemon Pledge."

I put a hand over my mouth but couldn't stop the giggles.

Vicky mashed her hands into her hips and mouthed, "What about the baby?"

Something about her over-the-top expression struck me as funny, and I dissolved into hysterics. An entire minute passed before I could form actual words. "I keep telling you, there is no baby."

"B-But—" Vicky sputtered.

My legs folded beneath me until I was sitting cross-legged in the middle of the floor at Magic Mike's unbelievably sexy feet. "I'm not even sure there's going to be a wedding anymore."

"What?" Vicky and Silvia shrieked in unison, drawing the naked magician's attention.

"Look." I pulled up the images I'd saved and handed my phone to Silvia. "While I'm here, dirty dancing with naked strangers, Vivian's trying to seduce my fiancé in New York!"

Unable to help myself, I panned up and down the magnificent specimen of manhood in front of me, carefully avoiding his impressive *attributes* staring me right in the face. As if it knew what I was thinking, his bulge twitched, and I blinked up at him. "I, uh, I'm sorry, but I'm engaged."

"Sweetheart, you're not my type." Magic Mike cooed as he looked over Silvia's shoulder at the photos of Cooper displayed on my phone. "Stop the presses. Who is that delicious hunk of man meat? Now, *he* is most definitely my type."

"That..." I let out a lemon-flavored sigh. "Is my fiancé."

With a sad smile, he held out his hand and pulled me to my feet. "Come on, honey, you can tell me all about it."

An hour later, I was still on the couch, cuddled up to the half-naked stripper with my head on his shoulder as I spilled my guts. "He knows I hate her. She's awful. I'll bet she drowns puppies on her days off."

"Or skins them for coats," Vicky tossed in from her spot on the floor.

"Yes!" I agreed. "I'll bet she has a whole closet of dead-puppy coats."

"Now why would your man want someone like that?" Magic Mike—or Sam, now that we'd been formally introduced—smoothed my hair behind my ear. "If what you said is true, he's one of the good guys."

"Mm-hmm, he is." I tried to imagine my new friend dressed in something more conservative than a shiny silver G-string. Like actual clothes. "How'd you get to be so smart?"

Sam beamed at me. "I'm almost finished with my masters in clinical psychology at Emory. I just do this on the side to pay the bills."

His revelation surprised me, and I looked up just in

time to see a half-naked sailor eating cheese dip out of a jeweled G-string. "Ewww, isn't that a..."

"Ryan!" Sam jumped off the couch, spilling me into the cushions. "Is that my brand-new NuttyBuddy?"

"It was this—" Ryan huffed as he held up his makeshift dip cup. "Or the *Mikasa*. And everyone knows you don't put *Mikasa* in the microwave!"

Something had crawled into my mouth and died there. *A squirrel maybe. Or a cat with poor hygiene.* Whatever it was, it needed to go. And according to the telltale pressure in my bladder, so did I. Every inch of me throbbed, and my limbs were as stiff as week-old roadkill. My left arm had gone numb from sleeping on it, and my hips ached where they pressed against the hard floor.

*Wait... the floor?*

The night before came back to me in flashes, and I groaned. *Cooper... Vivian... telling my life story to Magic Mike-slash-Sam, the naked psychologist.* With my eyes squeezed shut, I prayed for the room to stop spinning. I knew I'd eventually have to open them, but if the pounding in my head was any indication, total destruction surrounded me.

A rumble sounded on my immediate right. No, not a rumble... something else. Deep, rhythmic snoring... Cooper didn't snore, but there was definitely a warm body pressed against me. In fact, there was a warm body on either side of me.

*Oh, crappity crap crap!*

Somehow, I knew my luck wasn't good enough for even one of those bodies to belong to Cooper. Forcing one eye open, I winced at the stream of morning light that flooded into my foggy brain.

*Focus, Katie.*

A rock-hard arm came out of nowhere and caged me

against the floor. *Oh, God.* I recognized that hairy limb and the all-but-naked body attached to it. Sam held me in a bear hug with his face just inches from my mine. His stale morning breath fanned across my face as he mumbled in what could have been a foreign language for all I knew.

"Sam." I prodded his forearm with a finger. "Wake up."

A door slammed somewhere in the house as my worst nightmare imaginable came true.

"Katie?" Cooper called out to me from the kitchen.

I struggled to sit up, but Sam's iron grip on me tightened. "This can't be happening! Someone, please tell me I'm hallucinating."

"If you're hallucinating, you may as well take off all your clothes." Vicky groaned from the other side of me.

"This isn't funny, Vicky! Cooper's home." I ground out the words with as much composure as I could muster while a naked stripper drooled in my hair.

Like a jack-in-the-box springing forth, Vicky sat up and reached over me to slap Sam in the head. "Come on, Magic Mike. This may be your last chance to get out of here alive."

Sam stirred but failed to release me from his grasp.

"Oh, please, wake up," I whined, trying to slide out from under his burly arm with no luck. *Who knew strippers were so freaking strong?*

Cooper muttered obscenities from the next room, but I couldn't manage the appropriate level of concern for whatever he may have found there, when I knew what he would find if he managed to make his way into the living room any time soon.

"Who installed a damn—" His voice cut off just as his shadow fell over me. "What the hell?"

"I-I can explain," I grunted with another valiant attempt to extract myself from Sam's clutches.

"Somebody had better start explaining!" The vein in his neck pulsed in time with my fluttering heart.

"Cooper, what on earth happened in... oh!" Vivian strolled into the room looking as starched as ever. "So much for greeting you with open arms."

"This is not at all what it looks like." Sam rolled away as if I were a fire-ant mound and quickly cupped his sparkling package. "I swear I didn't touch her."

Cooper growled at Sam like a werewolf in the throes of a full moon.

Sam took several steps back, bumping into a chair. "Honestly, dude. I'm gay."

After processing Sam's declaration, Cooper turned his anger on Vicky. "I guess this explains why there's a stripper pole in my dining room."

She shrugged.

"I hold you completely responsible for all of this." Cooper paused as if running everything though his head. "Gay strippers, Vicky? Really?"

"Hey, you made the rules. I just followed them." Vicky smirked. "And trust me. Not one of these guys hit on your fiancée."

Vivian stood off to the side like a spectator at a multi-car collision until the anger simmering just below the surface bubbled over. "I can't believe you people! Is no one going to say anything about Katie, once again, drinking herself into a stupor? And you." Her voice rose to a crescendo as she pointed a claw at Vicky. "You let a pregnant woman drink?"

Cooper's mouth dropped open as a look of horror took over his features. "Viv, I told you that in confidence."

"Why does everyone keep saying I'm pregnant?"

No one bothered to acknowledge my question.

"Come on, Cooper. Let's get out of here." Vivian grabbed Cooper's sleeve and tugged.

He gaped down at where her fingers gripped his shirt then ripped his arm from her grasp. "I'm not going anywhere."

"So you don't care that your pregnant fiancée got drunk last night and slept with a gay stripper?" Vivian's voice ratcheted up a notch as she whirled on me. "And you! I have absolutely no idea what he sees in you."

"I'm sorry, man," Sam pleaded with Cooper as he tugged on his cutaway trousers. "I swear. All we did was sleep. And for the record, I had no idea she was pregnant."

"Oh. My. God!" I sat up and had to grab my head to hold it together. "For the last time, I'm *not* pregnant! Where did you even get that idea?"

While Cooper gave Vicky a non-verbal trouncing, I kept my eyes glued on Vivian and waited for her head to explode. *Hey, a girl can dream, right?*

"Well, *you* may not see it, but I certainly do." Vivian glowered at me as she spoke to Cooper. "You're far too good for this—"

"That's enough!" Something dark and foreboding flashed in Cooper's eyes.

"I'm serious, Cooper." Vivian didn't take the hint. She kept going, rattling off her laundry list of reasons why I was an unsuitable mate for her boss. "From the first moment I laid eyes on her, I knew she'd drag you down, and it looks as if I was right." Vivian stared at me with her upper lip curled up in distaste. "She's neurotic, immature, and decidedly middle class."

*Middle class? She's so lucky my mom wasn't invited to this fiasco.* Too stunned to respond, I simply stayed seated while Cooper rounded on Vivian.

"I said that's enough!" With his body rigid with tension, the muscles in Cooper's jaw popped, and his hands tightened into fists.

Oblivious to Cooper's meltdown, Vivian continued her unstoppable rant. "Oh, I figured you'd have your fun... get her out of your system, and move on... but no." Her jet-black curls bounced around her face in mad disarray. "You had to propose to the gold-digging whore!"

A chorus of gasps filled the air.

Before Cooper did something I knew he'd regret, I scrambled to my feet as a shot of adrenaline spiked through me. *Hello, backbone! So nice to finally meet you.* "Gold-digging whore? Well, aren't you the pot calling the kettle black? What about you? Gallivanting all over New York City with *my* fiancé? I'll bet you even tipped off the paparazzi to get those lovely photographs my mother and her friends saw splashed across the Internet."

Cooper's eyes bounced between Vivian's face and mine as if he were watching a heated tennis match. "What pictures?"

Vicky grabbed my phone from the couch cushions and cued up the photos before shoving it into Cooper's hands. "These."

Cooper's frown deepened as he flipped through the images. When he let out a breath with a loud whoosh, I knew he'd found the most incriminating of the bunch. "Jesus, Viv. I knew you weren't that clumsy. You spilled your drink in my lap on purpose, didn't you? Just so you could, what? Hurt my fiancée? Katie, I'm so sorry. I had no idea..."

"What? That you'd get caught?" Vicky snarked.

"Well, to coin the phrase of the morning..." Cooper flashed a grim smile. "This isn't at all what it looks like."

For the first time since I'd seen the horrible pictures, I could breathe again. My heart hammered behind my paper-thin cami as Cooper handed my phone to Vicky. Despite what some might consider overwhelming evidence, I had the utmost faith in Cooper.

He turned and took my ice-cold hands in his. "It would appear I owe you an apology."

"You what?" Vivian shrieked. She'd worked herself into a wild frenzy.

Ignoring Vivian and looking completely chastened, Cooper squeezed my hands. "I shouldn't have dismissed your concerns about Vivian as petty jealousy. As you said, you're a far better detective than I've given you credit for."

"I forgive you," I whispered. "And I've decided to take you up on your offer to come work for you."

His fragile grin spread into a full-blown smile. "Well, that's fantastic news because as it happens, I've just fired my publicist."

I wasn't sure what sound caught my attention first, Vicky's sharp intake of breath or Vivian's bloodcurdling wail.

For just an instant, I worried Vivian might actually transform into a fire-breathing dragon the way Maleficent did in *Sleeping Beauty*. But no fire spewed forth when she opened her mouth, only a rancid stream of vitriol. "You. Can't. Fire. Me!"

Cooper relaxed at my side, tossing an arm over my shoulder. "Actually, I can. You're fired. See how easy that was?"

With another earsplitting scream, Vivian stormed out of the house, slamming the door so hard behind her the windows rattled.

"Wow." A ginger head popped up from behind the couch. I didn't remember his name, but before taking it all off, he'd been dressed like a cowboy. "Y'all throw one hell of a party!"

# Cruise Queens

I'D OFFICIALLY LOST MY MIND. With less than two weeks to go before the wedding, and despite Cooper's best attempts to convince me flying was the safest way to travel, I was about to board an ocean liner for a week-long transatlantic crossing.

With my mother.

Since I'd waited until the last minute to come clean, and Cooper had already arranged to be in London during the two weeks immediately preceding the wedding, he couldn't go with me. But my ever-protective fiancé refused to allow me to travel alone, leaving me with no other choice but to accept my mother's oh-so-generous offer.

Before I'd even come up with a semi-reasonable protest, she'd booked the trip, paid for the tickets, and made arrangements to meet me in New York in time to board the ship. My hands, as they say, were tied.

"Katie, we need to go." Mom pressed her bony hands into her narrow hips and glared at me from behind her vintage Wayfarers. I couldn't see her eyes through the dark lenses, but I felt the icy chill boring through my forehead, nonetheless. In her crisp navy-blue capris and white blouse—complete with a huge navy bow—she looked like a retro ad for cruise wear. "You know how I hate to be late."

"Just a minute, Mom. You go on. I'll catch up to you, as soon as I say good-bye to Cooper."

With an exaggerated huff, her shoulders sank, and she

gave up. "Fine. But don't be long. You're not a good enough swimmer to catch us if you miss the boat."

Cooper gave my hand a squeeze and bit back a grin. "It's not too late to change your mind, you know. I bought you a seat on my flight, just in case."

I buried my face in his chest with a shudder. "I want to. You know I want to, but I can't."

"I know." Cooper's lips brushed against my temple. "Hey, it'll be fine. The week'll fly by. You'll see."

"Eight days." I groaned.

"What?" His chest rumbled against my cheek.

"It's not a week, it's *eight* days." I tipped my head back to peer into his sparkling beach-glass eyes. "And eight excruciatingly long nights."

"You'll have so much fun you won't even have time to miss me."

"You're right." I nodded, fisting the back of his shirt and holding him against me. "I'm sure with all the handsome sailors aboard, I'll barely notice you're not there."

Cooper pulled away and frowned down at me. "Oh?"

"It's not so funny when the shoe's on the other foot, is it?" I wrapped my arms around his neck and pulled his face down to kiss him.

He surrendered to my lips. "Not nearly."

"Well, if it's any consolation, I'm sure I'll miss you so badly, I won't even want to eat any of the gourmet delights served morning, noon, and night, and I'll end up needing someone to take in my wedding gown once we reach London."

"That's more like it." His face broke into a wide smile. "You have your phone?"

I held up my iPhone with a nod.

"Good. I've already checked, and other than a few places where the signal strength varies, mobile services should work fine on board. I added international calling to your phone, but the ship also has WiFi, so even if you lose the signal at sea, we should be able to keep in touch the whole time you're gone. Maybe we can even FaceTime?"

"Video chat? Sounds naughty." A zing of excitement shot through me.

He nuzzled my ear. "Only if we do it right."

"You're killing me." The ship's whistle blew out a warning, and I cursed under my breath. "I need to go."

With one last kiss, he released me. "I know. I love you."

"I love you too. Just think, in less than two weeks, we'll be married."

"I can't wait."

"How did you *not* know?" My jaw practically unhinged as I gaped at my mother. As usual, her unflappable countenance annoyed the hell out of me. It didn't help that we were wedged into our stateroom like a pair of bloated sardines, and she'd applied way too much of her tuberose perfume for such close quarters.

"I stumbled across the brochure at the salon and..." For the first time since I'd confronted her, my mother's composure cracked. "Have you any idea how much a transatlantic cruise typically costs? Cruise Queens was almost half the price! How could I pass up a deal like that?"

"Well, I guess we know why it was such a good deal, now, don't we?" I stared at the queen-size bed, the *only* bed in the tiny room. At least we had an ocean view, even if it was through a window smaller than a pizza box.

She huffed. "There's absolutely nothing wrong with our room."

"It's an absolutely adequate room... for a *couple*! Not so much for a grown woman traveling with her mother."

Mom squeezed between the mattress and the wall and rearranged the pillows on what I assumed would be her side. "It's only for a few nights."

"Eight nights." I dropped to the edge of the bed, banging my knees on the wall as I continued to mutter to myself. "Eight long, sleepless nights."

She blew out a breath. "I told you I'd gladly pay for another room."

"Yes, I know. *If* they had another room, which they don't. You've already said so a dozen times." I didn't mean to snap. I really didn't. But it was our first day at sea, and I already regretted not taking Cooper's last-minute offer. I should've sucked it up, downed a few of Vicky's Valium, and gotten on the damn plane.

"I've also said I'm sorry at least a dozen times. It was an innocent mistake. I must have missed the fine print advertising 'couples only.'"

"We should have just taken Cooper's offer to pay for our crossing on the *Queen Mary Two*. The staterooms are enormous. We wouldn't have had to share a bed. And—"

"And it's tradition for the bride's family to pay for these sorts of expenses."

"Mom—" I could tell by the way her chin jutted out that I'd wounded her pride.

"No, hear me out..." She sat beside me with a groan. "Good lord, this stiff mattress will wreak havoc on my sciatica."

"It's a good thing we're saving so much money. It'll help pay for your chiropractor bills."

"Oh, be quiet." Mom swatted me like a bee as she dug herself out of the mattress. "Cooper's family is taking care of the lion's share of this wedding, and that's not how it's done."

"That doesn't matter to—"

She folded her arms over her floppy bow, and her eyes narrowed to slits. "It matters to me."

"Fine. It's not like we can grab a water taxi and switch boats at this point, anyway. We may as well make the best of it." I wrenched myself from the uncomfortable bed and resigned myself to get ready for the welcome dinner. "The food had better be spectacular."

We hadn't even set foot in the dining room when the combined aromas of grilled steak, tangy tomato sauce, and garlic shrimp practically sent my salivary glands into cardiac arrest. Then the first whiff of hot, buttered roll hit me, and my stomach groaned with anticipation. Forget *hello*, the mysterious Cruise Queens had me at *fresh bread*.

With the words "maybe this trip won't be that bad, after all" on the tip of my tongue, I caught movement in my peripheral vision. "Is it just me, or are people staring?" I scanned the dining room. Unless I was mistaken, Mom and I were the only women in a room filled with well-dressed men. Before I had a chance to ask where all the other women were, Mom interrupted.

"Well, of course they're staring. Look at us." She smoothed an imaginary wrinkle from the skirt of her lemon chiffon dress.

"That's not what I—" As usual, I didn't get my entire sentence out before my mother set her shoulders and made a beeline for the *maître d'*.

While Mom charmed the host, I attempted to deflect the uncomfortable stares directed my way and discreetly checked to be sure I hadn't somehow tucked the back of my dress into my panties or something. Then I slid my phone from my shiny clutch and tapped out a quick text to Cooper.

*Me: Something fishy going on in the Atlantic.*
*Cooper: Besides the actual fish?*
*Me: So it would seem.*
*Cooper: Keep me posted, Nancy Drew.*
*Very funny.*

I swallowed a laugh and tucked my phone back into my purse.

Across the dining room, the host seated my mom at a large round table with four middle-aged gentlemen, and I hurried to catch up.

As I approached the table, the *maître d'* eyed me up and down with a barely suppressed snicker then disappeared without another word. At close proximity, the stares were even more obvious. All four of our middle-aged tablemates watched us with matching puzzled expressions.

As the awkward tension threatened to suffocate me, one of the gentlemen—a distinguished man who, other than the thick salt-and-pepper mustache, reminded me a little of my father—cleared his throat. "You'll have to excuse our shock. We didn't expect to dine with such lovely ladies this fine evening."

My mother actually blushed at his compliment. "You're too kind, Mr..."

"Oh, my apologies!" The mustachioed man stood just enough to extend a hand over the table. "Brumfield. Steven Brumfield. And this is Dave Handler, Mitch Boss, and Eddie... uh."

The blond man at the far end of Steven's group waved. The man—or perhaps Nordic god in disguise—looked like the youngest of the four, but he still had to have been in his late forties. His icy-blue eyes gave me an unexpected chill. "Edwin Voorhees, but my friends call me Eddie."

"Very nice to meet you all." Mom nodded to the men as she spread her napkin across her lap. "I'm Grace James, and this is my daughter, Katie."

"Mother and daughter?" Mr. Handler muttered to himself as if trying to work through a difficult puzzle. "Curiouser and curiouser."

"What Dave means is"—Steven shot a glare at his spray-tanned companion—"we don't often see many lovely ladies such as yourselves at these functions. May I ask what sold you on this particular cruise?"

Mom perked up at the chance to regale our new friends

with my shortcomings. She launched into her explanation with a dramatic eye roll. "Well, my daughter had the *brilliant* idea to get married in England but neglected to tell her fiancé she's terrified of flying. So we're on our way to London for the wedding. As for this particular cruise, I saw the brochure while getting my hair glossed, and how could I pass up a deal like that?"

"What a deal, indeed." Dave grinned from ear to ear, leaning forward onto both elbows, and flashed two perfect rows of shiny white veneers.

"So..." Steven's expression wavered between amused and confused. "You just saw a sweet deal and booked your tickets? You didn't stop to check out the fun activities or featured entertainment?"

The way he'd stressed "fun activities" struck me as odd.

Mom didn't seem to notice anything strange about Mr. Brumfield's question. She hummed out her answer as she sipped the wine our waiter discreetly poured while we got acquainted with our group. "I've been on several cruises before. Aside from the occasional deviation, they're all about the same, don't you think?"

"Oh, I don't know. This one's quickly becoming one of my favorites." Dave threw back his drink with a shudder. "I'm guessing you booked your tickets online?"

"I did! I'd never done that before, but when I called my travel agent, he said I needed to book directly on the website. I didn't expect it to be so simple."

"A little too simple, perhaps," Eddie added under his breath.

"And you didn't notice anything..." Dave made a dramatic sweep of the dining room with his eyes before whispering, "*Unusual* after boarding?"

"Unusual?" Mom furrowed her brows, then something clicked, and she laughed. "Well, ideally, we wouldn't have booked a couples cruise."

"I wouldn't think so." Dave threw an arm over Steven's shoulder and winked at me.

*Wait... couples cruise?* I whipped around to scan the dining room with fresh eyes. I had no idea how I'd missed it before. Everywhere I looked, I saw couples: men of all ages, laughing, talking, drinking. Openly celebrating their love. And not a single woman among them.

Apparently, Mom had come to the same conclusion I had, and as understanding dawned on her, her eyes widened comically. "Oh. Oh! Couples!"

Dave leaned back in his chair, the self-satisfied grin threatening to crack his face in two. "Bingo!"

"You mean this is a-a..." Mom struggled for the words.

"A gay cruise?" Steven completed the thought with a smile, saving Mom from herself.

"Yes." The word came out on a sharp exhalation, and I could practically see the wheels turning in her narrow little mind. "I-I had no... are we... you don't think they'll kick us... are we even *allowed* to be here?"

Shrinking into my chair, I swallowed a groan. I'd unwittingly subjected four unsuspecting innocents to my mother. I wondered if this was a crime in the international waters of the Atlantic.

Mitch, who'd stayed mum until that moment, held up his wine glass in a toast. "As far as I'm concerned, you're more than welcome aboard, Grace. Hell, the more the merrier. I haven't had this much fun since my mother discovered my porn collection."

Several courses and too many drinks later, I patted my stomach—and the distended food baby inside—stuffed beyond belief. Not even a hot slice of caramel-slathered chocolate lava cake could tempt me to swallow another bite. "At this rate, I'll need a shoe-horn to squeeze into my wedding gown."

Eddie raised his fork in a salute. "I'm sure someone on this boat knows his way around a sewing kit. We've got you covered."

"Such a sweet boy." My mother reached out and squeezed Eddie's free hand. "But don't you worry. I've already arranged for a personal trainer to whip her into shape, starting first thing tomorrow."

"Mother!" The word ripped from my throat before I could stop it.

"Close your mouth, Katie." Mom used her index finger to shove my chin up, much to the delight of our dinner companions. "No one wants to see your molars."

Despite a rocky start at the top of the dinner hour, Mom and our tablemates—the self-described Queens of Hearts—had become fast friends. My sharp-tongued mother had somehow managed to charm everyone but Dave.

"...so I'd finally gotten used to the idea of my daughter being a lesbian, and she goes and gets engaged to an assassin!" Mom's voice grew louder and louder with every fabrication.

I'd given up trying to explain. My version of truth was far less exciting than hers, and the wine had been flowing far too long to reason with anyone.

"Mom, don't you think you've had enough?" I reached for her glass, and she slapped my hand away.

"Oh, fiddle-faddle. I'm a grown woman, and I'll drink as much wine as I like. It's not as if I'm driving home."

"You won't be walking very far either, by the looks of you," I muttered.

Apparently, my warning fell on deaf ears, because Mitch clinked his glass to Mom's and waved the waiter over. "The next round's on me!"

"Thank you, Mitch." Mom flashed a toothy grin and patted his stubbled cheek.

"Tomorrow night, I'm dragging you to see the Meat

Packers. I still can't believe you've *never* seen male strippers." Mitch shook his head.

Dave grinned at Mom as he swirled the ice in his glass. "They don't have those in your posh little corner of the world, Grace?"

"You know, I've always wanted to see a Chippendale show." Mom's eyes widened as something clicked in her head. "And to think, my first time will be on a gay cruise! Oh, if Bette Wilcox only knew."

She giggled like a schoolgirl.

"Okay, Mom, time for bed." I hauled myself out of the comfortable chair and attempted to drag Mom from hers.

"No," she whined like a four-year-old resisting bedtime. "I'm having too much fun!"

"Come on, Grace. We'll walk you." Mitch helped Mom to her feet.

She didn't fight *him*.

"You simply must tell me more about the onboard entertainment. I don't want to miss a single event!" Mom linked arms with Eddie and Mitch, letting them lead her from the dining room. I couldn't hear what they'd said to her, but she threw her head back, her laughter bouncing off the walls.

I turned to Steven as we made our way toward the exit. "I feel as if I should apologize for my mother."

"Don't you dare," Steven admonished me. "Dinner with your mother was the most fun I've had in ages."

I cringed. "She tends to say all the wrong things."

"At least she's honest," Dave said. "I imagine she's a lot like a toddler, running around spouting uncomfortable truths everywhere she goes."

I had to laugh. Dave had hit the nail on the head. "That's her."

Ahead of us, my mother's voice carried down the hall as she, Eddie, and Mitch broke into the chorus of "Lady Marmalade."

Steven chuckled. "For your sake, I hope she's asleep the minute her head hits the pillow."

"And doesn't wake up 'til last call for breakfast," Dave added.

Steven stopped me at the end of the hall. "So you had no idea she'd booked a gay cruise?"

"Not a clue."

"Oh." Steven chuckled. "This is going to be a fun week."

# The Meat Packers

SOMETHING HARD AND FORCEFUL JUTTED into my lower back, and for a moment, I imagined I was back home in bed with Cooper. Then I heard a low moan, like the pitiful howl of a large animal caught in a trap, and I remembered where I was.

*Crap.*

I shoved my mother's knee out of my back and rolled over. "I'm so glad our window faces the sunrise today. I always wake up after less than five hours of sleep."

"Please tell me this a nightmare." Mom's voice cracked, and she pulled her pillow over her face to block out the morning light. "Or have I contracted some horrible exotic disease? I feel I may be dying."

I almost laughed but managed to rein it in at the last second. "You're not dying, though you may wish you would when last night comes back to you."

"Oh, dear God." Mom tossed the pillow aside and gripped both sides of her head as if she were testing a melon for ripeness. "So we're really on a cruise with hundreds of gay men? I didn't fall asleep during a *Will and Grace* marathon?"

"Mom, where would you even *find* a *Will and Grace* marathon? As far as I know, it isn't even on Netflix." I pulled my legs toward my chest and wrapped my arms around them, resting my chin on my knees. "Besides, I'm pretty sure even *Will and Grace* couldn't've cooked up something *this* outrageous."

"Your father bought me all eight seasons on DVD for Christmas. And I'll have you know—" Mom stopped mid-thought to groan again. This time, the sound seemed to climb all the way from her toes up her throat. "Please don't tell me I actually did a cartwheel in the passageway."

"Okay." I snorted out a laugh. I'd almost forgotten about the cartwheel. "I won't tell you."

Mom closed her eyes and nodded, sucking a deep breath in through her nose. "I really think that's best."

"I'll just send up a silent thanks to the makers of Spanx for preserving your modesty under pressure."

She exhaled in what came out as a cross between a croak and a belch, surprising both of us. "I certainly hope it was at least a halfway decent cartwheel."

"It wouldn't've earned a medal or anything, but it's probably safe to show your face at breakfast." I threw my legs over the side, abandoning the warmth of the bed for a hot shower and a change of clothes. I reeked of Mom's perfume and lemontinis. "Now, Mitch on the other hand... I doubt we'll be seeing *him* at breakfast."

Mom lifted her head from her hands. "Mitch? Why?"

"He *wasn't* wearing Spanx." I shuddered at the memory of Mitch flopping around inside his thin dress pants like a shoe in the dryer. Then his crotch seam tore open with a *rip* worthy of firecrackers on the Fourth of July, exposing what looked like an unbaked Pillsbury crescent roll. "Yeah, I saw *way* too much of him last night."

Mom clapped a hand over her mouth. "That wasn't the imagery I needed this morning."

"Serves you right for drinking so much."

"How ironic that *you* should chastise *me* for drinking too much. Have you messaged your boyfriend to gloat? Perhaps he can include my misfortunes in one of his far-fetched love stories."

Her question froze me in place, and I glared at her. "No,

Mother. Sadly, I've been unable to contact Cooper since last night."

"Oh?" She smirked at me, and for an instant, I thought maybe she'd remembered what she'd done, but the glimmer of recognition evaporated just as quickly. "And why is that?"

After years of telling my mother I'd broken my cell phone just to avoid talking to her, Karma had finally caught up to me. "Because you threw my phone overboard last night."

Another memory—this one of my shiny iPhone flying through the air, Cooper's handsome face grinning at me from the display until it disappeared into the black abyss below.

I never even heard a splash.

I'd spoken too soon about Mitch. He *did* show up for breakfast as if nothing had happened the night before. He didn't seem the least bit concerned that I'd gotten an eyeful of his less-than-impressive manhood. Then again, maybe the guy was a grower, and since I wasn't exactly his target demographic, he hadn't been inspired to impress.

After breakfast, we split up into two groups of three. For the rest of the afternoon, Mom sat poolside, nursing her hangover and playing third wheel to Mitch and Eddie, while Steven and Dave dragged me to the gym to work off last night's dinner.

As it turned out, Dave was almost as big of an Elizabeth Jayne fan as I was. Or rather, a Cooper Maxwell fan, since Cooper had finally gone public with his identity. When Dave discovered I was *marrying* Cooper, he declared himself my new best friend and spent nearly the entire morning quizzing me on the film adaptation and upcoming Immortal Blood series finale. When I told him Cooper wouldn't be writing another book, Dave went all Kathy Bates on me, and Steven had to escort his inconsolable partner back to their stateroom, leaving me to my own devices for the rest of the afternoon.

Good on his word, Mitch showed up at our door at eight o'clock sharp. "Ladies, we have a show to see, and I intend to get there with plenty of time to get a seat down front."

For the record, I didn't want to go. I felt weird seeing male strippers with my mother, especially strippers known as "The Meat Packers." But Mitch refused to take no for an answer. "It's an experience you simply can't miss," he'd said.

So I dressed in my most club-worthy outfit, donned my only pair of red pumps—*with underwear, thank you very much!*—and pulled my hair into a simple ponytail. "Okay, Mitch, you win. I'm ready."

"Wait for me!" Mom's muffled voice came from the other side of the bathroom door.

"Come on, Gracey. Eddie's waiting on the Promenade deck. But *he* won't fight for the best table, so we need to hurry."

Mom stepped through the door, and my jaw dropped. "What the hell are you wearing?"

"Do you like it?" She beamed, sneaking onc last peek at herself in the mirror.

Choking back a fit of giggles, I blurted out the truth before I could stop myself. "No! Where did you get that? You've been drinking again, haven't you?"

Mom didn't reply. Instead, her pale eyebrows angled down in a sharp V over narrowed eyes.

Despite her stern countenance, I found it impossible to take her seriously while she was clad in head-to-toe leopard print—from the thick headband holding back her platinum bob to the wedge-heel sandals and the belted plunging V-neck jumpsuit hugging her slender frame in between. She looked like she'd escaped from a low-budget Tarzan movie. Or lost a bet. More likely, she'd seen the trendy ensemble in one of the onboard shops and couldn't resist.

"Don't listen to her. You look fabulous!" Mitch kissed the air to either side of my mother's pinched face then took her by the hand, tugging her out the door.

"Thank you, Mitch." With one last scathing glare in my direction, she turned her back on me and marched off.

With my lips pressed together to keep from laughing, I followed them to the elevator, and we rode to the Promenade deck in silence.

The line in front of the Playhouse blocked the entrance to the casino and stretched so far back, I couldn't see the end. Much to my horror, Mom's God-awful getup wasn't the worst of the night. In addition to several retro *Miami Vice* linen suits and a few pairs of khaki shorts paired with black socks and dress shoes, several men stood in line wearing nothing but neon Speedos with leg warmers, and at least one man wore hot-pink zebra print.

"Oh no!" Mom stopped in her tracks, gripping Mitch's arm like a vine. "We'll never get a good table."

Mitch gently shook her off and nodded to the front of the line, where Eddie stood with his back to the wall, a look of trepidation etched across his face as he repeatedly checked his watch. "This is exactly why I sent him on ahead of us."

Eddie must've had super-hearing, because his blue eyes darted up at the sound of Mitch's voice, and he relaxed his stiff posture. "Finally! They're just about to open the doors."

We'd barely made it to the front of the line when the Playhouse doors swung open, and we were swept forward with the rushing current of people eager for the best seats in the house.

Like a man on a mission, Mitch abandoned us with Eddie and pushed his way through the crowd to a large six-seater right in front of the stage. He plopped down in a chair and leaned over the table with his arms stretched wide, laying claim as clearly as if he'd planted a flag in the center. "Come on, Gracey. Let's get our drink on before the show starts."

Half an hour later, the drinks were flowing, the room was packed, and the show was running late. Despite my better judgment, Mitch had already coaxed me into tossing back an appletini and a shot of Fireball while we waited. The anxious crowd—the men in our group included—clapped and stomped, chanting "Meat, Meat, Meat!" on a constant loop. Even Mom got in on the action, chanting right along with them.

"So how many cats did you have to skin for that outfit, Cruella?" Dave threw back an amber shot. After his embarrassing outburst that afternoon, I hadn't expected him and Steven to show up, but I'd completely underestimated Dave's tenacity.

Mom popped up an eyebrow and stared Dave down. "Apparently, one too few if you're still here."

Dave choked out a laugh. He hadn't mentioned Cooper or *Immortal Blood* again, but I could tell by the way he shot glances in my direction that he hadn't given up hope. "Aww, come on now. Did you wake up on the wrong side of the jungle this morning?"

"Ignore him, Gracey. He's just jealous." Mitch stroked a hand down Mom's arm to soothe her.

"That's right, Grace. You know I only wanna be like you-oo-oo," Dave sang.

With one last scowl, Mom turned back to the stage, where the lights were finally dimming for the show to start.

Dave snickered into his glass. "You make it too easy, Grace."

Maybe I'd give Cooper a little nudge to write one more book after all. I didn't care how annoying Dave had been, anyone who could get the upper hand on my mom deserved some sort of reward.

While I was brainstorming ways to compensate Dave for putting my mom in her place, our frazzled waiter zipped around the table with another round for everyone.

A single spotlight illuminated center stage, and I threw back the spicy cinnamon whiskey Mitch had ordered me as a man dressed in a crisp white Naval uniform strutted out. He reminded me a little of the ship's captain, and for half a second, I thought he was there on official business.

I'd briefly seen the silver-haired captain when we'd boarded. He was no Richard Gere, but for an old guy, he wasn't bad looking. The man in front of me was younger and taller and more muscular. Okay, so he looked nothing like the captain, especially with his dress whites straining to contain the bulk beneath. And after three drinks, even *I* was drooling over his hotness.

The officer and a gentleman's lips twitched as he surveyed the rowdy audience, but he said nothing. Instead, he stood stock still in the middle of the stage, bowed his head as if praying, and clenched his hands in front of him. I couldn't help thinking there was something really familiar about the guy, but with his hat sloped down over his eyes, I could only see his square jaw and full lips.

At least half a minute went by with nothing but the sound of the chanting crowd filling the space between us before the first strains of an electronic beat sounded. The fake Naval officer snapped his fingers along with the rhythm but kept his head down. The music built until the sound rumbled through my bones and echoed off the walls. I recognized the intro but couldn't quite place the song until George Michael's voice filled the air. And with the first lyrics of "I Want Your Sex," the pseudo-sailor came to vivid life, gyrating to the rhythmic beat as if his life depended on it.

"Whoooo!" My mother stood with her half-empty cocktail and let out a raucous whoop.

"Not yet, Gracey." Mitch grabbed Mom's arm and tugged

her back into her seat. "Give the man a chance to take it all off first."

Mom nodded, draining the rest of her drink before fumbling around in her purse. She squealed again as she pulled out a wad of one-dollar bills and waved them in the air as if hailing a taxi. "I'm ready!"

Ignoring my mother, I focused my attention on the man on stage. The feeling that I knew him hit me again, and I decided I had to have seen him somewhere on board. Dinner maybe. Or—I glanced at his rippling muscles yet again—it was probably the gym.

As he peeled away each layer, I tried to remember where I'd seen the impressive eight-pack abs or the anchor tattoo—probably a fake—etched into his side. My eyes stretched wide as he reached between his legs, and with little more than a flick of his wrist, ripped his pants clear off his body.

And that's when it all came back to me in a sudden flash. I would've recognized the sparkling G-string covering his super-sized manhood anywhere, even if the last time I'd seen it, it was filled with cheese dip.

The name Magic Mike popped into my head as I let out a deep breath. "Sam?"

His eyes snapped to mine, and his choreographed steps faltered slightly before he collected himself. Before anyone even noticed his slip-up, Sam quickly caught up. As he worked the room, he kept me in his peripheral vision, shooting me curious glances here and there. Halfway through the song's extended mix, Sam's lush lips spread into a wide grin, and something wicked flashed in his eyes. The big jerk winked.

Without as much as a nod to warn me, Sam leaped from the stage, landing right in front of me with a grunt. He cupped my chin in his hand, and his cocky grin got even wider. "Of all the gin joints on all the gay cruises, you end up in mine."

"Hi." With a little wave and a nervous giggle, I stared up at his nearly naked form. I might have drooled a little. If anyone noticed, I'd blame the Fireball. Besides, I was engaged, not dead. And unless I was mistaken, there was no crime in looking.

"Hello, sweetheart." Sam pulled off his hat and tugged it onto my head before straddling my knees and shoving his bare stomach in my face. "Come here often?"

My lips fell open as I stared at the ridges of Sam's rock-hard abs, following them down until I could almost count the tiny hairs trailing from the man's belly button to the top of his sparkly cup. "What are you doing?"

He smirked as he arched into me, bringing his sweaty hips forward to gyrate them against my midsection. "Putting on a show."

"Well..." Horrified, I darted my eyes around the room.

Everyone was laser focused on me and what Sam appeared to be doing to me, which he wasn't *really* doing, but as simulations go, it was pretty convincing. Even I almost believed it.

"Do it somewhere else!" I whisper-shouted. "Aren't you supposed to be entertaining the guys?"

"Aww, Katie, you wound me." His eyes followed the same path mine had just completed. "They're eating it up. Just go with it."

*Go with it? Is he crazy? Nice girls don't go with it. Girls less than a week away from getting married do not go with it. Do they?*

Sam planted a bare foot on each side of my seat then grabbed the back of my chair to haul himself up. His skin smelled like salty, hot buttered popcorn and cotton candy, and I had to restrain myself to keep from licking him as he hovered over me.

I leaned as far away from his naked body as I could get without capsizing my chair. The guy didn't play fair. I groaned. "Sam!"

"Oh, that's good." He chuckled as he thrust his hips toward my flaming face. I hissed out his name again under my breath, and he repeated the action, quickening his strokes. "Now say it louder..."

My stomach bottomed out, more from mortification than anything else. The man was attractive, but even if I wasn't madly in love with my fiancé, Sam and I were far from being compatible... with him being gay and all.

Beside me, my mother waved her wad of cash, lingering far too long as she shoved dollars into Sam's G-string. She hooked a finger into the front of his pouch, and Sam shrieked like a little girl.

Once he'd untangled himself from my mother's clutches, Sam leaned forward, his hot breath washing over me as he brought his lips to my ear. "Grab my ass, sweetheart."

"What?" I jerked my head up to gape at him. He had to be joking. "You're kidding, right?"

He laughed at my horrified expression. "Come on. Just do it."

Nothing in his face said he was anything but serious, so I shrugged. *What do I have to lose?* With trembling fingers, I reached around him to cautiously cup his glistening—and amazingly tight—butt cheeks.

As if I'd inadvertently hit some sort of release valve, Sam tossed back his head with a moan and bucked his hips forward, clipping me under the chin with his sparkly crotch. My head exploded with bright pinpricks of light, leaving me dazed while the crowd went wild. And as everyone around me surged to their feet with thundering applause, I could've sworn I heard the click of a camera shutter.

# Mission Improbable

THE ICY NORTH ATLANTIC WIND blew across the deck, sending a shiver down my spine. I tugged my sweater tighter around me and thanked the weather gods it wasn't raining again. Staring out at the gray ocean, I searched the whitecaps cresting over the top of the water for possible icebergs. The captain had made an announcement that morning that we would pass over the final resting place of the *Titanic* sometime that evening, but not even visions of a twenty-two-year-old Leonardo DiCaprio could chase away the dark shadow hanging over me.

For all of half a second, I wished I hadn't been a coward. I wished I'd said to hell with my pride and just marched into that dining room with my head held high as if I didn't have a care in the world. Unfortunately, I *did* have a care in the world. Half the people on the damn ship had seen me nearly knocked unconscious by a jewel-encased penis. And the other half found out through the ever-growing onboard gossip chain. I was pretty sure a bout of Ebola would've been better contained.

At three days post *penis-gate,* I'd expected the novelty would've worn off. It hadn't. Not even a little. In fact, I was beginning to think I'd never live it down. Mitch and my mother brought up my humiliation every chance they got, and each time they did, the story grew to more and more outlandish heights. Only last night, when I'd gone to score the only box of tampons available in the gift shop, I heard how I'd been slapped across the face by Sam's naked peen in a botched blowjob attempt, something that—as far as I knew—could only happen to Vicky. I'd paid for my stuff and got out of there before my entire body went up in flames.

As for the others, Eddie tried to appear unaffected, but I caught him giving me the side-eye every time we shared breathing space. Dave and Steven only stopped making jokes after Sam stepped in to defend my honor, but honestly, that seemed to make things even worse. For reasons that completely escaped me, they'd branded us "the love birds" from that moment on.

And that was the people I actually knew. Every time I walked into the dining room, a hush fell over the crowd before the furious whispers shot around the room like an autumn wheat field going up in flames. If Mitch hadn't sworn on Barbra Streisand's life, I'd have thought someone other than my mother had captured my humiliation on film, and the very thought had me shaking in my Uggs.

It didn't help that I was still sporting a penis-shaped bruise. I rubbed the tender spot under my chin.

"Still sore?" Sam winced as I tilted my head back to expose the greenish-yellow blob. "I'm really sorry, sweetheart. Me and my big dick just keep getting you into trouble, don't we?" He never passed up an opportunity to remind me how massive his package was.

"Don't worry about it." I flashed a smile for his benefit. Even though I suspected Sam actually enjoyed all the attention his wayward penis brought us, he'd spent most of the week making up for what he'd referred to as the NuttyBuddy incident. "It hardly hurts at all."

Sam tilted my face to the side so he could get a better look and shot me a cheeky grin. "Think of it as a badge of honor."

"Right." My eyes narrowed in his direction. "Because old bruise will go so nicely with my wedding colors."

His face fell. "Shit, I forgot. I'm sorry, sweetums. I should've been more careful where I was swinging my dick. I got so wrapped up in the spectacle of the whole thing."

"Yeah, well, you're just lucky Cooper wasn't there to witness your massive..." I waved a hand toward his crotch. "*Thing* swinging in front of my lips."

Sam smirked. "Is it wrong that I wish I'd been straddling him instead of you?"

I snorted out a loud laugh as an image of Cooper's horrified face popped into my head. "Don't make me picture that."

"So what did your hot fiancé say when you told him about your close encounter of the peen kind?"

Another blast of laughter bubbled past my lips. "Nothing."

"What?" Sam scrunched up his face.

"I didn't tell him yet."

"Why not?" Sam's smirk made a reappearance. "Afraid he'll turn all caveman again? Lordy, that man is hot when he's angry."

"True." I sighed. "But no. I would've told him if my mother hadn't thrown my phone overboard."

Sam gasped, pressing his huge hand to his chest in an exaggerated gesture. "She didn't!"

"Oh yes." Once again, I envisioned Cooper's grinning face flipping through the air on the phone's display as it dropped into the dark ocean. "She did."

"That bitch!" Sam managed to keep a straight face for all of thirty seconds before dissolving into hysterics.

Bringing my coffee to my lips, I giggled right along with him. "Exactly."

"I'd gladly let you use my phone, but sadly, I don't have international calling."

"Thanks, but it wouldn't help me. After firing the wicked publicity witch, Cooper had to get a new number, and I haven't memorized it yet. I never anticipated my mother sending my poor iPhone to live with the fishes."

"Was the witch crank-calling him?"

"I wish. She's way more creative than that. She posted his number on a fanfiction site."

"Clever bitch." Sam nodded.

"Here you are!" Dave cried out as he stepped through the door onto the deck. "Hell, Peenerella, I was just about to put out a maritime alert." He fell into the chair beside me, placing his steaming cup and a mouthwatering blueberry Danish on the table in front of him.

"Peenerella?" Sam's eyebrows shot up.

"Yeah." Dave shrugged. "You know... Peenerella dressed in yella, went to the dance to find her fella. Made a mistake, got punched by his snake, how many drag queens does it—"

"You're sick." I shoved Dave hard enough to rock his chair to the side, and he burst out laughing.

Sam didn't seem the least bit amused. "So where's the rest of your little posse?"

"Oh, Mitch and Grace refused to eat outside." Dave choked back his laughter and waved a hand in the air. "*It's too cold,*" he said, perfectly mimicking my mother's snooty voice.

"What about Steven?" I took a sip of my coffee and made a face. The air wasn't the only thing that was too cold. Maybe Mom was right. I cringed at the thought. I'd sooner turn into a block of ice than admit that out loud. Especially after... I shook the thought away with a shudder and turned back to Dave.

Dave checked over his shoulder. "Oh, he's loading up on sweets, and then he'll be out."

*Sweets.* The bane of my existence until Cooper and I left for our honeymoon. I was fully prepared to gain at least fifteen pounds *after* the wedding.

"So what's the plan for the rest of the day?" Dave asked. "You lovebirds hiding out here until we reach London?"

"Is that an option?" I drooled over his Danish. "I'm tired of being the resident Kardashian on this ship."

Sam followed my eyes to Dave's plate. "You hungry, sweetheart?"

"Who me? No, I'm good." My stomach rumbled loudly, making a liar out of me.

They both laughed.

"Come on, kid. Eat." Dave slid his plate toward me. "You can't starve yourself all week."

"Actually, yes, I can. If my dress doesn't fit when I get to London, I don't exactly have time to have it let out."

"Just one bite." Dave tore the pastry down the middle and sank his teeth into his half while he dangled the other half in front of me like a golden carrot. The aroma of blueberries and butter assaulted my senses, drowning out the salty ocean air. "Mmm, delicious. Sure you don't want some?"

With a groan worthy of a porn star, I snatched the uneaten Danish from his fingers and shoved half of it into my mouth before biting down. I hadn't even finished chewing before devouring the other half. "So good," I mumbled around a mouthful of gooey goodness.

"I think you've created a monster." Sam laughed.

Dave just shrugged.

"Katie!" Steven shouted as he came barreling through the door carrying a tray loaded with assorted pastries and fruit. "Oh, thank God I found you. You've been dodging us for two days."

"I know." I wiped my sticky lips with the tips of my fingers then licked them clean. "It was on purpose."

"Your mother said you haven't been back to the room since the morning she—"

I held up a hand to stop him. The last thing I wanted to remember was the sound of my father's boisterous laughter coming over the line when he told me about the photo Mom had sent him: a picture of my hands gripping Sam's ass while his jewel-encrusted penis hovered just a hairbreadth away from my open lips. My mother hadn't just told Dad what had happened. She'd sent him proof, in high definition, no less. And my smart-ass father had been impressed.

I shuddered. "And I'm not going back, either. She crossed a line."

"Could be worse," Dave said. "She could've posted it on Facebook."

I sucked in a quick breath. "Bite. Your. Tongue."

My only saving grace was my mother's inability to navigate social media from her mobile device. It was a wonder she'd figured out how to send the picture to my father. When we reached London, I'd get Dad to delete it from her phone. Until then, if she got even a whiff of how important it was to me not to spread it around, I'd be doomed for sure.

"Well, I don't know about everyone else, but I'm dying to know where you've been sleeping," Steven asked as he looked around the open deck. "I don't see any blankets out here, so I don't think you've been squatting on the deck."

I watched Dave's face shift into an unreadable mask as his eyes darted between Sam and me.

"It's not what you think," I added quickly. "Sam offered—"

"I'm bunking with Ryan so Katie can crash in my room." Sam squeezed my hand under the table. At least someone around here had my back.

Steven barked out a laugh. "I couldn't care less what you two lovebirds do behind closed doors. You know what they say. What happens on Cruise Queens stays on Cruise Queens... besides, I'm sure things'll die down before we hit London. By then, everyone will have seen the picture anyway."

My saliva went down the wrong pipe, and I practically hacked up a lung just to take a breath. "What?" I leapt to my feet, spilling my cold coffee across the table.

Steven flinched away from the flow. "I assumed you knew—"

"That my mom was sharing the photo with everyone on board? *No!* I had no idea. How does she even know how to do that? It may as well be on Facebook! What if..." Frantic, I turned to Sam for moral support.

Instead of offering words of encouragement, a deep furrow lined Sam's forehead.

Defeated, I dropped back into my chair and covered my face with my hands. I didn't dare hazard a guess what would happen if Cooper saw it before I could explain what had really happened. "This is worse than the time I passed out at karaoke or the morning I woke up wrapped around a male stripper on his living room floor." I lifted my head, blinking back tears. "He'll never forgive me... he just went public with his identity. This could end up causing a scandal. And... oh, God. I'm meeting his *diplomat* parents for the first time in less than a week!"

Steven flashed a bright smile, and I wanted to bash him in his cheery face. "Hey, it's not like she sent out a memo."

"She shared that horrible picture with the whole boat!" I shrieked.

"No." Steven held up a finger. "I didn't say that. I said she *showed* the picture to practically everyone. She didn't *send* it to them."

"Wait." I sat up straighter. "You mean she literally just held out her phone and showed people?"

"Yep," Steven said, popping the P.

"So let me get this straight." I drew in a deep breath then let it out. "My mom's been holding court in the dining room, entertaining hundreds of people by waving her phone around like the Oracle of Delphi or something?"

Steven nodded.

Sadly, I could see my mother doing exactly that. She'd found a way to position herself as the center of attention, and she gladly took it. "That's... *better*? I guess?"

"As long as no one suggests she send it to the Marcy Michaels show or something, I suppose." Dave stuck a big fat pin in my happy balloon.

The thought of Marcy Michaels posting my face across the screen sent a shiver of epic proportions down my spine. "We need to find that phone and destroy that picture before my mother can send it anywhere else."

"Someone needs to distract Mom while I grab her phone." The *Mission: Impossible* theme played inside my head as we slunk along the passageway toward the stateroom I shared with my mother. My plan, as lame as it might have been, was to grab her phone, delete the image, and pretend the whole thing never happened.

"Already handled," Dave whispered.

The words had no sooner crossed his lips than Mitch came strolling down the passageway from the other direction. He wore a bright-yellow Speedo and black flip-flops and had a thick white towel tossed over his pasty shoulder. He paused outside our door, shooting a tentative smile in our direction, then lifted a hand to knock.

"How'd you pull that off? Isn't Mitch in Grace's back pocket?" Sam asked.

Steven chuckled quietly. "Mitch has a few dirty little secrets he'd rather Eddie didn't discover. It didn't take a lot of prodding to get him to agree."

Curiosity almost got the best of me, but I pushed it back to focus on the task at hand. "She's not going to leave that damn phone behind," I hissed.

This had been our third attempt to separate Mom from her phone that day. The first two had failed miserably. I had no idea the woman was so attached to her technology.

I was beginning to think she slept with it tucked into her underwear or something.

"She doesn't have to. Unless it's waterproof, she'll have to leave it on a deck chair while she's in the water. That's when we'll grab it."

Dave grinned, nodding at Steven with pride. "Brilliant plan."

"And what if she doesn't get in the pool?" I wondered. "She's like a cat. She hates to get wet."

"Why doesn't that surprise me?" Dave snickered under his breath.

"Mitch is under strict orders to see to it that she gets into either the pool or the hot tub," Steven said.

"Why doesn't Mitch just grab the phone?" I pressed my back against the wall and watched as Mitch linked his arm with my mother's and led her back the way he'd come. "He can get closer to her than any of the rest of us."

"Because..." Steven rolled his eyes. "Mitch is terrified of your mother. He doesn't want her to know he had anything to do with it. If he's in the pool with her, she won't suspect he was involved."

"Pussy," Sam muttered.

We all nodded in agreement.

As soon as Mom and Mitch disappeared around the corner, Dave started down the passageway ahead of us. "Let's get this party started."

Like a squad of teenagers on a scavenger hunt, the four of us crept through the ship toward the pavilion pool, the only pool on board that was both heated *and* offered a retractable glass cover for cooler weather. No way would Mom venture out on deck in a bathing suit unless it was at least eighty in the shade.

Dave reached the door first and pressed his face to the glass. "Yep, you were right... they're in there. Grace just spread her towel out over a lounge chair and she's... wait... no... yep. She's lying on her stomach."

"What's Mitch doing?" I tried to see around Dave's big head. Nervous energy tied my stomach into knots. All I wanted was to get in, grab the phone, and get out, but like everything else in my life, it didn't look like it was going to be that easy.

Dave cupped his hands around his face. "Well, I *hope* he just squirted a glob of sunscreen on her back. Otherwise—"

My lips fell open, and a horrified squeak forced its way up my throat. "Don't even go there. She may drive me insane, but she's still my mother!"

Dave tossed a smirk over his shoulder. "Sorry, Peenerella. Couldn't help myself."

"So what's the plan?" Sam clapped his big hands together.

Steven shoved Dave out of the way to take his place at the glass. "We wait for Mitch to get her in the water, then we go in."

I didn't have a watch, but I was certain the minutes ticked by excruciatingly slowly. While I waited, my thoughts were plagued with close-ups of my horrified face splashed across the pages of the *National Tattler* or *TMZ* and Cooper's disappointed face as paparazzi descended on our wedding ceremony, whirling helicopter blades blowing pristine reception tents into a nearby duck pond. I had no idea if there even *was* a duck pond nearby, but the mere possibility festered in the pit of my stomach, fermenting like sour milk.

Finally, Steven perked to life again. "Okay, Katie. You're up!" He reached out to grab hold of my sleeve, dragging me in front of him as he pulled the door open just enough for me to slip through.

I'd stepped into a tropical paradise. The air inside the pool area was easily a sweltering ninety-plus degrees, and I'd already started to sweat. With a thick pane of glass between my co-conspirators and me, I took one tentative step forward, then hit the deck when my mother's vacuous laugh echoed off the glass ceiling.

*Shit!* Except for Mom and Mitch—and one very old man lying facedown on a teak lounge—the pool was deserted. Hiding behind a chair of my own, I watched the leathery man sun himself under the glass ceiling. He looked dead. For one, his lime-green thong disappeared between his shriveled ass cheeks, practically sawing him in half, and I couldn't begin to imagine leaving it like that if I was still breathing.

Ignoring my mission, I kept my eyes on him, waiting for any telltale signs of life. For all I knew, he could've been there all night—slowly decomposing. The overpowering stench of chlorine would probably mask the smell of death for at least a day. Maybe two.

A few moments later, an inhuman groan rumbled from the corpse, and he rolled over. A scream lodged in my throat as I caught a glimpse of the swollen front of his shimmery thong growing like Pinocchio's nose after a string of lies. He'd obviously sheltered *that* particular part of him from the sun. It wasn't nearly as withered and dehydrated. Tearing my eyes away before singeing my retinas, I shuddered convulsively and began the short crawl toward the only other deck chairs currently in use.

Mitch had managed to coax my mother into the Jacuzzi and somehow made sure her back was to me. I'd have to remember to thank him later. Until then, I prayed the sound of the jets would keep her distracted while I dug through her bottomless beach bag.

*What the hell?* For some inexplicable reason, my mother appeared to be channeling Mary Poppins. Inside her bag, I found two jumbo-sized tubes of sunscreen, a travel pack of wet wipes, three tubes of red lipstick, pepper spray, a rolled-up wad of one-dollar bills, a stun gun, a pair of wool socks, several packs of mints, and an adult diaper, but not one cell phone.

I wanted to scream. There was no way she'd left it in the room. *No. Way.*

Crouching beside her chair, I dumped the contents of her bag onto the towel and went through it more thoroughly. *Why does she have so many paper clips in here? It's like she knocked over an office supply cabinet. And who keeps a red pen in their purse? Is she grading people on their etiquette?* As I pawed through my mother's belongings a second time, I came across more bizarre items but still no phone. Shoving everything back into her bag, I had to blink back tears. What if I never found it?

Somewhere in the tangled mess I'd made of Mom's purse and her towel, I heard a chirp. Not like a bird, but more like a friendly robot, sending me some sort of signal. I shoved her bag under the chair and patted the towel for the phone I knew had to be hidden within the folds.

*Jackpot!*

"Katherine Grace James, what on *earth* are you doing?"

I whipped my head around at the shrill sound of her voice and waved. "Oh... hi, Mom."

She raised one perfectly arched brow and focused her attention on the hand I held up. "Is that my phone?"

My eyes darted to the side to discover I'd waved at her with her phone still in my hand. *Crap.* "Uh... is it?"

"Yes." She rose up in the water and sloshed her way to the ladder. "Why do you have my phone?"

Something about her tone of voice and the way she bore down on me, water sluicing over her skin and dripping from her trendy black one-piece, reminded me of the Sea Witch climbing out of the briny depths of the ocean. I shuddered. I wasn't going to sing my way out of this one.

"I'm..." *I'm what? Taking what's mine? Making sure you can't post my picture on social media for all the world to see?*

"Is this because I threw your phone overboard? I told you it was an accident." She paused for a moment, cocking her head to the side. "Well... not an *accident* exactly, but more of a byproduct of too much alcohol. A decision I regret but, unfortunately, can't erase."

As apologies went, hers sucked, though I hadn't expected an apology. And I wasn't after revenge. But her assumption gave me an idea. I threw my shoulders back and pushed my chest out. "Yes! I'm taking your phone as retribution."

Mom stopped cold, her hands drifting to her hips as she stared me down. "You're being childish."

"So!" With my mother just a few yards away, I took a step back, preparing to run as the child buried deep inside me took over.

She huffed out a breath and rolled her eyes. "Katie, put my phone down."

I had two choices. I could put her phone down as she asked. Or I could run like the coward I was and wipe the images then bring it back to her when I was finished.

I didn't choose either option. I bet everything on door number three and made a break for the side exit, the one that led straight for the open-air deck.

"Don't. You. Dare." She called after me as I shoved through the door and headed for the railing.

Before I'd fully considered the repercussions of my actions, my hand had already cocked back and started the forward motion, launching Mom's phone over the side to join the *Titanic* at the bottom of the ocean.

And immature or not, I'd never felt more satisfaction in all my life.

# Diplomatic Hilarity

W E'D FINALLY ARRIVED IN SOUTHAMPTON, and I never thought I'd be so happy to see dry land. I was fully prepared to kiss the ground as soon as we stepped off the ship. Our allotted disembarking time was nine o'clock, and at exactly 8:59, I was bouncing in place, waiting to be reunited with Cooper after the longest eight days of my life. Being trapped on a boat for a week with my mother had officially cured my fear of flying.

After I'd hurled her phone into the ocean, Mom refused to speak to me. At. All. Even something as benign as "pass the salt" turned into an epic stare-a-thon where Mom would roll her eyes and turn to Mitch. "Would you ask my daughter to pass the salt?" And even then, I'd have to pass it to Steven, who would pass it to Eddie, who would pass it to Mitch, who would hand it to my mom. Any necessary messages were handled the same way. It made dinner a little awkward, but I wasn't going to complain about the sudden silence.

I'd known my mother for almost thirty years, and for at least half of those years—since I hit puberty—I'd barely managed to get a word in, let alone the last word. It felt pretty good to say my piece without having her cut me off.

As for my fifteen minutes of fame, it'd faded as quickly as my bruise. By our last night on board, the discoloration under my chin had gone from a mottled purple to a dull yellow, and someone else had become the center of attention.

Sadly, the leathery sunbather from the pavilion pool *did* actually die on his teak lounger a few days after I saw him, unwittingly stealing my thunder. Not that I minded losing the top spot on the ship gossip chain. Not in the least. The man went peacefully in his sleep, but it took half a day for anyone to realize he was dead. Rumor had it he'd died with the world's biggest boner. But as Sam reminded me more than once, *dead men don't get boner*s. According to Eddie, the guy had some sort of automatic penis pump that had been triggered when he'd rolled over. That actually explained a lot. I'd seen him after he'd rolled over, and it was horrifying and impressive all at once. I wasn't going to ask Eddie how he knew about the pump... or how to trigger it. All I knew was, with that one inappropriate hard-on, a huge weight had been lifted off my shoulders.

With Sam on my arm and Dave at my side, I walked into the farewell dinner with my head held high. I couldn't do anything about the people who'd seen my embarrassing photo, but in tossing Mom's phone overboard, I'd effectively prevented anyone else from seeing it. I suspected people still whispered about me, but I no longer cared.

As soon as I'd taken my seat, Steven slid into the chair beside me. "Katie, you have a new message from your beloved."

"Cooper?"

"Unless you have another beloved I'm unaware of." He snickered.

With my head cocked to the side, I stared at him.

"Oh, fine," he grumbled. "He's apparently tried to call you every night since your phone met its untimely demise, and you haven't responded."

"He has?" I turned my attention to my mother as she slowly chewed her dry chicken. "Why didn't you tell me?"

Mom grunted but didn't reply.

"Now who's being childish?" I narrowed my eyes at her.

She flashed a sardonic grin and took a sip of her Cabernet.

"Whatever." I turned back to Steven. "Is that all he said? He's been trying to reach me?"

"Uh, no. He said he'll be waiting by the curb at nine a.m. sharp, and..." Steven looked toward the ceiling for a second then snapped his fingers before rushing through the rest. "He's looking forward to hearing you dig your way out of this one."

*Dig my way out of this one?*

"Is he mad because I never called him back?" I glowered at Mom again. She could have at least given me the messages. A sudden—horrifying—thought hit me. "He doesn't know I've been sleeping in Sam's stateroom, does he?"

Steven cleared his throat and glanced at Mom. "You wouldn't do something that mean spirited, would you, Grace?"

"I haven't said a word to him about anything." And those were the last words my mother spoke in my presence.

The instant we were given clearance to leave the ship, I grabbed Sam's sleeve, pulling him forward, leaving my mother, Mitch, and Eddie in our dust. I hadn't seen Steven or Dave since breakfast, but if they accepted my last-minute invite to the wedding, I'd see them again in just a few days.

"Come on." I shoved Sam ahead of me toward the front of the line. "Don't let anyone cut you off."

Low laughter rumbled in Sam's chest. "It's not a race."

"The hell it's not! I haven't seen Cooper in over a week and haven't even talked to him in almost as long. I'm in a hurry!"

With our luggage in tow, Sam and I headed toward the pickup zone. Through the crowd of passengers, I saw him—Cooper—all six feet two inches, dark wavy hair, and blue eyes of him. I could already feel the ghost of his lips on mine, and my heart kicked like a mule in my chest, leaving me breathless. God, I loved him. In less than a week, we'd be married, and I. Could. Not. Wait.

"Cooper!" I jumped up and waved to him.

Cooper slowly made his way to me, his posture stiff and uncomfortable. He did a double take when he saw Sam. I met him in the middle, launching myself into the air to collide with him, smashing my chest against his. He grunted at the impact.

Breathless, I kissed every square inch of his face. "I've missed you so much! I'm sorry I didn't call you. My mother tossed my phone overboard and... Oh my God, I have so much to tell you. It's been a crazy week."

"You can say that again." Cooper's lips—the full, kissable lips I'd dreamed about for the past week—pressed into a hard line.

His unreadable expression sent my stomach plummeting toward my toes. "What does that mean? Are you mad at—"

Before I'd gotten the whole sentence out, Cooper turned to Sam with a tight smile. "Sam."

"Cooper," Sam replied with a stiff nod.

Cooper held up his phone toward Sam. "I'm guessing this is you?"

Sam blanched, and my entire life—okay, so the last *six months* of my life—flashed before my eyes in a loop. And then both Sam and I were talking at the same time, Sam trying to explain why his sparkly G-string was mere inches from my nose, and me trying to explain why my hands were latched onto Sam's ass. I told Cooper about the bruise and the rampant rumors that escalated into several covert missions to erase the offending image, my grab-and-dash in the pavilion pool that ended with my mother's phone taking the same trip as the Heart of the Ocean, and even the dead guy in the Speedo. In the end, Cooper ended up laughing so hard I thought he might pee himself.

When the explanations were over, and I'd said my good-byes to Sam—nearly breaking down in tears more than once—I asked Cooper exactly how he managed to get a copy of the picture I'd thrown into the freaking Atlantic Ocean.

"Vicky." Cooper said her name in the same tone one might say "diarrhea" or "toxic waste."

I felt my mouth drop open like a bigmouth bass's. "How did—"

Cooper shrugged. "How does she do half the things she accomplishes?"

"Facebook." My mother let out a haughty grunt. "And you could have at least told me which direction you were going. I've been dragging this suitcase behind me for half a block!"

"Well, if you'd been speaking to me, I might've told you." I growled. "And what do you mean 'Facebook'?"

Mom shoved her hands onto her narrow hips. "I had a very good reason for not speaking to you, and Facebook is where Vicky saw the photograph. I posted it the night I took it!"

"Since when did you learn how to post pictures to Facebook?" My voice climbed another octave as I shouted at my mother in the middle of the arrivals lane. "And why on God's green earth are you friends with Vicky?"

Mom let out another passive-aggressive grunt and rolled her eyes. "I added her when I thought the two of you were *involved*. I was being supportive. And Mitch showed me how to post to Facebook so I could share all the wonderful photos from our trip."

"And *that's* the picture you decided summed up our entire trip?"

Mom just grinned, and I knew. I knew in that one bright, shining instant she knew *exactly* what she'd done. And she was proud of herself. I had to wonder what I'd done in a past life to deserve Grace James as a mother. Whatever it was, it must've been bad.

"Come on." Cooper grabbed my hand, slipping his fingers between mine with a smile. "Let's get in the car before you two make an even bigger scene."

We stepped up to a shiny black car—one of those fancy, old-fashioned things you'd see the villain in an old James Bond movie driving—and the trunk popped open. An older man in a crisp black suit and horn-rimmed glasses stepped out of the driver's seat to help with our bags.

"Where are your parents?" I whispered.

Cooper cleared his throat and reached up to scratch his cheek. "Uh…"

Before he'd finished the thought, the chauffeur strolled up to me, sweeping me into a bone-crushing hug. Then this total stranger did the unthinkable. He pressed a chaste kiss to my shocked lips. "Katie! I'm so delighted to meet you!"

"Come on, Dad." Cooper groaned. "Don't scare off my fiancée before I have a chance to marry her."

*Dad?* I pulled back from the kiss and did my best to wipe the shocked expression from my face. Up close, I could almost see the resemblance. His hair was more gray than brown, and his eyes were more green than blue, but the smile was the same. And I could see where Cooper had gotten his amazing bone structure. They were definitely related. "Mr. Maxwell?"

"Oh, pish. Call me Colin." He gripped the tops of my arms, giving them a squeeze before turning to my mother. His already-wide smile cranked up a notch. "And this must be your lovely mother."

Mom returned his smile. "It's so nice to finally meet you, Colin. I've heard so much about you."

"The pleasure is all mine." Colin clasped my mother's hands between both of his and raised his eyebrows suggestively. "And *I've* heard so much about *you*, Grace."

Cooper choked on a laugh, coughing to mask it. "Uh, Dad? We're blocking traffic."

"Yes, yes. Of course." Colin nodded, releasing Mom's hands to reach for her bags. "Your mother is quite looking forward to meeting your beautiful fiancée. And I'm sure Grace is anxious to be reunited with Hank. A wonderful chap, I must say."

"Wait." I darted my eyes between Cooper and his father. "Dad's already here?"

Colin nodded. "Oh yes, he arrived late yesterday. He'd booked a room at the Park Plaza, but I insisted he stay with us. We have more than enough room."

Once Cooper and his father had finished loading our luggage into the trunk, Cooper held the door for me to climb into the back.

"Come, Grace." Colin stopped Mom before she could follow me into the backseat and pulled open the front passenger door for her. "Sit up front with me. I'm sure the kids would like to get reacquainted."

Mom's smile wavered slightly. "What a wonderful idea."

Once we were all buckled in, Colin jerked the wheel, pulling out in front of several cars.

"Careful, Dad," Cooper warned as he grabbed my hand, giving it a reassuring squeeze.

Colin chuckled. "Ah, how our roles have reversed. Not so long ago, I was the one giving driving advice."

"Actually," Cooper said with a smirk. "Chambers, the chauffeur, taught me to drive."

"Well, yes, but on my orders."

"You had a chauffeur?" I didn't dare mention I'd mistaken Colin for the chauffeur moments ago.

"Yes." Colin looked over his shoulder, taking his eyes from the busy road ahead. "Until very recently, actually. When I left Her Majesty's Diplomatic Service, I let our driver go. I find I enjoy driving immensely." He'd barely turned around again before accelerating and cutting over two lanes to a chorus of loud honking.

Cooper stiffened beside me but said nothing. I wondered how often he'd held his tongue on the trip to pick us up.

"I find it fascinating to hear you were a diplomat," Mom gushed.

Colin shot a grin in her direction. "It's only a job, Grace, albeit with a few added perks, but a job nonetheless. I'm infinitely more satisfied with my life since leaving."

"Oh? And what is it you do now?" As Mom shifted in her seat, turning to face Colin, a strange noise sounded from somewhere under her. Her lips fell open, and her pale cheeks brightened like two halves of a ripe tomato.

*Oh my God. Did my mother just fart in front of my future father-in-law?*

The sound repeated, louder this time, and Colin cocked his head to the side. "Well, isn't that interesting?"

I shifted in my seat, wondering if the leather was prone to squawking, but the movement was blissfully silent.

"That..." Mom's face blanched that time, and she opened and closed her mouth before spitting out the words. "That wasn't me!"

The inside of the car went deadly silent.

And then Colin laughed. "I dare say not, unless you're harboring a chicken in your bag, that is."

"Certainly not," Mom huffed.

With one hand still on the wheel, Colin leaned over and reached between my mother's legs to fish under her seat. Mom flinched back at the unexpected invasion of her personal space. After a few tense moments, Colin's hand reappeared with a gray-and-silver chicken at the end of it. He held the bird by its feet then placed it into Mom's lap. "Hold this for me, will you?"

Mom swallowed a squeal as the chicken flapped its wings in her face.

"Lizzie will be livid when she discovers our dinner

decided to stow away in the car." Colin narrowed his eyes at the chicken. "Naughty Prudence."

"W-Why do you have a chicken—" Mom shrieked again as the bird flew from her lap to her headrest then to the back, where it perched on the seat beside Cooper. With the chicken a safe distance from her, Mom visibly relaxed. "It reminds me of a hat I once had. I loved that hat."

I remembered the hideous hat well. I didn't miss it. At all.

I must have made a face, because Colin's eyes lit up as he glanced at me in the rearview mirror. "I could save the feathers for you, if you like?"

"No. But thank you," I said.

Much to my surprise, Cooper snatched up the chicken from the seat beside him, stroking the silky feathers as if he'd done it a thousand times before. "Poor Prudence. You didn't want to become dinner, did you?"

"Are we really eating your pet?" My mother's eyes zeroed in on the contented bird on Cooper's lap.

Colin clicked his tongue against the roof of his mouth. "Well, it doesn't appear so, now does it? She's gone and been naughty. I'm sure Lizzie was forced to take another bird out of rotation."

*Poor Prudence, indeed.* I cringed inwardly. The idea of eating something I'd actually met didn't sit well with me. "Cooper's parents live on a farm, Mom. I'm sure they frequently eat the residents."

"Well, that sounds ominous, doesn't it?" Colin chuckled and caught my eyes in the rearview again. "I heard you had a vivid imagination. I'll have to keep both eyes on you, won't I?"

"A farm?" Mom spun around in her seat, one sculpted eyebrow arched above cold eyes. "You said they lived in a country estate."

"Estate, farm, who's keeping track?" I shrugged.

Mom narrowed her eyes at me. "I'm sure it's lovely either way."

I'd known my mom long enough to read between the lines. *It had better be a lovely place with the five-star amenities she expected from any hotel she stayed at.*

Cooper squeezed my hand again. "The estate used to be owned by a baron, back in the day. When Mum and Dad bought it, it was in various stages of disrepair. They restored the house and converted the grounds into an organic farm."

I smiled as I remembered Cooper telling me this story on one of our first dates. "That's how you know how to milk a cow."

"You remembered."

"How could I forget?"

"How far is the estate from London?" Mom asked.

"Oh, a bit over two hours," Colin said.

My muscles locked up. *Two hours? From civilization? With my mother?*

It was going to be a long week.

# Chickens and Goats and Cows, Oh My!

WE TURNED ONTO THE PRIVATE road leading to the Maxwell estate, and I unbuckled and slid forward in my seat to get a better look. I had to be dreaming. Either that, or I'd somehow wandered into the set of a Jane Austen movie. Rows of flowering trees exploding with tiny pink-and-white blooms lined the long gravel drive. In the distance, reddish-brown cows grazed in the grassy field, and fluffy white sheep roamed closer to the house.

*And oh my God, the house.*

The three-story weathered gray-stone mansion had to have been there for centuries. Ivy climbed up a wall, reaching across the front like eager fingers, and sunlight reflected off three rows of windows, highlighting the wavy glass. The place was so magnificent, I half expected Mr. Darcy to come strolling out the front door in his sexy white shirt and tight pants and dive into the shimmering duck pond.

"Cooper, it's beautiful."

He leaned in, his lips brushing my ear and sending a tingle down my spine. "I know they aren't your favorite, but wait until you see the rose gardens. My mother treats those bushes as if they're her flesh and blood."

Colin honked the horn. As soon as we'd come to a complete stop, Cooper grabbed my hand, towing me from the car before Colin had even cut the engine. We'd barely stepped onto the gravel drive when the front door flew open, and a petite woman came rushing out of the house. Her dark, curly hair was pulled up into a loose topknot, and she had a smudge of dirt across her cheek as if she'd been tending the roses Cooper mentioned. I had no doubt she was Cooper's mother. He had her sea-glass blue eyes.

"Mom." Cooper dragged me forward. "I'd like you to meet—"

"Katie!" Cooper's mom wrapped me in a hug, swaying from side to side as she held me long past the point of polite introductions. But I didn't mind. She smelled like roses and hot peppermint tea. "I'm so happy to finally meet you. Welcome to the family."

"I'm so happy to meet you, Mrs. Maxwell." I blinked back tears.

She scoffed and wiped a tear from my cheek with her thumb. "Who is this Mrs. Maxwell person? Call me Lizzie."

I caught my mother's raised eyebrows as Mrs. Maxwell—Lizzie—pulled me into another hug. A hot flush climbed up my neck. I wasn't used to such warm affection, especially in front of my standoffish mother.

"Katie," Mom said with a barely veiled twinge of bitterness in her voice.

I turned to my mom. The iciness in her voice had nothing on the frost in her eyes. "Hmm?"

Her mouth opened then promptly snapped shut as my father's voice bellowed from behind me.

"Grace?" I spun around to see my dad standing in the open doorway. His eyes were locked on my mom in an epic stare down. "We discussed this."

"Yes, of course, dear." A fragile smile withered on Mom's lips as she deflated like a popped balloon.

"Daddy!" I ran to give my dad a big hug. "I'm so glad you're here."

"Me too, pumpkin." He patted my back. I couldn't see his face, but something told me he was still watching Mom.

Cooper cleared his throat. "Sorry to interrupt the

family reunion, but I need to steal my fiancée for a few minutes. I promise to bring her back as soon as I show her the gardens." Without another word, Cooper grabbed my hand, dragging me away from our grinning parents. Well, *his* grinning parents. My mother was anything but smiling as my father shot her another one of those "behave" looks of his. She looked downright pissed. I was all too happy to escape the drama.

"Thank you," I said once we were finally out of earshot.

"For what?"

"For rescuing me from *that*." With my head resting on his shoulder, I hooked a thumb back toward the front of the house. "I have no idea why my mom is so..."

Cooper glanced behind us. "Intense?"

"I was actually going for bitchy, but intense works."

He laughed, but his arm tensed where it wrapped around me. "I don't know, Katie. I wish I did."

We walked for several more minutes without talking. Cooper took me to the cutting garden, where cottage flowers of every variety grew wild. As he rattled off the different species of plants, he took every opportunity to touch me—innocent little gestures like brushing my hair back from my face, slipping his fingers between mine to stroke the side of my thumb with his—and I soaked up the attention. I'd been starved for affection for over a week.

He showed me the kitchen garden, where his mother grew herbs and vegetables. He picked fresh peas from the pods and fed them to me. After that, we skirted the duck pond to double back around toward the rear of the estate. At the western corner of the massive house, Lizzie's famous rose garden was tucked into its own secret hideaway. At the entrance, thick vines flush with pale-pink blooms climbed up and over the arbor gate like sentries. The entire area was hidden behind a low stone wall. I'd never been a huge fan of roses—they were just too ordinary for me—but

I'd never seen so many different varieties—or colors. The scent was intoxicating.

"This really is amazing," I said on a sigh.

Cooper hummed out a reply as he pulled me toward an ornate iron bench and lifted me to sit across his legs. He nuzzled my cheek. "I missed you."

"I missed you too." I shifted until I straddled his lap, my knees pressing into the hard bars across the back. "It was the longest week ever."

"But you survived." He studied my face carefully, tracing a finger across my jaw. "Relatively unscathed."

"Barely." I debated bringing up the circumstances of my fading bruise and thought better of it. "My injuries have practically healed."

"Thankfully. And..." Cooper brought his lips to mine but didn't kiss me. His hot peppermint breath warmed me to my toes. "We're getting married in less than a week."

I nodded, making my lips brush his. "We are. And then we're going..." I let my thought trail off, hoping Cooper might finish the sentence for me.

"Not so fast, Nancy Drew." He kissed me quickly then stood, forcing me to slide down his body to put my feet on the ground.

"Oh, come on," I whined. "Just a hint?"

Cooper shook his head, grinning from ear to ear. "No hints. And don't pout. I promise it'll be worth it."

"Fine." I huffed out a breath as I followed him toward the stone barn. I tried and failed to decipher the mysterious expression on his face. "Are we...?"

"Are we what?" He smirked.

I turned my head in both directions, making sure we hadn't been followed by one or more of our parents. "Are we going to have sex in the barn?"

Cooper scooped me up in his arms, tossing me over his shoulder. "I guess you'll find out in a minute, won't you?"

I didn't have a mirror at my disposal, but I was pretty sure I had hay in my hair and probably a few other places I didn't want to think about until after I'd had a nice hot shower. Cooper wrapped his arms around me from behind, stilling my nervous hands.

"Hey, I need to—"

"Nope." He nuzzled my neck with his cheek, and I all but melted from his touch all over again.

"Nope what? I need to straighten my clothes and pick the hay out of my hair, or everyone will know what we've been—"

"So what?"

I turned my head so I could see the grin on his swollen lips. "So? Those are my parents in there. They still think I'm waiting until my wedding night."

Cooper laughed, a full belly laugh that did things to me where we rubbed together. "Katie, they're not stupid."

"Yes, they are!" I argued. "I mean, my dad's a doctor, so obviously, he isn't *stupid,* but I like to think he's at least clueless. And my mother, well... The jury's still out on that one. But Cooper, my father still thinks I'm his sweet little girl."

Warm lips pressed against my throat on a steady path to my collarbone. "You'll always be his little girl, but he's not an idiot. They know we—"

I spun around, gaping at him with my mouth open so far I could taste grass and oats and a touch of something else I didn't want to think about. "In five days, they can think whatever they want. But until then, they're clueless, got it?"

"Whatever you say, babe. "Cooper swallowed a snicker and kissed me full on the mouth. "Come on."

We left the barn through a side door and made our way back toward the house. Behind me, soft footsteps closed the distance. A cold nose pressed against the small of my back. I flinched and let out a shrill scream.

Cooper pulled me behind him then burst into loud laughter. "Katie, it's only a goat."

Eyeing the horns on the dog-sized animal, I took a half a step back. "Don't ask me why, but I don't trust them."

His eyebrows climbed up his forehead. "Them?"

"Goats." I narrowed my eyes at the shifty beast. "I heard someone talking about—it doesn't matter. I just don't trust them."

With a chuckle and a shake of his head, Cooper grabbed my hand and towed me toward the house. "You and your wild imagination..."

Inside, Cooper's parents were entertaining my mom and dad in the grandest living room I'd ever seen. The ceilings had to be twelve feet high, and the fireplace was easily large enough for Cooper to stand inside without ducking. Cooper tugged me toward a worn leather sofa. He sat first then pulled me down beside him.

"Did you give Katie the fifty-cent tour?" Colin leaned forward in his wingback chair, his eyebrows climbing up his forehead as he looked us over. I could swear he saw right through the calm facade I attempted to portray.

Who was I kidding? I probably looked as guilty as a teenager with a joint in my pocket. My face went up like a tinderbox.

Giving my hand a squeeze, Cooper grinned at his dad. "No, we only made it as far as the barn before heading back."

"Oh?" Colin turned his gaze on me. "And how did you find our stables, Katie?"

What was I supposed to say? *Surprisingly comfortable? I really enjoyed myself? Wouldn't mind having another go if I get the chance?* My already-hot face burned even brighter.

"Katie isn't fond of the goats." Cooper jumped in, saving me from responding.

"Lizzie showed me around this morning," Dad said. "I wouldn't mind having a few chickens and a goat or two."

"That would go over well with the homeowners' association." Bitterness rang from Mom's voice.

Dad chuffed. "Davis Sherwood and his band of old cronies can bite my—"

"Thank you, Lizzie!" My voice came out a little too loud and way too high as I attempted to head off my dad's next remark. I suspected he'd been sipping more than tea when we walked in. "For planning the wedding. And just... everything."

"Oh, it was my pleasure!" She beamed at Cooper. "It's not every day my only child gets married."

"Speaking of the wedding..." Mom injected herself back into the conversation without missing a beat. "It was my understanding the ceremony would take place in a London church."

"Yes." Lizzie cleared her throat and schooled her features into a tight smile. "I was waiting for Cooper and Katie to come back so we could discuss the wedding. I *had* planned for the ceremony to take place at Saint Pancras Old Church in Camden Town. Our family has ties to the church going back centuries."

Mom actually looked impressed. "That sounds wonderful."

"Yes. It would've been." Lizzie shifted in her seat. For the first time since we'd arrived, I sensed nervousness coming from her.

It took a moment, but finally her words sank in, and my stomach did an uncomfortable flip. "Would've been?"

The smile fell from Lizzie's lips. "Well, yes. Unfortunately, we've hit a bit of a snag."

"Snag? What kind of snag?" Cooper's forehead wrinkled, and he sat forward just a smidgen.

That infinitesimal movement sent a jolt of panic rushing through my veins. I put two and two together, and it hit me. "We don't have a church?" I tried to stay calm. I really did. But panic always made my voice all shrieky.

"We do! Of course we do, sweet girl." Lizzie rushed over, sitting on my other side and taking my hand in hers. "Just not exactly as originally planned. We're all booked up for the church... on Friday."

Mom let out a dramatic gasp, and my insides churned. "But the wedding is scheduled for Saturday."

"Can't they just switch days?" I asked, but in the pit of my stomach, I knew where weddings were concerned, nothing was that simple.

"I'm afraid not." Lizzie cringed. Her grip on my hand tightened. "I've already spoken with—"

"All the invitations have gone out." Mom stood, her voice getting higher and higher with each word. "Flights and hotel rooms have been booked!"

"Well, yes." Lizzie patted my trembling hand. "That does present a bit of a problem. But I have it all worked out."

"Worked out?" Mom's eyebrows shot up. "How?"

"We'll just have the ceremony a day early, and then—"

Mom cut Lizzie off again. "Katie can't get married on Friday! That's not part of the plan. We have people coming." Mom turned to Dad, her pulled-together facade melting faster than ice cream in a heat wave. And with every panicked word out of her mouth, my composure slipped a bit little farther south. "Hank, tell her!"

"Cooper?" Tears burned my eyes as I gazed at my fiancé. The concern in his face worried me more than Lizzie's nervousness or my mother's complete meltdown.

As if he sensed *my* imminent meltdown, he leaned in to rest his forehead on mine. His voice was like a soothing balm to my frazzled nerves. "Hey, it'll be fine. I'd marry you in the barn if you'd still have me."

My thoughts flashed back to the dusty old barn. *Maybe with a little tidying... and some flowers... Maybe a few chairs. It might not be so bad.*

"Okay." I nodded. If it came to that, I supposed I'd be fine. Come hell or high water, in five—make that *four* days, I would be walking down an aisle somewhere in England whether or not anyone was there to witness it. Nothing and no one would stop me from becoming Mrs. Cooper Maxwell.

# Dead Men Recite No Vows

"I JUST SAW HIM LAST WEEK!" Lizzie paced the stone kitchen floor. Her dark curls spun out of control around her head as she flailed her arms. "He seemed so..."

"Don't you dare say healthy." Colin crossed the room with his tea and a plate of scones. He sat across from me at the antique breakfast table overlooking the gardens. "I'm telling you, I've seen healthier looking cadavers in the morgue."

"Don't be daft, Colin." Lizzie let out a loud sigh. "He didn't look *dead*. He looked *old*. He was eighty-three."

Colin's cup clattered against the saucer as he abruptly set his tea down with a barely masked snicker. "The man looked like a walking corpse when I saw him in April. Clearly, all it took was a few months for the rest of him to catch up."

Lizzie stomped across the room to repeatedly stab a finger into her husband's chest. "Don't. Make. Fun. Of the dead. You'll be old one day... sooner than you think... and then it won't be so funny."

Colin snatched her finger from the air and pressed a kiss to the tip. "Yes, dear."

With just four days to go until my fairytale wedding, not only did we not have a church booked for the right day, but as of an hour ago, we were officially short one ancient priest to perform the ceremony. And according to Lizzie, at the height of wedding season, the likelihood of finding a replacement in just a few days was nonexistent.

"What are we going to do now?" My voice barely carried above the sound of Lizzie's shoes slapping against the stone floors as she continued to pace, a harried expression marring her delicate features. We'd already scrapped the idea of the church wedding in favor of a quiet ceremony in Lizzie's rose garden. And now...

"We'll figure it out," Cooper said.

The situation seemed hopeless. My stomach swirled like a flushing toilet. "When my mother finds out about this..."

"Don't worry about your mom." Cooper took my hand in both of his and squeezed. The action wasn't the least bit comforting, not when his hands trembled as badly as mine.

"Do you know what she'll say? She'll say this is a sign we shouldn't get married." Despite her initial happiness when she found out we'd gotten engaged, my mother's enthusiasm had steadily declined the closer we got to the actual wedding. If I hadn't known better, I would've thought she'd found someone else she wanted me to marry. The thought was preposterous. She just didn't want me to be happy.

"It's not a sign." Cooper dropped my hands and stood to pace alongside his mom. "It's a setback. But not a sign."

I gaped up at him from my spot at the table. "I *know* it's not a sign. I love you. I'd gladly marry you in front of one of your stupid goats if it came to that. But my *mother...* I can hear her now. 'How many setbacks do you have to have before we take it as a sign?'"

"Katherine Grace James..." My full name on Cooper's lips sent a wave of electric shocks through me. "We're getting married in four days if I have to tie your mother up in the wine cellar to do it."

"Wait... You have a wine cellar?"

Cooper ignored my question and stalked back to me.

He planted his hands on the table behind me, caging me in. "Four. Days. Do you hear me?"

A slow grin spread across my face, and I nodded. I sort of loved it when Cooper got all alpha male on me.

Cooper kissed me—*hard*—sweeping his tongue across my lips. "And not even a dead vicar will prevent that from happening."

Dad walked into the room, his gaze flicking around the room like a cat stalking a laser pointer. "What the hell happened now?"

"The priest died." Colin dropped the bombshell in between sips of tea.

Dad slid into the chair beside me and reached for a blueberry scone as if we were discussing the weather or what to have for dinner. "So get a new one."

"Dad, I don't think it's—"

"Of course!" Lizzie stopped pacing and ran over to hug my father around the neck, earning a chuckle from him. "A *new* one. Why didn't I think of that?"

"What are you carrying on about, Lizzie?" Colin asked. "I thought you said we couldn't find a replacement on such short notice?"

"Well, not an established priest, no. But what's stopping us from dashing down to the diocese to get a newly ordained one!"

"Brilliant plan, Mum." Cooper's smile lit up the room.

"Thank you." She beamed for a long moment before jumping back into action. "Now... this will take a bit of finessing. First..." Lizzie glanced at her faded floral capris and chambray button-down. "I'll need to wear something a little less pastoral, perhaps. Colin, you'll have to drive me... and—"

"My goodness, I heard the racket all the way upstairs. What on earth are you people so enthusiastic about at this hour? I must still be on New York time." My mother sashayed into the room in a cloud of her cloying perfume, wearing a cream silk sheath and peep-toe pumps. *On a farm.* She stopped in front of the teakettle and frowned. "What? No coffee?"

Instead of being annoyed, Lizzie broke into a wide smile. "Grace, I believe I may be in need of your services this morning."

While Colin read the paper in the driver's seat of his Bentley, I sat wringing my hands in the backseat. "This is a bad idea, as in, the *king* of all bad ideas."

Without looking at me, he turned the page then shook out his paper with a loud *crack.* "Just leave everything to Lizzie. It'll all work out."

"I have the utmost faith in Lizzie." And I did, even if she had booked the church for the wrong day and hired a man on his deathbed to perform the ceremony. In her defense, neither of those things were entirely her fault. The parish wrote the date down wrong, and the priest had a massive stroke—totally unrelated instances—it could happen to anyone. *Or just me.* But my faith in Lizzie aside—this was about my mother. "Lizzie doesn't know my mom the way I do."

That time Colin looked up from his page and smiled at me in the rearview. "I think Lizzie knows exactly what she's getting by asking your mother to assist."

My lips fell apart as I watched Colin's grin get even wider, so I wasn't paying attention when the passenger door jerked open. I jumped as my mother slid into the seat beside me.

"Close your mouth, Katie. You look like a fish."

I'd barely registered my mom's words when Lizzie climbed into the front.

"Now," Lizzie started, spinning around in her seat to face me. "When we get there, I'll introduce myself, but after that, I think we should let Grace do the talking."

"What?" My shriek vibrated against the glass. I cleared my throat and brought it down a notch. "Don't you think *you'd* be better suited to talk with whoever's in charge? This is your country. Your rules. I'm not at all opposed to begging if necessary. I can beg with the best of them."

"Actually..." Lizzie threw a sly glance at my mother. "I think your mum would do a bang-up job securing us a new priest."

*A bang-up job? Really?*

While I was busy letting Lizzie's assertions sink in, Colin hit the gas and tore down the driveway like a Formula One driver. Over an hour later, we pulled into the diocese office governing the parish. Lizzie apparently knew the bishop by reputation if not in person. I had no idea if what we were about to do was considered remotely appropriate or if we were about to walk into a hornet's nest. I followed closely behind Mom and Lizzie, letting Lizzie, dressed in her "diplomatic special" as she'd referred to it—a neat blue skirt set and crisp white blouse—take the lead. I'd honestly hoped to blend into the scenery, but in my hot-pink sundress and matching hot-pink sandals, I stuck out like a Post-It note on a whiteboard. I hadn't thought to pack anything appropriate for a visit with the bishop.

Lizzie maneuvered the revered hallways as if she knew where we were going, and after a maze of turns, we landed in a large office. Wooden shelves and a simple desk overflowed with books and loose papers. Lizzie knocked on the doorframe, drawing the attention of the white-haired man behind the desk. He was dressed far more casually than I'd expected—dark dress pants and a gray shirt under a dark blazer. The only indication that he was, in fact, a priest was the white rectangle at his collar.

The man looked up from his book and slid his glasses down his nose. "Yes?"

"I'm looking for Bishop Franklin."

The man shuffled his papers, clearing a spot in front of him. "I'm Andrew Franklin. How can I help you?"

"Splendid," Lizzie said with a wide smile. She held out her hand to the bishop, and he reluctantly took it. "My name is Elizabeth Maxwell, and these are my dear friends, Grace and Katie James. We're here at on the recommendation of Eleanor Platts at the Saint Pancras parish office."

"Oh yes, Eleanor." The priest gave Lizzie a warm smile. "How is she?"

"She's doing quite well." Lizzie let out a long, dramatic breath. "Though I dare say she's in need of more help at the office. The poor woman works seven days a week. And you know, she's getting on in years. She should really take at least one day off."

Bishop Franklin nodded. "I'll see what I can do to get her more help. How can I be of assistance to you today, Mrs. Maxwell?"

"I—that is to say *we*—have a serious dilemma." Lizzie motioned to Mom and me. "My son, Cooper is marrying dear, sweet Katie here in just four days' time, and poor Father Tom at Saint Pancras has gone and died unexpectedly."

"I see." The old priest made a clucking noise with his tongue. "That is a dilemma, though I hardly think it was unexpected. Father Tom has been ill for as long as I've known him."

"So it would seem, but... Perhaps Grace can explain better than I can. Grace?" Lizzie waved a hand toward my mother and stepped back.

Mom cleared her throat, unfolding what I knew was a list of demands. "The loss of Father Tom seems to have left a vacuum at the local parish level. It would seem there is no system in place in the event of an emergency such as this. The church has made their position known. They don't have anyone else who can perform the ceremony on Saturday, but that is simply not acceptable."

"Excuse me?" His white eyebrows made the long climb up his forehead.

Mom arched a single brow. "We need a new priest immediately. We have people coming from out of the country. Flight reservations have been made. Hotel rooms booked. My husband is a very important doctor, and he absolutely *must* return to the United States in a week's time. We cannot wait for the next available date. We need you to assign a new priest for this wedding. My preference would be someone with a good deal of experience, perhaps someone older, and yet not someone so old as to drop dead on us without a moment's notice. And in that vein, someone in good physical condition would be ideal. A good dresser. I'm sure you can understand why—I'd rather not have to crop him out of photographs…"

"Mom!" I whisper-shouted from the corner of my mouth. "I don't care what the man looks like. I'm not planning on dating him!"

"Oh, Katie. Trust me. You'll care when you get your photographs back, and the priest looks like he just came from a Super Bowl party, covered in a sheen of sweat, with Cheetos dust ground into his trousers and a bad comb-over."

I suspected there was more to her vivid description than met the eye, but I dropped the whole train of thought before I ended up choking my mother in the diocese office. While Mom rattled off the rest of her list of expectations, Bishop Franklin's eyes stretched wider and wider, until I worried they might roll right out of his head. He shot a quick glance at Lizzie, who shrugged, motioning again to my mother, who was still going on about the qualifications she expected in a priest.

"…and furthermore, I think someone with a full head of hair, but without any facial hair would be preferred. Again, this is in order to keep the photographs consistent.

You'd be surprised how casually some priests behave on formal occasions."

"Is that all?" Bishop Franklin seemed to be dumbstruck by my mother's audacity.

"I believe so." Mom turned to Lizzie. "What do you think, Elizabeth?"

Lizzie wiped the grin from her lips. "Oh, I think that should do nicely."

"I—" The bishop's mouth dropped open, and I almost told him to close it before my mother called him a fish, but I held my tongue. "Things don't work that way, Mrs... I'm sorry, I've forgotten your name."

"James. Grace James."

"Mrs. James, we aren't an... an *escort* service. You can't just come in and order a priest from a catalogue and expect one to be delivered on a specific day and time as demanded. These things must be planned in advance. We have specific protocols that must be considered."

"Protocols?" Mom asked.

"Yes." The bishop slid his glasses back onto his face and riffled through the loose papers on his desk until he found what he was looking for. "There are forms to fill out. Pre-wedding classes. At the very least, the priest in question would need to meet with the—"

"Cooper and I already met with father Tom over FaceTime."

Bishop Franklin blinked at me. "FaceTime?"

"It's a..." I took in his glazed-over expression and decided against a modern technology lesson. "Never mind. But we did complete all the pre-wedding formalities over a month ago. Our paperwork is in order, we have all the necessary licenses, and...we're very much in love."

"This is *completely* irregular..." The bishop huffed.

Lizzie cleared her throat and stepped forward again. "Bishop Franklin, in the interest of time—yours and ours—look at Katie's face."

Once again, my mouth fell open, and I stared—stupefied—at the bishop.

Lizzie slid an arm around my shoulder and pulled me tightly against her side. "I don't suppose you have any newly ordained priests who would be willing to perform the ceremony for this poor sweet girl? Someone who could use extra practice perhaps? We would be willing to give a handsome donation to the parish of their choosing."

"A donation?" Bishop Franklin perked up. "I-I suppose I could ask if anyone was willing... for a donation. The parish of their choosing, you say?"

"Yes, of course." Lizzie grinned.

That one smile sealed it, and I knew. She'd planned this all along... using my mother's overbearing tendencies to our advantage rather than our detriment. My future mother-in-law had just Jedi mind tricked a bishop. *Check and Mate.* The woman was a genius.

# I'll See Your Vicar and Raise You One Tart

THE MORNING OF MY WEDDING had finally dawned. In fact, the sun had barely crested the horizon when a trio of roosters made sure I knew about it. My brain must have been numb, because I rolled out of bed the same way I did every morning. I took a shower and shaved my legs the way I did every morning. And after slathering on moisturizer and brushing my teeth, I sat on the side of the bed, wrapped in the fluffiest white towel I'd ever had wrapped around me, and contemplated getting dressed... for the last time as a single girl.

"Holy shit! I'm getting married in a few hours." Instantly overwhelmed, I fell backward into the plush mattress and gaped up at the ceiling. Marveling at how not a single cobweb stretched between the ornate moldings at least ten—if not twelve feet—overhead, I mused, "How the hell do they keep that so clean?"

"Hey, hooker. I appreciate the view, but don't you have a wedding to get ready for?"

Vicky's abrasive—yet oddly comforting—voice infiltrated my panic attack, and I sat bolt upright, closing my legs and dragging my towel tighter around me. "Vicky!"

She kept her eyes fixed on my covered crotch for a moment longer then lifted her eyes to my face. "Looks as though it healed nicely. No more sparkles?"

"No... no sparkles." Her unexpected appearance had me more than a little flustered. "When did you get here?"

Vicky flopped down beside me with a huff and tossed her fiery curls over her shoulder. "Speed Racer picked us up from the airport late last night, but Cooper said you were wiped out, so we had to wait until this morning to disturb you."

"Us? Does that mean Silvia's here too?"

"Yep. She's probably antagonizing your mother as we speak." She rolled her eyes, but I could see the smile lurking behind them.

"What about June and Phil?"

"June is getting the farm tour with your sister. I had no interest in seeing the inside of a barn. And Phil and his wife aren't staying here. They booked some little B and B down the road. Pretty sure he doesn't want her to know how much he actually likes us."

"You're staying here?"

"Surprise!" She widened her eyes comically. "Cooper said you'd want us close to help you get ready so you weren't forced to face the ice queen all alone."

If I didn't love him already, I would've fallen hard at that moment. My eyes brimmed with unshed tears. "Thank you."

"Hey, don't mention it." Vicky ducked her head with a sniffle then jumped up to look out the window. "So what's the plan?"

"Well, the ceremony is scheduled for noon, followed by a wedding breakfast or something."

Vicky scoffed. "What is it with the Brits? Explain to me what ungodly reason they have for getting married so early in the day. I could have done without the whole waking up at dawn's ass crack."

"Tradition?" I stood and hiked the towel under my armpits. "Besides, we're already bucking tradition with the venue. Lizzie had to pull more than a few strings to get approval for us to get married in the rose garden."

"So I heard." Vicky rolled her eyes again. "It's a stupid rule if you ask me, but whatever. I guess we'd better get cracking if we want you to look halfway decent by the time the orchestra plays 'Here Comes the Bride.'"

"They're violinists, and they're not playing 'Here Comes the Bride.'"

"What?" Genuine shock registered on Vicky's face. "Forget all this noon ceremony crap. *That* is tradition."

I shrugged. "On daytime TV maybe. We picked something by Bach."

Vicky shook her head. "So hair or makeup first?"

"First, you eat," Lizzie said from the doorway, carrying a tray of assorted pastries.

Silvia came in behind her, carrying a second tray with a porcelain tea set. "English breakfast tea, anyone?"

"Silvia!" I waited for Silvia to put the tray down before embracing her.

"Hello, sweetie." Silvia chuckled as she hugged me back. "You're gonna lose that towel if you're not careful."

"Yeah, I guess I'd better go..." I pointed toward the en suite bathroom.

"Hurry back!" Lizzie called after me. "We have a schedule to keep."

"Beautiful." Lizzie clasped her hands under her chin as she gazed at me with glassy eyes. "Oh, Grace, isn't she simply stunning?"

With my sister, Lauren, playing mediator between us, Mom had been quiet all morning. She barely spoke a word while the hairdresser twisted and teased my hair into an elegant updo, but when the makeup artist stepped back to admire her work, I caught the ice queen blinking back tears of her own.

Lauren—a near carbon copy of the younger version of our mother—nudged her with her elbow. "Mom?"

"Yes." Mom dabbed at her eyes with a tissue. "I was about to say you look lovely, Katie."

"Thank you both." I beamed at my own reflection. For the first time in my life, I felt like a princess. Unlike Mom and Lauren, I didn't have the pretty blond hair or the ballerina figure. I had my dad's dark hair, and curves that seemed to come out of nowhere. But standing in front of that mirror, I felt like the most beautiful girl in the world. And I hadn't even stepped into my dress yet.

Silvia freed the blush-colored gown from the satin garment bag, and Lizzie and Mom helped me step into it. It would seem the unbearable hours spent in the onboard fitness center weren't wasted after all. Exactly as I remembered, the silk folds fit snugly across my breasts, cinching my waist. The gauzy fabric of the full skirt draped around me like delicate tissue roses, puddling at my feet. The cathedral train unfurled behind me as I stepped into a pair of matching satin shoes.

Silvia, June, and Vicky hovered close by, fluffing the fabric roses while Lauren pinned the tulle veil to my hair.

Lizzie drew in a sharp breath. "Oh, Katie. My boy is going to shed actual tears when he sees you."

"Don't make me cry." I laughed and sniffled at the same time. "My makeup will run."

"Where's your bouquet?" Silvia asked.

I looked from Mom to Lizzie then back to Silvia. "I don't know."

"I think I saw it in the kitchen," June said.

"I'll go get it," Vicky offered.

I knew what she was doing—escaping before I commented on the unapproved alterations to her platinum-gray bridesmaid dress. She looked like a freaking tart with the new plunging neckline and overly snug silhouette. But not even Vicky could spoil this day for me.

"Katie." Lizzie drew my attention from Vicky's retreating figure. She picked up a long black velvet box from the bedside table and held it out to me. "I'd love it if you'd wear these today."

I opened the box. Inside was a triple-strand choker of pearls. The gold clasp looked antique. My eyes instantly filled with tears. "Lizzie, these are..." The gesture left me speechless.

"I wore them when I married Colin thirty-two years ago."

"I don't know what to say. Are you sure you want me to wear them?"

"Absolutely. I don't have a daughter of my own, so seeing you wear them when you marry my son would truly warm my heart."

"I'd be honored." I held out the necklace, and Lizzie helped me put it on.

Once the pearls were secured around my neck, my mother cleared her throat loudly. "Katie. Could I have a word?"

My head snapped up in her direction, and one look at her flinty eyes chilled my blood. "Yeah, sure."

Lizzie gave me a shaky smile then corralled everyone else from the room. "Come now, ladies. Let's give them some privacy."

"*Be nice.*" Lauren mouthed the words to my mother before following the others out the door.

Keeping my eyes locked on my reflection under the guise of primping, I waited for my mother to say her peace.

Mom eyed the pearls around my neck with blatant distaste. "How dare you agree to wear Elizabeth's jewelry?"

"Uh..." I opened my mouth, but no intelligent response would come. How did I begin to answer that question? "I'm marrying her son."

"So? Your father isn't down there offering up fatherly advice to Cooper on the morning of his wedding. Do you know why?" She didn't wait for me to respond. "Because that privilege belongs to *his* father. Not yours. You should be wearing *my* pearls, not hers."

My throat dried up as if I'd swallowed a cup of sand. "You didn't—"

"I didn't what? Interrupt her offer with one of my own? Publicly embarrass her in her own home? No. I didn't. You should have refused."

"Mom..." She was being unreasonable. *Wasn't she?* "I had no idea you wanted me to wear your pearls."

"That's not the point."

"Wait..." The horrible reality of what she *didn't* say hung in the air. "Were you even going to offer me your pearls?"

Mom fixed her hair in the mirror, avoiding my eyes. "No."

"What the hell?" I almost laughed, but nothing about the situation was remotely funny. "Why are you even mad then?"

"Because you didn't know whether or not I would offer my jewelry. You should have refused on principle."

"Why do you hate me so much?" The question had burned my soul for longer than I could remember. Saying it aloud both relieved and gutted me. A hot tear slid down my cheek to rest on the corner of my lips. "You've treated me differently since the day I got my first period, and you made me ask Lauren how to use a tampon. What did I do wrong?"

An unladylike grunt erupted from my mother's throat. "I don't know what you're talking about."

I stepped into her field of view, blocking her reflection and forcing her to confront me face-to-face. "No. Seriously, Mom. Tell me. What have I done to earn your constant animosity? You don't treat Lauren that way. You don't second-guess her every decision, criticize her every choice. For most of my life, I've felt like Cinderella seeking the approval of a disapproving stepmother, but you gave birth to me. So why do you hate me so much?"

"I—" Mom opened and closed her mouth a few times then cocked her head to the side and blinked. "I didn't realize..."

"How could you not? Everything I do is wrong. Even Cooper. He's everything you've ever said you wanted for me, and still, you act as if I picked an unemployed musician to marry. Not that there would be anything wrong with that, but Mom, he's wonderful. And his family is wonderful. I can't begin to tell you how it felt to have his mother welcome me the way she did and to offer me her pearls as if I'd always belonged—while my own mother looked at me like the chimney sweep. I could swear you were happier when you thought I was a lesbian."

"Katie... I..." Mom stammered for another moment, and I saw the wheels turning in her head as she attempted to reconcile her own actions to herself. Finally, she found her voice. "I don't hate you. I've never hated you."

I slowly released a breath, letting my question tumble out with it. "Then why are you so much harder on me?"

Mom shrugged and turned to perch on the edge of the bed, careful not to wrinkle her gray silk gown. "You were always a such spirited child. When you girls were young, Lauren followed me around, always begging to wear my shoes or my lipstick. But you..."

Like a magnet drawn to metal, I soaked up her words, moving closer until I sat beside her.

She glanced over at me with a fragile smile. "You were your father's child. No one could make that man smile the way you did. Even now, that hasn't changed. The two of you have always been so close, I suppose maybe I felt left out."

"Mom." My voice cracked.

"Jealousy is an ugly trait, but admittedly, I'm jealous

of you, of your independence, your spirit, your refusal to live up to the standards I set for you."

Another tear snuck past my lower lashes, and my mother caught it with her thumb, swiping it away before it left a trail.

"But never once have I *ever* hated you, Katie. I love you as much as I love your sister, but unlike Lauren, you don't need me. And I guess I didn't deal with that particular truth very well."

"Oh, Mom. I've always needed you. You just didn't realize it." I went to hug her, and she flinched away from me.

"Let's not get carried away, shall we? You'll wrinkle my dress." Her soft expression faded into the stern countenance I'd become accustomed to, and she huffed out an exaggerated breath. But under all the bluster, I noticed a faint smile that hadn't been there before. "And we'd better get that makeup girl back in here. You've gone and ruined your makeup already."

"Right." I nodded, but I couldn't contain my smile. "I guess we'd better..."

"Yes, we had better. We're going to be late, and you know I loathe being late." Mom got up and walked over to the door. With her hand on the knob, she turned back to me. "Those pearls really do look lovely with your dress. I think you should go ahead and wear them. You've already fastened them, and it would be a shame to get married with a bare neck."

"Thanks, Mom."

She nodded once then slipped out the door, closing it behind her with a quiet *click*.

My quiet didn't last long. First, the makeup artist arrived to touch up my face and chastise me for crying before the groom had even seen me. And then my room was a flurry of activity as June, Silvia, and Lizzie buzzed around me like flies at a picnic. It didn't take long to notice they weren't helping me get ready as much as distracting me.

"Okay, what's going on?" I narrowed my eyes at the three of them.

I'd never seen my future mother-in-law so nervous—not since the priest died, anyway. "It's nothing really... Just a minor delay."

"A delay? Wait... What time is it?" A quick glance at the clock told me we were running about fifteen minutes behind schedule. And then my worst fear sucker punched me in the gut. I couldn't breathe. "It's not Cooper, is it? He doesn't have cold feet, does he?"

"No! Oh, no." Lizzie grabbed my hands and squeezed. "Cooper very much wants to marry you. And he will, as soon as we locate the priest."

"The priest didn't show up?" I let out a shriek. "But Bishop Franklin promised!"

"See, that's the thing..." Lizzie started. "Colin sent a driver for him. He was picked up at the local diocese and dropped off at the house. He's here... somewhere. Last I heard, he was in the kitchen, but no one can seem to find him."

"How do you lose a priest? He's not a toddler. It's not as if someone would take him!" Silvia coughed, and I whirled to face her. "What?"

"What do you mean 'what'?" She avoided my probing gaze.

"You know something."

Silvia shook her head, making her caramel hair bounce.

I stalked up to Silvia, looking her straight in her shifty eyes. "Don't you dare lie to me."

She let out a loud sigh. "Vicky's missing."

"I really can't worry about Vicky being missing when I'm trying to find the—"

"Katie...?" Silvia's eyebrows slowly climbed her forehead, and her eyes widened.

"No. Not the *priest*. That's. Just." Visions of Vicky flirting with Bishop Franklin flooded my thoughts. "Gross. Even Vicky wouldn't stoop so low as to come on to an old man. Would she?"

Silvia doubled over laughing. "No, I don't imagine she would, but sweetie, the priest isn't an old man."

"Don't you remember? We asked Bishop Franklin to assign a newly ordained priest," Lizzie reminded me. "He can't be more than in his late thirties, I wouldn't imagine. And based on the description the driver gave us, he's younger than that."

*Crap!*

I bunched up my skirt and took off like a shot with my entire bridal party—minus one—chasing after me.

"Katie, wait!" June yelled. I heard her and the rest of them huffing behind me, but they were far from catching up. "You don't want to run into Cooper before the ceremony. That's bad luck."

"There won't even *be* a ceremony if we don't find the—" I came skidding to a halt in the kitchen.

Standing directly in front of me, looking like a pair of recalcitrant teenagers, were Vicky and the missing priest. Vicky's red hair stuck out like a wild mane around her head. Bits of hay poked out from between the tangled strands. The man beside her looked nothing like the priest I'd envisioned. First of all, he was exceedingly tall, at least six feet two or three. And though he was clean shaven, the rest of him looked like he'd be more comfortable in front of a camera rather than behind a pulpit. His artfully disheveled sandy-brown hair actually had style. And for a priest, he filled out his clothes a little too nicely.

"What the hell, Vicky!" I shrieked at her. "You kidnapped my *priest* before the ceremony?"

Vicky's eyes popped wide, and she whipped her head around to look at the man beside her. "You're a priest? Why didn't you tell me?"

He shoved his hands into his front pockets and shrugged. "You really didn't give me a chance to say much of anything before dragging me into the barn."

"Holy shit, I'm going straight to hell." Vicky threw her head back and laughed. "I just had the best sex of my life...with a priest! And God help me—it was sooo worth it."

"Oh my God! You had *sex* with my *priest*?" With my skirt hiked up to my knees, I paced the stone floor in the kitchen, shooting glares at my disheveled bridesmaid and her ruined paramour. My missing bouquet lay in a crumpled heap on the table beside her. I wanted to slap the satisfied grin from Vicky's lips, but since I was hyperventilating, my fingertips had gone numb. "How did you miss the freaking collar around his neck?"

Vicky shot a glance toward him and snorted. "I wasn't exactly looking at his neck."

For his part in the train wreck that my fractured fairy-tale wedding had become, Father Loose Zipper had turned the shade of a ripe tomato.

Lizzie, June, and Silvia formed a half circle behind me, and I looked to Lizzie in a state of near panic. "Can he still marry us, or did Vicky break his vows? Please tell me she didn't break him... We don't have time to find *another* new priest!"

Lizzie bit the inside of her cheek. "While I'm certain his behavior is frowned upon by the church..."

The priest—appearing thoroughly chastened—slipped a finger between his neck and his collar as if to loosen the noose.

Narrowing her eyes at the handsome clergyman before turning her comforting gaze on me, Lizzie continued. "Anglican priests aren't required to take a vow of celibacy, so no, your friend hasn't broken Father Luke's vows."

I heaved in a giant breath.

"Father..." With a sigh, Lizzie gave him one last withering

look. "I really should report you to the bishop. But since I'm more than certain you weren't the instigator in this whole affair..."

Vicky had the good sense to keep her wayward lips locked.

"I won't say a word." Lizzie waited for his reply.

Father Luke cleared his throat. "Th-Thank you, ma'am."

"I trust we won't have any further delays?" Lizzie gave him a quick once-over. "Perhaps long enough for you to clean yourself up? And I'm so sorry, Katie, but I think you're going to get your embarrassing photos after all."

It took a moment for her meaning to sink in. Then I noticed the dirty hand print on the front of the priest's trousers and several missing buttons on his shirt.

"I don't even care about pictures." I groaned. "Can we just get married already?"

# I Now Pronounce You

THE SOFT STRAINS OF THE violins carried through the air, bringing the sweet fragrance of Lizzie's garden with it. The familiar tune managed to tie my stomach even further into knots as I stood outside the house, staring at the rose-covered arbor half-a-dozen yards away.

In keeping with the American wedding traditions I'd dreamed about since I was a little girl, Vicky, June, and Silvia each took their turn walking toward the music, disappearing, one by one, as they stepped through the gate ahead of me. My pulse skipped as I remembered Cooper was somewhere inside that secret garden, waiting for me.

"Katie, breathe." Dad grabbed my trembling hand and tucked my arm in his, giving it a gentle pat. "You look beautiful, pumpkin."

Smiling up at him reminded me of every father-daughter dance, every stolen Saturday morning at the bakery, every bedtime story. "Thanks, Daddy."

Dad took a step forward then stopped to search my eyes. "This guy. You love him, right?"

"I really do." I beamed.

With a nod, Dad turned back toward the rose garden.

The violins went silent, and the sound of my own heart thundered in my ears until the first notes of Bach's "Air on a G String" began to play. "That's our cue."

"Just remember," Dad whispered as he took my arm and led me forward. "There's cake at the end of this whole thing."

Too nervous to laugh, I let Dad pull me along. Inside my head, I heard the *click, click, click* of a roller coaster making the slow climb up the tracks, inching ever closer to the sharp drop. We stepped close enough to the arbor that I could see the texture in the velvety pink petals in each cluster of blooms, and the sudden sensation of falling over the other side sucked the air from my lungs. My stomach dropped to my toes, fluttering like a scarf in the wind.

I could taste my heartbeat as Dad walked me up the crushed-stone path to Cooper. Along the way, I barely registered the faces of my friends and family. Somewhere in the back of my mind, I knew the guys from the cruise were there: Steven, Dave, Eddie, and Mitch—and Sam, beaming at me from the back row of the bride's side like a proud father. But the only face I wanted to see was turned away from me. For reasons I didn't understand, English tradition dictated that Cooper keep his back to me, and I was dying to see his expression.

Following behind my unorthodox trio of bridesmaids, my attention was completely riveted to Cooper's back as he said something to the man beside him—John or Sean. I'd met him briefly at the rehearsal, but all of a sudden, I couldn't remember his name. Somehow, even with my head trapped in a fog, my feet carried me forward until we reached the front, and Cooper finally turned to face me.

My breath caught in my throat.

"Katie." Cooper's voice floated to me like music as his trembling hand took mine from my father's. "You're so beautiful."

*Lizzie was right.* His eyes shimmered with unshed tears. And then he smiled that dazzling smile of his, and I fell in love all over again. *He's all mine now.*

Father Luke said something, and my dad responded, but I wasn't listening. How could I possibly pay attention to anything but the man beside me? My God, I thought I'd seen Cooper at his best—*so many times*—but I'd never seen him in a tuxedo until that moment. He was the beautiful one.

Father Luke cleared his throat and began in his low, soothing voice. "Love is patient; love is kind; love is not envious or boastful or arrogant or rude. It does not insist on its own way; it is not irritable or resentful; it does not rejoice in wrongdoing, but rejoices in the truth. It bears all things, believes all things, hopes all things, endures all things..."

Cooper squeezed my hand, anchoring me to the present. The whole week had been a whirlwind that I knew I'd never really remember, but at the same time, I also knew I'd never, ever forget it. Before I'd even caught my breath, we'd repeated the vows, exchanged rings, and then Father Luke said the words I'd been waiting for since the first day I met Cooper Maxwell: "...husband and wife."

"This is the best damn cake I've ever tasted." Dad was on his second piece by the time I caught up to him. "But don't you dare tell Mrs. Cohen. I'll deny every word."

"I wouldn't dream of it, Dad. She'd totally cut you off from your baklava."

"And that, right there, would be a damn tragedy." Dad stabbed another bite of cake, but instead of bringing it to his lips, he slipped his fork under the edge of the table. A pink tongue poked out from beneath the tablecloth seconds before a furry snout snapped up the cake.

"Is that...?" I peered under the table. A small white goat peered back at me.

Dad pointed his empty fork at me. "Not a word to your mother."

"My lips are sealed."

I was still laughing when I worked my way back through the crowd to Cooper.

He took my hand, slipping his fingers between mine

and rubbing his thumb over my platinum-and-diamond wedding band. "Are you having a good time?"

"The best." I tipped my head up, and he met me in the middle with a soft kiss. "But I'm ready to have you all to myself."

He let out a quiet groan and gripped my waist in his hands. "Soon."

"Not soon enough."

I'd barely gotten the words out when his mother dashed over to us, interrupting our moment. "I need to steal my son for just a minute. Do you mind, Katie?"

"Sure, that's fine." I smiled. What else could I say?

"Cooper, come say hello to Emily. She's just heartbroken now that you're married. The poor girl's had a crush on you since she was twelve." Lizzie winked at me as she hooked her arm in Cooper's. "We won't be gone but a minute. I promise I won't let her sink her claws into him."

Cooper shot me a pleading glance then disappeared into the crowd with his mom.

*Not nearly soon enough.*

Like Cooper, I'd been passed around the reception tent at least twice, meeting every member of the Maxwells' extended family and friends Cooper hadn't spoken to in years. But for the first time in my life, I didn't feel the least bit insecure about my appearance, not even when I watched the beautiful blonde cozy up to my husband. God, I couldn't stop thinking the word: *husband, husband, husband.* Cooper's eyes never left me the whole time he talked with her. I felt his gaze searing into me no matter where I went.

While I waited for Cooper to finish his mandatory socializing, I managed to wander into a discussion between Colin and Cooper's crazy aunt, Edna. After he introduced me, she took it upon herself to enlighten me about Cooper's youth.

"It's amazing he turned out so well, really. We worried

the boy might eat himself into a coma," she said around a mouthful of cherry tart.

"Come, Edna. I think you missed a tray of chocolate éclairs." Colin dragged her off with a wink.

"James!" Phil came trotting over to me, his wife, Candace, in tow. "You look lost... at your own wedding. Why doesn't that surprise me?"

"It's a bit overwhelming." I laughed.

"No kidding. I just saw your mom doing the YMCA with a couple of guys. And did you see Vicky with the priest?"

I'd already seen my mom dancing with Mitch and Eddie, so I followed Phil's gaze to the edge of the tent, where Vicky and Father Luke had their heads together, intently discussing something. Vicky's cleavage acted like a tractor beam, holding the priest's eyes captive.

"Am I the only one who finds that hilarious? You ended up with an authentic Tarts and Vicars party. How very British of you." Phil cracked himself up.

"Philip, stop." Candace shot him an icy glare, and Phil immediately clammed up—a neat trick I would definitely have to share with June. "Why must you always antagonize your staff?"

"Katie doesn't work for me anymore, remember? She's officially fair game again."

With an apologetic smile clearly meant for my benefit, Candace grabbed Phil's arm and shook her sleek black bob. "I can't take him anywhere."

As Phil's wife dragged him toward the bar, my attention went back to the conversation between Vicky and the priest. I had to admit, Father Luke had done a beautiful job on the ceremony, but I couldn't help imagining him with his snug pants around his ankles while he serviced Vicky on the same bale of hay Cooper and I had used just a few days earlier.

"Peenerella!" Dave called out to me, loud enough to draw the attention of half of Britain. "You clean up nicely."

I turned to see not just Dave, but Steven and Sam strolling forward, wide grins and champagne flutes all around. Mom had clearly called dibs on Eddie and Mitch for the entire reception.

"Leave the girl alone." Steven shoved him aside and grabbed me in a hug. "You. Look. Beautiful!"

"Aww, thank you," I said. "I'm glad you guys could make it."

"We wouldn't have missed it." Dave drained his drink and reached for a fresh glass from a passing tray. "You promised to introduce me to your writer husband, remember?"

*How could I forget?*

"Stop with the stalking already, David. You already got to meet Katie's pretty husband, and it was rude of you to flirt with him like that at his own wedding. Would you excuse us for just a minute?" Steven didn't wait for a response before pulling Dave toward a quiet corner.

"Those two have been bickering all morning." Sam laughed then sobered as he took me in from top to bottom. "My God, but you really do look absolutely stunning." He leaned in to kiss my cheek, and for half a second, I wondered if he'd been lying about being gay. "Cooper's a lucky guy."

"I can't argue that fact." Cooper reappeared, wrapping his arms around me from behind. He pressed his lips to the same cheek Sam had, lingering long enough to erase the other man's touch. "I am most definitely a very lucky man."

Without a word, Sam quietly excused himself to mingle while Cooper kissed his way down my neck.

"We've eaten. We've danced... We've mingled until I think my mingling gene is permanently damaged. We've even had cake," he whispered, biting the soft spot between my shoulder and my neck. "Can we escape now?"

He'd rendered me virtually speechless, and I couldn't manage more than a breathless, "Please..."

"Come on." Cooper took my hand and led me through the throng toward our parents with enthusiasm I'd never seen before.

"You in a hurry?"

"You betcha." Cooper grinned. "I'm anxious to have sex with my wife."

"Oh." I felt myself blush. "Then let's say our good-byes and get the hell out of here."

When I was a teenager, I used to imagine my wedding day—and my wedding *night*—in graphic detail. Well, as graphic as a fourteen-year-old virgin could get. Today had completely surpassed my wildest dreams and even my worst nightmares in some ways. *Vicky.* But as I stood in the marble bathroom in our suite at the Hever Castle Bed and Breakfast, every notion I'd had before had been swept out of my mind. I was in brand-new territory. I wasn't a virgin anymore. And I wasn't a little girl. But apparently, my insides hadn't gotten the message, because my stomach was teeming with butterflies. And my legs felt like Jell-O.

"Katie?" Cooper called my name through the door. "Baby, are you okay? You've been in there for a while."

"I'm fine!" I yelled back, willing my knees to stop shaking. "Be right there."

I gave myself a quick once-over in the mirror. My green eyes were too bright, my skin too flushed. *This is Cooper,* I reminded myself. *We're far from strangers. We've done this dozens of times already. So why am I so nervous?* Something about *this time*—in *this place*—made everything seem more important somehow. Did I undress before walking out there? It wasn't like I was still wearing my wedding gown. I'd already changed out of that before we left his parents' house. Should I dispense with the simple ivory silk sheath and put on one of the sexy nighties I'd packed for this occasion? Or let him do the honors? How was I supposed to know? I'd never been married before.

"Hey," Cooper's soothing voice came through the door again. "Did I ever tell you the moment I knew I was going to marry you?"

I glanced at the simple wooden door separating us and whispered, "No."

"It was the day you introduced me to your imaginary cat."

"Very funny." I laughed.

"I'm serious," he said with a chuckle. "You were so adorable, whispering across the desk as if you were giving away state secrets."

"It was a big deal. Can you imagine if Vicky or Silvia ever found out? Or worse... Phil?"

"They still don't know?"

"No way! I never told anyone but you. They would've ridiculed me daily and enjoyed every second."

"See..." I heard a thump and realized Cooper must've rested his head against the door. "That's exactly why I fell in love with you that day. You invited me into a place no one else was allowed. And I've never wanted to leave."

He didn't say anything else, and the silence filled the space around me. "Cooper?"

When he didn't answer, I opened the door.

Like an impossibly perfect Greek statue, Cooper leaned against the doorframe in his dressy black pants and nothing else. Behind him, votive candles flickered on every flat surface. Cooper had gone all out for our wedding night, booking us a suite in a freaking Tudor castle. With the candles, the ornately carved furniture, the dark mahogany-paneled walls, and the trefoil ceiling moldings, I felt like a queen. Cooper watched me with his arms crossed in front of his bare chest.

I took another step closer until our noses almost

touched and reached up to run my fingers through his light dusting of dark hair. "I don't know the exact moment I fell in love with you, but I think maybe I'm still falling in new and exciting ways every day."

Without waiting for me to chicken out again, Cooper cupped my face in his hands and brought his mouth to mine in a toe-curling kiss. "I love you, Mrs. Maxwell."

"I love—"

Before I could finish, his lips were on mine again, steering me across the room toward the carved canopy bed. Desperate to feel all of him, I slid my hand down his chest, over his taut stomach, and his muscles jumped under my fingers. I fumbled with his fly, shoving his trousers over his narrow hips. Cooper stopped walking to step out of his pants, and we stood there in the middle of the room, surrounded by dancing shadows.

Kissing his way across my collarbone, he reached behind me to slowly slide my zipper down my back and over the swell of my rear. Skimming his hands over my exposed shoulders, he pushed the slippery fabric from my body, leaving me in nothing but sheer lace lingerie.

"Jesus." Cooper hissed out a breath. "I didn't think you could possibly get any more beautiful. You take my breath."

I *felt* beautiful with his eyes roaming over me from head to toe like a caress.

With trembling hands, he unhooked my bra and let it drop to the floor. His lips fell open, and he mouthed the word "gorgeous."

My skin pebbled under his intense gaze, and I groaned out his name. "Cooper, *please...*"

He cupped my breasts in his warm hands. Cooper's mouth latched onto the spot between my neck and shoulder, kissing his way back to my swollen lips as he walked me backward to the edge of the bed. My heart hammered behind my ribs as he guided me down, crawling over me until his delicious weight pressed me into the mattress. The hard length of him settled between my open thighs, nothing but two scraps of fabric between us, and I shifted beneath him, hungry for more.

"I want you," I said, and my words seemed to spark something inside him.

He snaked a hand between us, pushing his boxers down his legs and kicking them free. With a devious sparkle in his eyes, Cooper poked his fingers into the whisper-thin crotch of my lace panties until they ripped through. He tore them from my body with a wicked grin. "They were in my way."

I swallowed, nodding furiously as his fingers continued their intimate exploration.

"Katie..." Cooper said my name between kisses, his hands searing my skin where he touched me.

I groaned into his mouth. "I'm about to spontaneously combust."

"We can't have that." Cooper trailed his free hand down my arm, lightly grazing the side of my breast with his fingertips. He continued down my stomach and over my hip until he grabbed my leg, hitching it up to his side. His mouth came down hard against mine, his peppermint breath coming out in short pants as he filled me for the first time... as my husband. "I love you, Mrs. Maxwell."

"I love you, Cooper."

# Back to the Future

A THROAT CLEARED, DRAGGING ME FROM the blissful memory of my wedding night, back to the Paris police precinct and my present predicament.

Inspector Gaspard's mustache twitched with the threat of a smile. "When I said to start at the beginning, I meant when you arrived in Paris."

"Oh." I blinked at the grizzled detective and felt an unpleasant twinge low in my belly—well, lower than that, really. "I was just getting to that part... but, uh, do you mind if I use the restroom first? My bladder doesn't seem to hold as much as it used to."

Gaspard nodded reluctantly and ushered me to the restrooms. His bushy eyebrows climbed up his forehead as he pointed to his feet. "I'll be waiting for you right here, so don't get any crazy ideas."

"Crazy ideas? Me? That's ridiculous." Rolling my eyes, I pushed open the door and hurried to the closest stall to take care of business. Once my bladder had been sufficiently emptied, I stood in front of the dingy mirror to wash my hands.

I placed a hand across the barely noticeable swell of my belly, tilting my head from side to side to check out every angle. "Cooper was right." I smiled. I didn't really feel any different. Other than being a little nauseous, I was still basically me. Well, except for the fact that the once-flat planes of my stomach curved outward as a new life grew within me. It came to me in a rush how much had changed in such a short time.

How much I'd changed.

I turned sideways, arching my back as I tried to imagine what I'd look like in a few months. My lips twisted to the side in an expression almost as unflattering as the reflection brewing in my imagination. *I wonder if they have maternity prison wear.*

A month ago, I was convinced the worst thing I had to look forward to was getting fat. Now I wasn't so sure.

A loud bang brought me back to my senses as Gaspard pounded on the bathroom door.

"Mademoiselle, must I come in there to check on you?"

"No! I'm coming," I shouted through the door before rolling my eyes in the mirror. "Geez, can't a girl pee without being harassed in this country?"

After escorting me back to his desk, Gaspard resumed tapping his pen on his pad. "Tell me how you happened to come to Paris."

The memory of that morning swirled through my brain as I sorted the parts I could tell Gaspard from the parts I couldn't. "The whole trip was out of character for Cooper."

"Explain."

"Well, for starters, he was extra secretive when he booked us on the first morning flight, and I had no idea why."

I crawled across the mattress and shook my wet hair over him, getting the exact response I was looking for. He reached out and hooked his arm around my waist, pulling me on top of him, setting off a round of giggles from me.

"You showered without me." He croaked in his husky morning voice. His dark waves stuck out in every direction, and several days' worth of stubble dotted his chiseled jaw. "Why didn't you wake me?"

"Because you booked us on a morning flight, and we'd never make it to the airport on time if I'd woken you up to shower with me." I kissed him quickly, before he could drag me down for more, and rolled off his chest, settling into my spot beside him. "Now go. If you don't shower now, we'll be late."

"In a minute." He kissed his way across my shoulder, nipping my skin then soothing the spot with his tongue. "Mmm... you smell good. Like peppermint and Katie."

"Will you still love me when I'm fat?" I blurted out the words, cringing at the whiny tone of my voice. Damn it, I wasn't that insecure girl anymore. *Must be all the raging hormones.*

Cooper's lips curved against the hollow of my throat, his deep voice vibrating against my skin as he resumed kissing his way up my neck. "You aren't going to be fat. You're pregnant. It's not the same thing."

"I will." I'd almost reconciled myself to the fact. Acceptance is half the battle. "I'll be fat. Allison Stanley gained sixty pounds with her baby. Sixty! And she said she still hasn't lost it all."

Cooper's lips froze against my chin. "Allison who took over for you at the bank?"

"Yes, her."

"I don't know what she looked like before the baby, but if that's fat, bring it on."

I whipped my head around to glower at him.

"Stop worrying." Cooper choked back a laugh. "I married you because I love you, not because you fit into a specific dress size. I'd still love you if you got as big as a house. There would just be that much more of you to love. But..." He cupped my cheek. "For the record... you're not fat."

Smiling despite myself, I wriggled out of his grasp. "Here..." I took his hand and placed it against the slight swell between my hips. "Can you feel that little bump?"

He gazed down to where his fingers spread across my

stomach, his eyes reflecting wonder back at me. "Our baby's in there somewhere."

"Well, yes." His dazed expression caught me off guard, and I scrambled to find my way back to my thought process. "But I'm going to get fat... and it's already happening."

"How many times do I have to tell you? I'll love every expanding inch of you, Katie Maxwell." He kissed my pouting lips and tugged me into his arms. "Stop worrying so much."

I wasn't really worrying. Having Cooper's baby delighted me to no end, but I'd researched all the gory details about the different stages of pregnancy and wasn't thrilled about losing my body in the process.

"I've been Googling pregnancy and childbirth, and I'm a little nervous about the whole thing. There's so much to be concerned about." I turned in his arms until I was staring down at him. "For example... did you know changing a cat box is dangerous to pregnant women?"

"Katie..." His lips twitched as he brushed a strand of hair from my face. "You have an imaginary cat. He doesn't use a box."

Oh. Right. I sank into his arms again. "Well, that's true... but so many other things can go wrong. I couldn't sleep. I spent all morning surfing the Internet for everything pregnancy related. You're lucky the second trimester is the safest time to fly."

"Hmmm. Surfing the Internet all morning?" He ignored my remark about flying while pregnant and rested his chin on the top of my head. "Were you watching me on YouTube again?"

"No. Don't be ridiculous," I lied, biting the inside of my cheek to keep the smile at bay, but my lips curved upward at the memory despite my best efforts.

I'd sprung the news that we were expecting during Cooper's appearance on the *Marcy Michaels Show*, and now the entire world—myself included—could watch his reaction over and over again.

Naturally, I always fast-forwarded past the moment I tripped—I didn't need to replay that. I'd burned it into my permanent memory along with all the other times I'd managed to embarrass myself publicly. And there were plenty of those. I'd much rather savor the look on Cooper's face when he found out he was going to be a father. It was better than almost any other memory from my entire life.

But I didn't have time to think about that now. We had a flight to catch.

"We're going to be late," I groaned as Cooper's lips went back to draining every drop of willpower from me. If anyone had told me a year ago that I'd willingly trade make-out time with Cooper Maxwell to get on an airplane, I'd have called them crazy. "Don't forget, you're the one who booked the flight, not me. Maybe if you told me why we're leaving the country so suddenly—"

"No." His answer came out clipped, and his fingers bit into my hips as he gripped me tighter, but he barely slowed his attack.

Using both hands, I shoved against his chest until his lips froze a millimeter from mine. Something flickered in his eyes as if he had something on the tip of his tongue but refused to voice it. "Well, if you won't tell me why you were so anxious to leave the country that you didn't even book a nonstop flight, you'd better go get ready."

"You, Mrs. Maxwell, are a taskmaster," he growled, flopping back against the pillows with a heavy sigh. "Is it wrong that I don't care if we're late? I just want to make love to my wife."

My heart pounded against my ribs, and I bit back a grin, refusing to let him see how much he'd affected me. "You should probably make that a cold shower. We don't have time for any more distractions. You may be famous now, but I seriously doubt the TSA will be impressed."

He gave me one last breathless kiss before grumbling all the way to the bathroom. I listened for the water and nestled into the warmth of his pillow, breathing in his wonderful scent. I drew in another deep breath, telling myself I'd rest for just a minute, but I couldn't help thinking about Cooper's reaction when I'd mentioned the trip.

Other than the unexpected announcement that he'd booked us two first-class tickets to Paris, Cooper hadn't breathed a word about our mysterious trip to France since he first told me last night. I knew we weren't going to see his parents. They were halfway to Madagascar for the next two weeks. And Vicky and her priest were on the outs, so that idea was a bust. I couldn't image any other reason Cooper would have for a last-minute trip to Europe.

Cooper's book—the story of how we'd met and fallen in love—currently reigned at the top of the *New York Times* bestseller list, and the first movie based on his Immortal Blood vampire series was box office gold, catapulting my husband to the top of the paparazzi's must-photograph list. Everyone from his agent to the movie studio eagerly awaited his next book, but that didn't explain his eagerness to leave the country, especially when he'd been so adamant that he wasn't interested in any of the production aspects of the movie. He'd been asked and asked, and each time, he refused to make the trip. So why change his mind so suddenly? As his publicist, I would've known if it had been work related. *Unless...*

The shower cut off in the other room as I replayed his words through my head again. *What is he keeping from me this time?* My overactive imagination scrambled to come up with all the different possibilities. Could I simply be overreacting? It certainly wouldn't be the first time.

Cooper stepped out of the CRWAT with one towel wrapped low around his narrow waist—his bare chest glistened with water, making my mouth go as dry as overcooked chicken—and he rubbed his dark waves with a second.

He cleared his throat, and my eyes snapped back to his knowing smirk. "Are you packed?"

I managed a faint nod before coming back to my senses. "I packed last night."

"Good." He stopped drying his hair long enough to kiss me full on the lips. Then he quietly went back to getting ready.

I knew he was keeping something from me, and I also knew I'd do whatever it took to figure out what.

"After flying all night long, we arrived in Paris early the next morning to a crowd of photographers."

Gaspard nodded, shuffling a stack of papers on his desk. He flipped the stack over, spilling an assortment of images across his desk. "I don't see you in any of these photographs."

I glanced at the pictures of Cooper arriving in Paris almost five weeks ago. Gaspard was correct. I wasn't in a single one. "Cooper knew we'd be mobbed. He had an assistant waiting to escort me to the car while he walked through the paparazzi."

"Hmm." The detective frowned, his bushy eyebrows pulling low over his eyes. "You seem to have every angle covered. And still, you offer no concrete proof of your identity. You expect me to take you at your word, to trust you on faith. And I must tell you, in my line of work, that faith is shattered time and time again."

Frustration turned my stomach inside out. "What more proof do you need? I've shared my life story with you. I've humiliated myself by telling you things I wouldn't tell my own mother. How can I convince you?"

Before Gaspard could answer, the same young officer who'd unshackled me earlier came charging across the room with a grim look on his face. His large, round eyes darted between my face and the detective's. *"Puis-je s'il vous plaît avoir un mot?"*

*"Oui,"* Gaspard answered the man, rising from his chair as he turned to me. "Excuse me for one moment."

The two men walked far enough away from me to have a conversation out of earshot. Not that it mattered. I didn't understand a word they'd said before they walked away. But there was no doubt in my mind. They were speaking about me. The young officer gestured wildly in my direction, and Gaspard's forehead furrowed deeper each time he glanced at me. Then with a series of nods, they split apart, and the older detective made his way back to me.

Gaspard sat, watching me for a long uncomfortable moment while tapping his lips with his index finger. Tufts of dark hair sprouted from his knuckles like grass growing between the cracks in a sidewalk. When he finally spoke, I could've sworn he forced back a smile. "You've been elusive as to why you were sneaking around a closed movie set this evening. If you can explain your reasons to my satisfaction, I may be inclined to believe you."

I blew out a breath and sank back in the uncomfortable chair. "My husband's been lying to me for weeks. I-I don't want to believe he would cheat on me, but—ugh! I thought if I could follow him without him knowing I was there, maybe I could figure out what he's been keeping from me."

Gaspard sat forward in his chair, resting his elbows on the desk in front of him. "Ah, this is something I understand."

"Cheating husbands?"

"Suspicious wives." He studied me for a moment longer. "What makes you think your husband has been unfaithful?"

Unfaithful. My stomach lurched. The mere idea of that word describing Cooper gutted me. "I have a horrible feeling

Cooper dragged us all the way to Paris to rendezvous with a woman."

Gaspard folded his hands in front of him and waited.

With an exasperated breath, I continued. "Despite the clause in his contract giving him limited creative control, Cooper had no interest in participating in the production of this movie. Then one evening—totally out of the blue—he gets a mysterious phone call... from a woman. Next thing I know, we're booked on a flight to Paris, and he won't tell me why. Since we've been here, I've caught him on the phone more than once with that same woman, and when I ask who he's speaking with, he gets all squirrelly."

"Squirrelly?"

"Suspicious."

"Hmm. Madame Maxwell"—Gaspard cleared his throat—"if that is your real name. Your story is the most outrageous tale I've heard in a long time, but I must admit, new information has come to light forcing me to reevaluate my initial position. Despite my better judgment, I find myself with no choice but to believe you."

Those three words—I believe you—rang out in my head like church bells. I rose up from my chair, ready to get the hell out of Dodge, when Gaspard brought my internal celebration to a screeching halt with one severe look.

"However..." he continued. "You have no identification, no passport. Not to mention the matter of trespassing—"

"I've already told you, my passport and other identification is back at the Ritz. If you'd just take me back to my room, I can show you my ID, and we can part company as friends." I tamped down the urge to stomp my feet. "I'll even score you an autographed copy of my husband's book."

"Bribery is a crime, Madame."

"I wouldn't dream of bribing you. Consider my offer a simple goodwill gesture for taking such good care of me during my stay in your lovely city." I flashed a wide smile.

"Hmm." Gaspard bounced his pen against his desk for an impossibly long time before facing the busy room. He cupped his hands around his mouth and bellowed out an order. "Rousseau! *Allez viens.*"

The younger officer bounded back to Gaspard's side. "*Oui?*"

The grizzled detective nodded toward me as he rattled off a monologue, every word of it in French. When he finished, Rousseau took off through the crowd again, disappearing through the door on the other side of the room.

Gaspard rose from his chair and walked around his desk to perch on the corner directly in front of me. I was close enough to smell the tobacco smoke lingering in his clothes. "A bit of advice, Madame?"

"Sure." I shrugged. Why not get advice from a total stranger in a foreign country? It's not like I had anyone else giving me worthwhile guidance as of late. "Go for it."

"Ask yourself why your husband would be unfaithful to such a beautiful woman and while you're carrying his child. Your answers may surprise you. And consider, perhaps your condition has tricked your mind into seeing things that aren't really there."

*Well, isn't he a regular Sigmund Freud?*

Gaspard's attention darted toward the center of the room again, and he stood. "It has been a pleasure getting to know you, Mrs. Maxwell."

"Am I free to—"

"Katie!"

I whipped my head around to see Cooper following Rousseau across the room. My mouth fell open, and I whirled on Gaspard. My voice came out in a shrill squeal. "You called him?"

"No, Madame," Gaspard whispered as he crossed in front of me. "I can assure you, I did not."

Cooper reached me in a few long strides, coiling his arms around me and lifting me off the ground in an epic hug. "Thank God you're okay! You left your phone and your ID in the hotel room. When I couldn't find you, I nearly went crazy. I called every hospital and police station in Paris."

"I'm sorry! I-I..." I shot a glance at Gaspard, and he winked.

"I'm afraid your wife got lost. She should really learn a few more phrases in our language before wandering the city alone."

I narrowed my eyes on Gaspard. The man had saved my ass while simultaneously making me look like an idiot. And if his grin was any indication, he knew I wouldn't say a word to contradict him.

"Baby, I told you I'd take you to see Notre Dame tomorrow." Cooper released me and extended a hand to the sly detective. "Thank you so much for taking care of Katie. I don't know what I would have done if anything had happened to her."

"The pleasure was entirely mine. Your wife is an interesting woman."

"Yes." Cooper gazed down at me. "She is."

One long cab ride later, we arrived at our hotel. Other than giving me strange looks the entire time, Cooper didn't bring up the police station or my bizarre appearance. But once he'd dead bolted us into our suite, he let the questions fly.

"So..." Cooper stood ramrod straight with his arms crossed over his wrinkled blue button-down. "Are you going to tell me why you're dressed as an extra on an Immortal Blood film, or should I take a wild guess?"

I froze halfway between the door and the bed and tossed a glance over my shoulder. I couldn't tell if Cooper was annoyed or amused. "Just experimenting with Paris fashions?"

"Uh-huh... Try again." Definitely amused—he fought a grin.

"A bad makeover at Lancôme? I really should learn to speak French while we're here."

Cooper released a drawn-out breath, and his shoulders slumped. "Katie..."

"Okay, fine. I tried to sneak onto the set with the extras and got arrested."

His eyes went impossibly wide, and his mouth followed suit. "You got arrested?"

I choked out a laugh. "They didn't charge me with anything."

"But you got arrested?" He gaped at me as if I were a stranger. "What were you thinking?"

Gaspard's words came back to haunt me. I had no rational reason for thinking Cooper would ever be unfaithful to me, and I'd lived under the veil of suspicion for long enough. It was time to let go of my fear and confront the elephant in the room.

I dropped onto the side of the bed and fought against the tears threatening to undo me. "You've been keeping secrets from me and sneaking around taking calls from someone I don't know."

"Katie..." Cooper took several long strides to reach my side and knelt on the floor at my feet, resting his hands over my baby bump. "I love you with every fiber of my being. I would never do anything to risk that. I thought we'd worked through the jealousy thing when I fired Vivian."

"I'm not jealous." If he'd asked the same question a couple of hours ago, I might have answered differently. "I'm not accusing you of cheating on me. But you are keeping secrets."

Cooper dropped his head to my lap and groaned. "Yes. I am."

"And we agreed. No more secrets."

"Yes." He lifted his head and locked his sea-glass eyes on mine. "We did agree."

I slipped my fingers into his thick dark hair. "So come clean already."

"Fine, I'll tell you, but first, you have to promise to stay calm. Okay? I've only kept this from you to protect you... and our baby." Cooper's hands flexed on my stomach. "This is something I've dreaded since the day you got those stupid roses..."

My insides clenched into a tight fist and punched me straight in the kidneys. "Roses?"

"The roses Dean sent you." Tension came off him in waves.

Was he still mad about the damn flowers almost a year later?

"That was so long ago." My voice came out in a squeak. I knew the instant I'd recruited Vicky into my insane scheme it would come back to haunt me. "Why bring it up now?"

Cooper swallowed hard. "Baby, do you remember what he wrote to you in those cards?"

My thoughts raced. I couldn't remember a single word Vicky'd come up with. At the time, I was too busy panicking, afraid Cooper would find out we'd staged the whole thing. Obviously, Vicky had gone completely over the top if he was still so affected. "No?"

"He said he was coming for you when he got out." Cooper heaved out a breath. "I couldn't let that happen, so I brought you here."

"But..." I was sure I looked as confused as I felt. "Dean's in jail."

Cooper pressed his lips together and shook his head.

"What? He's not? When? How?"

"It doesn't matter how. It's a long story. I found out the night I booked the tickets. I always knew he wanted you. The roses just confirmed my suspicions."

"So the mysterious phone calls... the sudden trip to Paris?"

"I've been keeping in touch with the DA's office. And..." He sighed. "I didn't know how else to keep you safe. I couldn't risk him making good on his threats."

"Cooper..." Panic gripped my insides, but not for the same reason it held Cooper in its grasp. I knew Dean had no real reason to come for me because I'd been the one who'd paid for those roses. Why hadn't I come clean when Silvia warned me to?

"Hey, it's okay. We're safe here." Cooper squeezed my hands, dialing the guilt up a notch. "He can't leave the country."

"It's not that... I'm not exactly afraid. I—" *I'm terrified, but not about Dean.* I slipped past him to stand, leaving him on his knees in front of the bed. I needed to tell him, but I had no idea where to begin.

"Then why are you so upset?"

"Dean..." *It's like pulling off a Band-Aid, Katie. Just do it.* "Dean didn't send me those flowers... I did. Well, I paid for them, but Vicky did the actual sending."

Cooper blinked up at me like a confused boy. "Vicky?"

Taking another step back from him, I continued my confession. "It was my idea to make you jealous, but she was the mastermind of that particular plan. I-I didn't know she was going to send them from Dean. I would've shut that idea down before she—"

"So Dean didn't send the flowers?" Cooper frowned, forming a deep furrow between his brows.

Lowering my eyes to the carpet, I shook my head. "No."

"You wanted to make me jealous?" Slowly rising to his feet, Cooper kept his laser focus on me.

"I... Vivian was there. She was... You didn't see the way she looked at me or how she looked at you!"

He stalked forward like an angry lion. Blistering heat flowed from his eyes, and my skin went up in flames.

"Cooper—"

Without a word, he shook his head, silencing me.

"But—"

"Katherine Grace James Maxwell..."

*Holy shit, he totally full-named me!*

Like a petrified rabbit, I stood stock-still while Cooper reached out and grabbed me. He spun me around so that my back was flush against his chest, and his lips were at my ear. "I don't know whether to strangle you or make love to you."

I shuddered, and a tingle ran entire length of me. "Do I get a vote?"

He chuckled, sliding a hand down to cup my baby bump as his hot breath fanned out over my neck. "I should be furious with you right now."

"You're not?" I tilted my head so I could see his face. Warmth radiated from his eyes as he gazed down at me.

"Surprisingly, no. I'm just so damned relieved that you're not in any danger."

That's where he was wrong. I was in horrible danger of spontaneously combusting from his proximity. "Does that mean you're going to make love to me?"

"Absolutely." Cooper kissed a path down my exposed throat to my collarbone. "At least until you've learned your lesson."

"Hmm. Have I ever mentioned I'm a slow learner?"

"I'm actually counting on it." Without so much as a word of warning, Cooper scooped me into his arms and carried me to the bed, depositing me in the center.

I grinned up at him. "What now?"

"Now..." He crawled over me. "We live happily ever after."

Dear Reader,

We hope you enjoyed *For the Love of Katie*, by Erica Lucke Dean. Please consider leaving a review on your favorite book site.

Visit our website to sign up for the Red Adept Publishing Newsletter to be notified of future releases.

# More Books by Erica Lucke Dean

Splintered Souls (Flames of Time 1)

Scattered Souls (Flames of Time 2)

To Katie With Love

Suddenly Sorceress (The Ivie McKie Chronicles 1)

Suddenly Spellbound (The Ivie McKie Chronicles 2)

Craving Caine

Ashes of Life (with Laura M. Kolar)

Diamond Duplicity (Jewels of Desire: Book 1) (with Eloise Delacroix)

Ruby Ransom (Jewels of Desire: Book 2) (with Eloise Delacroix)

# Acknowledgements

When I finished writing *To Katie With Love*, I knew the characters would stay with me far longer than the editing process. In fact, I had a feeling they would stick with me for many years to come. I even had this crazy idea about how to revisit them. I always wanted to tell the story of what happened in that missing year between the last two chapters, but writing *that* story was harder than I ever envisioned. First of all, I couldn't figure out how to make what would basically be a giant flashback feel fresh and new. And then the spark hit me. What are the odds Katie would suddenly stop sleuthing just because she married her dream guy? Slim to none. And what could possibly be more fun than talking her way out of a stint in jail? Nothing. And so *For the Love of Katie* was born...

I really hope you enjoy this book as much as I enjoyed writing it, because I enjoyed it thoroughly.

I'd like to acknowledge a few people who helped along the way, starting with Colleen Miller, who would *not* stop nagging me about a new book. Thank you from the bottom of my fuzzy pink heart, Colleen. Without your persistence, Cooper and Katie might be sitting at the bottom of a drawer today, with no hope of finding their way to the light.

As always, I want to thank my devoted beta readers, Karissa Laurel and Louise Flynn, without whom I don't think I'd ever finish a single chapter.

To Streetlight Graphics for the gorgeous cover. To my editors—specifically the amazing Karen Allen—and the staff at Red Adept Publishing for making me look so good. I can't imagine working with anyone else.

To the bloggers and fans who keep me excited about writing—and you know who you are!—thank you from the bottom of my heart. I do this for you! And to Alicia, Donald, Gail, Bette, and Candy for inspiring a few of my favorite characters.

As always, I'd like to thank my family for their continued support. I couldn't do any of this without them. I love you guys.

# About the Author

After walking away from her career as a business banker to pursue writing full-time, Erica Lucke Dean moved from the hustle and bustle of the big city to a small tourist town in the North Georgia Mountains, where she lives in a 90-year-old haunted farmhouse with her workaholic husband, her 180-pound lap dog, and at least one ghost.

When she's not writing or tending to her collection of crazy chickens and diabolical ducks, she's either reading bad fan fiction or singing karaoke in the local pub. Much like the main character in her first book, *To Katie With Love*, Erica is a magnet for disaster and has been known to trip on air while walking across flat surfaces.

How she's managed to survive this long is one of life's great mysteries.